SUNSETS AND HAPPY EVER AFTERS

Teresa F. Morgan

SUNSETS AND HAPPY EVER AFTERS

Published by Sapere Books.

20 Windermere Drive, Leeds, England, LS17 7UZ,
United Kingdom

saperebooks.com

ISBN: 978-1-80055-677-5

For Mary, a writing friend taken from us far too early.
In the short time that I knew you, thank you for your words of wisdom,
sharing your knowledge of champagne, the laughs, and being a huge
inspiration to me as a single, independent woman.
Every day, I aspire to be more like Mary.
xXx

ACKNOWLEDGEMENTS

This book has been on an incredible journey. It started out as an online dating book, to share some of the (horror) stories I've accumulated over the past few years since my divorce. However, it didn't work as well as I wanted it to for a romantic novel, so most of it was removed — so maybe one day they'll come out in another book! Ha ha!

Kittiwake Cove is a fictional town but the inspiration behind it is based on Polzeath, North Cornwall, where the boys and I holiday every year. A couple of years ago, I even sent them on surf lessons for research purposes for this book. My two sons, much younger when I first drafted *Sunsets and Happy Ever Afters*, have been the inspiration (if you can call it that) behind the children in this book. (Why do you think I gave Emma two boys!)

As ever, I would like to thank Romantic Novelist Fay Keenan for her support and continued encouragement. We met over Twitter, and I always remember my son saying, when he was much smaller and cuter, "But Mummy, you're not allowed to meet people over the internet…" Fay and I have usually journeyed together to Lacock for our RNA Chapter meetings, where we've bashed out ideas for our books. She created our very own Chapter — Weston to Wells, where I am (occasionally) Social Secretary. Over the pandemic, Fay and I frequently met on Zoom, both missing our writing community and our Frankie & Benny's brunch. But we kept each other going! It is only fitting that Fay's name should be on the cover of this book, too. I will always be grateful that we met on Twitter.

Author Jane Lark is another best friend in my writing world. We both started our journey together with One More Chapter. She has huge belief in me, as I do in her too. We are party buddies and share a love for Prosecco and *Bridgerton*. Thank you, Jane (aka Sandra — although it feels weird calling you by your real name) for your continued support.

Thank you to the team at Sapere for putting this book together and making it all the better. And thanks to my agent, Sara Keane, for all your hard work in helping me get this book to publication, too.

Lastly but not least, thank you dear reader for choosing *Sunsets and Happy Ever Afters*, and taking the time to read it. You are the reason why I love to write. I couldn't imagine life without writing now. I do hope you enjoyed your Kittiwake Cove adventure and the sunset.

PROLOGUE

Never in a million years had Maya Rosevear imagined that the day of her daughter's eleventh birthday party would end so badly. What could possibly go wrong at a pamper party for four pre-teen girls?

"Right, let me take a quick photo, girls!" Maya held her phone up and snapped a photo of Amber and her three friends looking ghostly with creamy white masks on their faces. They pouted and pulled silly faces, giggling infectiously. After twenty minutes, Maya set about removing the face masks before massaging some gentle moisturiser into each girl's face.

"Now, who's first for their nails?" Maya asked once the giggling had reduced to a level she could speak over.

Chloe's hand shot up. "Me, please!"

Maya led her over to the table where she'd set up the manicure station. She tidied the young girl's cuticles and filed her nails, in preparation for applying the polish. "What colour would you like?" she asked, massaging moisturiser into Chloe's left hand.

"That one, please." With her free hand, Chloe pointed to a glittery candyfloss pink colour which Maya knew would be popular with the girls.

"Great choice," Maya said and set aside the chosen nail polish, then swapped to massaging Chloe's other hand.

In the throes of a divorce, Maya wanted to get at least one thing right: being a good mother. She wanted her daughter's birthday to be perfect and, being a mobile beautician, she had agreed to hold a pamper party for Amber and three school friends, treating them to facials and manicures. She had deliberately kept the party small so that it was manageable — and affordable. As each girl was dropped off, she'd checked with their mums that it was okay to paint their nails and apply make-up.

Maya tried to block out the sound of the other three girls chattering and squealing from the lounge, where they were supposed to be watching *A Cinderella Story*. With four excitable girls on her hands, she was relieved that she had arranged for Lewis, Amber's eight-year-old brother, to be looked after by her best friend Emma. Owen, Emma's youngest son, was the same age as Lewis, so he could play with him and help Emma's eldest son, Finley, celebrate his eleventh birthday. Maya knew full well that Lewis would not want to be around four hyperactive older girls.

Maya already knew Amber's other two friends, Lottie and Hannah, but this was the first time she had met Chloe, who had only recently moved to Portishead. Their teacher had asked Amber to look after Chloe on her first day, and the two girls had quickly become 'best friends forever'. Chloe was a strikingly pretty girl with dark brown hair and brown eyes, in contrast to Amber's fairer features.

"It's my birthday, too, in two weeks," Chloe said, all bubbly and excited, yet somehow managing to hold her hand still.

"Wow, Chloe, that's not long to wait," Maya replied as she started to apply the gel nail polish. She placed each hand under the UV lamp between coats. "This dries it quicker than normal nail polish."

Once all four girls had immaculate nails to show off, Maya treated them to the application of some make-up, being careful to keep it minimal and age-appropriate. A little bit of eyeshadow, blusher and lipstick was enough to satisfy them. Again, Maya snapped photos of their faces.

To round off the party, Maya had prepared a high tea of delicate cakes and finger sandwiches, presented on three-tier cake stands as if they were in an expensive spa. To mimic champagne, she poured sparkling white grape juice into plastic flutes which the girls thought divine.

Before she knew it, six o'clock had arrived: the candles were blown out, the cake cut, and the tea devoured. Maya had managed to pinch only one of the sandwiches.

"Amber's mum, can you do me a pamper party when it's my birthday?" Lottie asked, the remains of chocolate cake at the corners of her mouth.

The doorbell rang, saving Maya from having to answer.

It was Lottie and Hannah's mums, arriving together. Before they'd even stepped into the hallway, they were forced to admire their daughters' nails and make-up, both girls waving their hands in front of their faces excitedly. It being the beginning of half-term week, the girls would get to keep their painted nails for a week before they went back to school.

"Wow, Maya, I might have to get you to do my nails," Lottie's mum said.

"Anytime, just give me a call. Here's my business card." Maya always made sure she had these to hand.

"I will. Thanks so much for having Lottie. I hope she was good."

"They all were."

"Catch you next week for my waxing," Hannah's mum said, waving goodbye. "Thanks so much for the party."

Closing the front door, Maya returned to Amber and Chloe, who were in the lounge choosing another film. With her newly painted nails, Amber tentatively held the remote control to flick through Netflix. Maya was about to explain that she didn't need to worry about smudging her nails, when her mobile rang.

"Hi," she said, seeing it was Emma calling. "How did you cope with ten boys? House still standing?"

"Yes, but we've had a bit of an incident. Lucas has had to take Finley to A&E."

"Oh, God, what happened?"

"I don't think it's anything serious, just a close encounter with a doorframe. But Lucas wants to make sure Finn's nose isn't broken."

"I'll come right away and get Lewis out of your hair."

"Thank you, and sorry." Emma sounded unusually subdued.

Maya put the phone down. She hadn't quite finished putting away all her make-up and nail varnishes, but she shut the lids on the cases, leaving them in the lounge.

"Listen, Amber, I need to pop out quickly to fetch Lewis from Emma's. Do not open the door to anyone, is that clear?"

Chloe's dad, who was collecting her, wasn't arriving until half-past-six, so Maya calculated she had ample time to drive round to Emma's house and be back before he arrived.

Twenty minutes later, she let herself back into the house. Her patience had been tested to breaking point all the way home with Lewis whinging. Exhaustion was starting to set in. She hadn't stopped all day and was ready to collapse on the sofa with a leftover scone. Plus a well-earned glass of wine.

"I'm back!" she called. Lewis went straight to the bottom of the stairs to take off his shoes.

"Mummy!" Amber came running into the hallway. "Chloe's daddy is here. Was it okay we let him in?"

"Oh, er, of course." Flustered, Maya plastered on a smile and entered the lounge. "Hi, I'm Maya…" Her cheery greeting faltered on her lips. Chloe's dad was sitting rigidly on the edge of her sofa, his expression thunderous, hands clasped, fingers twisting his gold wedding ring. He would have been handsome with his dark wavy hair and brown eyes if his face hadn't looked like it was made of stone.

In Maya's absence, Chloe and Amber had evidently found her make-up and dabbled further. Chloe was wearing bright purple and pink eyeshadows and cerise pink lipstick, and blusher was streaked across her face, all coarsely applied with the lack of finesse that only an eleven-year-old would manage. Amber was similarly daubed with blues and greens. The two girls looked like Toyah Willcox in her eighties heyday. Both eyed each other cagily. They knew they'd done wrong.

Before Maya could reprimand them, Chloe's dad stood up and said furiously under his breath, "I didn't think a 'pamper party' would leave my daughter looking like a tart." He beckoned to his daughter. "Come on, Chloe, let's go home and clean this mess off your face."

He ushered her out of the room, leaving Maya gobsmacked, unsure whether to apologise or stand her ground. The two girls had helped themselves to her make-up, after all.

"I did check with all the girls' mums whether they minded make-up —"

"My wife died four years ago, so I'm not sure how you checked with her." His eyes narrowed.

Maya blushed scarlet. She'd assumed that the woman who had dropped Chloe off was her mum. "Look, I'm sorry, I had to pop out for ten minutes to collect my son —"

"You were clearly gone longer than ten minutes." His angry tone shocked Maya into silence.

"I'm sorry." She wanted to explain about Emma and Finley and the trip to hospital, but she couldn't find the words. How dare this man assume that she was an irresponsible mother?

"*You* may feel it's okay to leave *your* daughter at home unattended, but I do not." He barged past Maya and opened the front door. "Come on, Chloe." She followed, waving at Amber sheepishly.

Maya slammed the door behind him, shocked and shaken. If she never saw that man again, it would be too soon. Her hands balled into fists. "What an utter bastard," she muttered. "I *hate* him."

CHAPTER 1

Three months later

Maya, tucked away in the corner of her favourite coffee shop with Emma, took a sip of her skinny latte. "If I go to another candle or card party, I think I might scream."

"Or another child's birthday party," Emma mumbled into her coffee cup.

"Exactly! Right now, it's my only form of socialising. It's the closest I get to going out."

"And you won't meet a new man at an Avon party!" Emma added.

Maya rolled her eyes. *Here we go.*

With it raining and blowing a gale outside, Portishead's seafront was looking particularly bleak and grey, and the café was a cosy refuge from the icy January wind. Maya warmed her hands around the latte glass as Emma fixed her dark brown eyes on her.

Emma Thear had been Maya's best friend since Amber and Emma's son, Finley, had been born within two hours of each other. Bedside buddies in the maternity ward in St Michael's Hospital in Bristol, they'd helped each other with breastfeeding and nappy changing, plus sharing the worries only new mothers had. Then, just over two years later, and three weeks apart, Maya had given birth to Lewis and Emma had had Owen, cementing their relationship further. Over the years they'd become quite a team; Emma was a mobile hairdresser, so she cut and coloured Maya's hair and in return Maya would give her perfect nails — or the odd, much-needed back massage.

Emma was Maya's physical opposite with her long auburn hair, brown eyes and voluptuous figure. And when out together, she always attracted the attention of men, even though she was the married one.

"Hmmm … I'm not sure," Maya said, ignoring Emma's comment. "But I do know the kids have a better social life than me. Every other week there's a birthday party to attend."

"You need a date!" Emma was always unfailingly forthright, and her current favourite subject was finding Maya a boyfriend. "It's been nearly two years now, Maya. You need to start dating again. New year, new you!"

They had an hour before they had to pick up their kids from school. This was their regular Monday afternoon treat: a catch-up over coffee. It had started years ago, when Amber and Finley were asleep in pushchairs, then as the children started pre-school, they'd meet at this café because of the play park outside. While Amber and Finley played, Lewis and Owen would be asleep in pushchairs — if timed right.

Now, they got to relax and talk, undisturbed. A small part of Maya did miss pushing the kids on the swings — it meant they'd grown up, and no longer needed her for some things. Today, however, with Emma's nagging, Maya wasn't finding the catch-up quite so relaxing.

"Emma, we've been over this. I'm not sure I'm ready. I'm quite happy being single," she lied. She did miss cuddles on the sofa, watching the TV, sharing a bottle of wine, the intimacy…

"You're not even forty." Maya would be thirty-nine in May. "You should be dating, being wined and dined…" Emma added.

"How am I going to meet anyone? I've got the kids, remember. Kyle has them once a month — if I'm lucky! And all my friends are happily married."

She knew a couple of friends who were also divorcing, but if truth be told, a heavy night out wasn't Maya's style. She'd been there, done that in her early twenties. Her days of burning the candle at both ends were over. She was too knackered running around after two kids.

She'd started to enjoy her girls' nights out with the mums from school, and she'd figured that if someone was going to come along, then they would. But those nights out happened rarely. Emma was right — she did miss the company of a man, but she could hardly afford to get dolled up and go out every Saturday night in the hope she might meet someone. And one-night stands weren't really her thing. Her ex-husband, Kyle, had only been her third boyfriend, and he had been the love of her life — until he'd cheated on her.

"You don't have to leave your front room, silly. These days, everyone meets online."

Maya screwed up her face. Emma had mentioned online dating in the past, but Maya didn't like the idea of it. It made sense in some ways, but she wasn't convinced it worked. She'd met all her previous boyfriends while out socialising, and they'd shared that instant attraction that had grown the more they'd been together. With Kyle, it had very quickly turned into love rather than infatuation. But back then, she hadn't had two children and responsibilities like a business and a mortgage.

Emma sipped her coffee, swallowed then said, "Why don't you ask Selina? She met her bloke online."

"I don't know…" Maya placed her empty latte glass on the coffee table.

"Talk to her tonight at the PTA meeting." Emma looked at Maya sternly. "Please, for me, give it a try."

Maya chuckled. "For you?"

"You know what I mean. I think you need to get out there. Be brave, Maya, like you once were."

"I am brave. I don't think I have the time — that's all."

"Excuses, excuses." Emma rolled her eyes. "You're beautiful. You'll be snapped up in a flash."

Maya doubted that very much. Yes, she was blonde with blue eyes, and didn't look too bad with make-up on — which she wore most days due to her work. But in all honesty, it was her confidence holding her back. But would she get any more confident leaving it longer? She feared finding no one once her looks were gone. She'd been with Kyle for so long he was all she knew — she hadn't had a relationship with anyone since he'd left. *Two years without sex.* She was too young to be celibate. But Kyle had loved her before children, when her breasts could stay up without a bra, and after, with the stretchmarks and post-pregnancy body.

"Go on, Maya, what have you got to lose?" Emma insisted. She wiped her hands on a napkin, then flicked her hair back over her shoulders.

Maya tried to think of excuses and couldn't come up with any. "Okay, I suppose I need to bite the bullet one day." She wrinkled her nose. She could at least hide behind the computer screen this way. And she could make time when the kids were in bed. "I'll chat with Selina first."

Emma beamed and glanced at her watch. "Oh, shit, we'd best get the kids."

"Oh, yes." Maya pulled on her coat and glanced out of the large café window across the park. The rain continued, making everything dark and miserable.

Tucked under Emma's huge golfing umbrella, Emma and Maya walked as fast as possible up the hill towards the school, leaving the dismal seafront behind them.

They entered the school playground and stood waiting for the bell to ring and their younger children to emerge. The older children would join them — in their own time. There was a scattering of other parents waiting under umbrellas or huddled up to the school buildings to shelter from the rain.

Emma nudged Maya as a smartly dressed man walked past. "Isn't that Chloe's dad?" Emma asked quietly. "Now he's your type of guy." With the umbrella restricting her view, plus her hood pulled up over her head, Maya hadn't caught sight of who it was, just his dark hair at the back of his head. He could have been anybody's dad. "He's talking to Candice's mum," Emma continued, coldly. "She's always in full make-up and heels — just to do the school run! I know we don't turn up in our pyjamas, but she always makes me feel like I'm slumming it."

"I expect she comes straight from work," Maya said.

"You can't work in four-inch heels, even in an office — can you?"

Maya was certainly not interested in Chloe's dad, even though Chloe was one of Amber's best friends. She'd avoided him like the plague since the disastrous end to Amber's birthday party. And fortunately, he'd done the same.

The man must have sensed that Emma and Maya were looking at him. He turned his head, caught Maya's eye, and then with an expression of contempt, he returned his attention to Candice's gorgeous mum.

"Anyway, you know how I feel about *him*." Maya scowled.

"That was months ago. He might have mellowed."

Emma couldn't have noticed how he'd just turned his nose up at them.

"Well, I'm not sure I'd fancy dating a dad from school. Anyway, I thought you wanted me to go online?"

"Yes, I do. And who knows, you might find someone as gorgeous-looking as Chloe's dad on there."

Before they could continue the conversation, the bell rang and the kids streamed out of the classroom like sheep fleeing their pen. Maya and Emma had to adjust and retune their ears from adult talk to the babble and squealing of excited children.

PTA meetings were held once a month on a Monday evening, usually at The Golden Lion pub, a local for Maya, which meant, weather permitting, she could walk there. Emma loathed the thought of being involved, but sometimes she attended the meetings to get out of the house. Tonight, Maya knew why Emma had come along: to make sure she spoke to Selina.

As the assembled group of ten women discussed the success of the Christmas Fair, and planned the next fundraising events, Maya found it hard to concentrate as to her mortification she spied Chloe's dad at a table in the opposite corner of the pub. He was seated next to a stunning woman, laughing and chatting with her and another couple sitting opposite them. She'd been caught watching them, that annoying sixth sense kicking in: Chloe's dad made eye contact with her. His smile dropped instantly, and they each awkwardly broke their gaze. After that, Maya made a concerted effort to focus on the school meeting. She shouldn't waste time overthinking his obnoxious rudeness. But it riled her that he continued to punish the girls; he still wouldn't allow Chloe over for tea with Amber.

Once all the items on the agenda had been discussed, and some of the mums had sloped off home, Maya caught up with Selina, who still had wine left in her glass and hadn't needed to dash off. Selina's eldest son, Toby, was in the same class as Amber, so they knew each other fairly well.

"Hey, Selina, can I have a quick word before you go?" Egged on by Emma, Maya moved round the table to talk to her.

"Yes, sure." Selina smiled.

"I hope you don't mind me asking, but I'm looking for some advice about online dating. I was wondering how you'd got on," Maya said as quietly as she could, not wanting everyone to hear.

"Hey, no problem. But it's been a while since I've done online dating."

"Oh."

"Yes, I've met someone. I've been dating Kelvin for five months now. Seems to be going well."

"I'm really happy for you."

"Yeah, I might have found the one." Selina crossed her fingers, looking happy. Maya hoped she would find that kind of connection again.

Selina named the dating site she'd used to meet Kelvin. "Might be worth dabbling with the free sites before thinking of signing up to a paid one."

"So, is it safe?" Maya couldn't help asking.

"Yes, but whenever I went on a date, I would tell a friend where I was going and who I was meeting."

"Yes, you can text me!" Emma interrupted.

"I would also text a friend that I was home safe," Selina said. "Just make sure you meet somewhere public, and that you chat a bit on the site first before moving it to text messages. A phone call before you meet them is a good idea too. But some don't like to chat on the phone. And some do." Selina shrugged.

"Okay, thanks for the info."

Selina finished her wine. "Good luck and let me know how you get on. You do have to sort the wheat from the chaff, but it's worth it!"

"Thanks so much for all your advice."

In the pub car park, Emma and Maya hugged.

"Right, Missus," Emma said sternly, "I want you to go straight home and take a look at that site Selina suggested. Let's get you dating!"

Maya sighed. "Yes, boss." She loved her best friend, and Emma was right. There was no point putting this off. She had to get herself back out there. Kyle had moved on, and so should she.

CHAPTER 2

"Chloe! Tea's on the table," Sam Trescott shouted up the stairs to his daughter. He knew she'd be plugged into her iPod, her music too loud for her young ears. Another minute and he'd knock on her door.

He returned to the stove and turned down the potatoes that were boiling, while reading a text from his mate, Daryl, asking if he was up for an impromptu game of badminton. Sam texted Daryl back: *Sorry, can't do tonight. No babysitter.*

Sometimes his mates forgot it was just him and Chloe. His sister Heather and her husband Tom stepped in as often as they could, but tonight wasn't their usual night to help.

OK mate, Daryl replied. *Have you tried that online dating site yet?*

Sam shook his head at the text. "Give me a chance, Daryl," he said out loud as he typed: *No, not yet.* Daryl had only mentioned it last weekend. Sam still wasn't sure, but Heather was also nagging him to start dating again. Now Joe, his younger brother, was settling down — much to the family's surprise — Heather was keen to see that Sam was too.

He'd been a widower for four years and still couldn't bring himself to think seriously about meeting another woman. He'd tried dating too soon after Jade had died from cancer. It had been disastrous. Every woman he'd met, he'd compared to Jade. It had just made him miss his wife even more. If it hadn't been for Chloe, he didn't know where his life would be.

Even now, he couldn't shift the thought that it would be a betrayal to his wife, to sleep with another woman. Daryl, younger than Sam and single, had told him many times that he was allowed to date again. Daryl didn't understand that dating any other woman felt like trying to find a replacement. Maybe it would feel different, if he'd been like some of his friends who'd divorced or separated, having fallen out of love with their partners. But his love for Jade hadn't died when she had.

"No, it's not!"

Sam turned to see Chloe, her expression disapproving with her hands on her hips. *Only a couple more years and I'll have a teenage girl to contend with*, he thought. He had never imagined the attitude would creep in from the age of eleven.

"No, it's not what?" Sam asked as patiently as he could, ignoring the tone his daughter was taking with him.

"You said tea was on the table. And it's not. *Clearly.*"

"Oh, right, sorry, no. I said that, love, because usually you take forever to come to the table. Have you washed your hands?"

"Yes," Chloe said with a huff.

"Chloe, less of the attitude please."

Sam heard another unladylike grunt from his daughter as she took her seat. Concerned he was running late to dish up dinner, he quickly drained the new potatoes, sharing them between the two plates. The steaks were done; he flipped them onto the plate from the frying pan, then shared out the baby carrots and green beans, and poured peppercorn sauce onto his own plate. He would leave Chloe to pour her own, so he placed the jug on the table.

"Can't I have tomato ketchup?"

"No, you can't have tomato ketchup and ruin a good steak."

"I want ketchup."

"You won't get anything if you forget your manners. What's the matter with you, anyway?"

"I want to go to Amber's next weekend." Chloe sat, arms folded, knife and fork still lying either side of her plate. "But you said I could never go to Amber's again!"

"Oh." Sam picked up his own cutlery. He had said that, very angrily, on the way home in the car after collecting Chloe, who had looked a mess. "I'll think about it."

"You always say that!" Chloe huffed. "And then you always say no." She glared. "You make some excuse we have plans, but I'd rather see my best friend!"

"Oh." Frowning, Sam cut his steak.

It had been a few months since *that* party, and Heather had lectured him enough over his overreaction to Chloe looking like some eighties rock chick. She'd laughed, saying how her girls always found her make-up. She'd been more disappointed Sam hadn't snapped a photo on his phone. He still wasn't sure about Amber's mother leaving the two girls unattended; his forgiveness wouldn't quite stretch that far yet. Heather seemed to think he was overreacting about that too — but he didn't agree. Although Jade had used to accuse him of being stubborn…

"Oh, Dad, please can I go? Amber's grandparents are taking them to Bristol Zoo. She's allowed to take a friend."

Maybe this would be a good test to build bridges with Amber's family. The two girls were clearly great friends, and Amber had certainly helped Chloe settle into her new life. In fact, she missed her mother less and loved school more these days.

And possibly Chloe needed to be rewarded. She was a good girl — mostly — and moving to Portishead could have gone one of two ways, but she was thriving.

Now eleven, this September Chloe would be moving up to secondary school. Maybe Sam needed to let go of the reins a bit and let his not so little girl gain some independence. Maybe Heather was right and he was being too overprotective. It was so hard to know what to do for the best — and he was the only one making that decision now, without Jade to discuss things with.

"Okay, you can tell Amber you can go," he said with a sigh.

"I can?" Chloe's thunderous expression cleared instantly.

"Yes. You can go this once. I can't always say yes, but we've no plans this weekend." He watched Chloe try some of the creamy peppercorn sauce and not screw her face up. "Is it a special occasion?"

"No, silly," Chloe replied. "It's just because we're best friends."

"I know you are." Sam smiled. He was relieved his daughter enjoyed her new school. Making the decision to move to Portishead to live nearer to Heather and Tom had been a difficult one at the time, but with the engineering project manager job coming up in Bristol, leaving Swindon had seemed the right thing to do. The job was stressful and demanding at times, but the balance of an easier home life and the easier commute outweighed the stress. "And in future, can you ask me before getting yourself into a state?"

"Yes, Dad."

Sam shook his head as he concentrated on his dinner, trying to understand why Chloe had been unable to ask him and instead decided the answer would be no, putting her into a foul mood.

The night time routine went without a hitch, and Chloe read for a while before turning her light out at eight-thirty.

With his own chores done, Sam walked into his study and switched on his PC. He looked up the couple of online dating sites Daryl had mentioned: Find My HEA (short for Happy

26

Ever After) or Soul Mate Search. Daryl had said these two had proved successful for him, although he was still single. But then Daryl was the kind of guy who liked being single. He argued he hadn't found 'the one' yet. Sam believed he was more of a player with his good looks and charm. His idea of 'success' was very different to what Sam wanted.

What the hell, he'd take a look. However, he soon realised he couldn't actually take a look unless he created a profile.

Sam's heart sped with trepidation. From his previous disastrous online dating experience, he remembered that he did already have an account on Find My HEA — but could he remember the password? His laptop remembered the username… But could he be bothered to look tonight?

No, he couldn't bring himself to do it. Not yet.

He logged off and picked up the photo of Jade on his desk.

He'd do it tomorrow.

CHAPTER 3

Bleary-eyed, Maya poured breakfast cereal into bowls and placed glasses of orange juice in front of her children and remembered why she needed a full eight hours' sleep — or at least seven. She didn't have the patience for the children's bickering. The whole school run was grating on her this morning.

She had stayed up past midnight again, opening an online dating account on one of the sites Selina had recommended — the one she'd met Kelvin on. Maya had thought it best to go with that one. Maybe there would be less chaff and more wheat.

It had taken up most of her evening, making her late going to bed. She couldn't afford to commit this level of time continuously. Maya normally used her evenings to order stock and read up on the latest beauty treatments and products in *Guild News* and *The Beauty Professional*, which she subscribed to. And then there were her accounts. She had a business to run! And she liked *some* downtime before bed.

Now she realised why she hadn't dated in so long. She simply didn't have the time.

This morning, Selina had booked Maya for some beauty treatments. Kelvin was taking her away for the weekend — their first break away together — so she wanted a manicure, pedicure and waxing.

"I'm so excited," Selina said, lying on Maya's massage bed, ready for her bikini wax. "Have you set yourself up online yet? How's it going?"

Maya was pleased Selina had broached the subject. She'd held off, unsure whether to raise it. "Yes, but I haven't put up a profile picture yet." She wasn't very good at the whole selfie thing — only girls in their teens and twenties had perfected looking beautiful while pouting at a camera an arm's length away. She'd only partly filled out the information the site requested.

Maya ripped at the wax and Selina gave a gasp.

"Oh, sorry, should have warned you that bit would hurt." Maya winced, forgetting how she was used to administering these treatments. *Concentrate.*

Before she'd had children, Maya had worked as a beautician in the spa at one of Portishead's luxury hotels, a job she'd loved. After the children had been born, she'd returned briefly, before agreeing with Kyle to convert a room in their large house and became self-employed. Clients had come to her and it had worked conveniently around the kids and school holidays. But after Kyle had left — or rather after she'd kicked him out — the family home had had to be sold to split their financial assets.

Maya could forgive Kyle for no longer loving her: after all, relationships faltered. But she'd never forgive him for cheating on her. If there had been problems, they should have discussed it.

Contrary to expectations, Maya loved her cosy semi-detached cottage. Every decorating decision had been hers. There had been no one to moan that the colour was too dark, or not to his taste — Kyle would have had magnolia throughout. It may have needed some cosmetic updating — which her dad had helped with — but it was comfortable. She and the kids had lived in it for just over a year now. The school was still within walking distance. It was more manageable, and a new start for the three of them. This way, Maya could live comfortably and affordably. But it meant taking her beauty business mobile.

She'd downsized the house but upgraded the car to an estate, so that she could fit in a massage bed and any other equipment she would need for her clients. To keep up with the latest beauty trends, she sent herself on courses and learnt new treatments: with Kyle no longer there to provide financial stability — apart from the child maintenance — she needed to stand on her own two feet.

"You never warned me how time-consuming it would be," Maya said, thinking of the lack of sleep she'd had last night as she pasted on warm wax, then ripped it off with strips of muslin.

"Yes, sorry, I forgot that," Selina said with a grimace. "Try to restrict when you go on the site. I would only go on in the evenings, once Toby was asleep."

Maya agreed. She wouldn't be in a bar at a lunchtime trying to pull, so maybe she needed to restrict her online search for a date to the evenings as well.

"Hey, but high five." Selina raised her newly manicured hand, and Maya slapped it. "You've done it, you've braved the internet and got yourself out there."

Yes, she had. Tonight, she would upload a photo and give this online dating thing a proper go.

CHAPTER 4

"Hey, have you eaten?" Heather greeted Sam as he entered her spacious, designer kitchen. Tall and slim, with brown eyes and long, dark, wavy hair similar to Sam's, she was a prettier version of her brother. "I've saved you some stew."

On Thursdays, Heather always collected Chloe from school, which allowed Sam to work late and play a game of badminton with Daryl.

Last April, Heather had convinced Sam to move to Portishead. She'd told him often enough how much she loved helping him out with childcare for Chloe. It also meant with less of a commute from Swindon to Bristol, he saw his daughter more too.

Heather lived in a similar townhouse to Sam; both were new-builds on the hill above Portishead marina. They were within walking distance of one another. Heather and Tom had a larger house, with four bedrooms, whereas Sam's was a three-bedroom.

"Oh, great. That would be lovely." Heather always fed Sam. Maybe she'd made another promise to Jade, or their own mother, that she'd make sure he ate well. These past four years had been tough, but life was getting steadily better, and had certainly improved once Sam made the decision to move away from Swindon and the home he and Jade had shared. He'd worried he'd lose his memories of Jade, leaving the house, but Chloe was a constant reminder of her mother.

As Heather dished up Sam's dinner, she called out, "Chloe, your dad's here."

"Leave her, sounds like they're having fun." He could hear the three girls laughing in the front room.

"Yes, they're playing Hungry Hippos. Daisy and Scarlett love that game." Heather pulled a face. "I do not. I *would* say it keeps them quiet…" She paused to listen. There was a bashing, scraping noise and lots of screaming and laughter. "But it's more that they play nicely together with it."

Sam tucked into his beef and ale stew. Heather had slow-cooked it and the meat was falling apart, moist and succulent.

"Sam…" Heather paused, eyeing the door behind Sam, as if to make sure the girls wouldn't disturb them. "Chloe confided in me today, on the way out of school."

"About what?" Sam's mind raced.

"Oh, don't panic." Heather gave a little chuckle, as if reading Sam's worried expression. "She talked about her mum and then said how she would like you to find someone else. I think she had been talking with friends at breaktime. Amber was discussing her mum. And Toby's mum, Selina, has got a new boyfriend, and Toby was saying how much he liked him. Chloe's worried you'll be lonely, and that her mum wouldn't want that."

"And what did you say?"

"I agreed that Jade wouldn't want you to be on your own, and I told Chloe I'd made her mum a promise. So, I told her not to worry: Aunty Heather has it all under control." Heather tapped her nose.

"Right." Sam forked another mouthful of stew. "Where's Tom?" he asked, wanting to change the subject.

Then there was a deep, manly laugh from the lounge, making the girls scream and giggle louder. Heather raised an eyebrow, with her hands on her hips. "He's winding up the girls. We've all eaten." Sometimes Tom got home from work at the same time as Sam arrived, and the two men would talk as they ate together. Other times, his work being flexible as a self-employed electrician, he was already home in time to eat with his family.

Tom entered the kitchen, wearing jeans and a polo shirt, and not his workwear, which meant he'd probably been home for some time. "Hello, Sam, I thought I heard you come in. Fancy a beer?" Tom kissed his wife, then went to the fridge and pulled out two bottles of Stella. Sam's brother-in-law was over six feet tall, with a stocky frame and blonde hair showing no sign of grey yet. He looked intimidating but was as soft as a teddy bear and had the growl of a kitten when it came to it.

"Go on, then," Sam said. "Thanks." With a pop and clink, Tom opened them up and placed one in front of Sam. Tom gave his wife an affectionate squeeze on the shoulder, then drank from his own bottle.

Sometimes Sam envied his sister and brother-in-law. Yes, they had their fair share of arguments like any ordinary married couple, but Tom seemed to keep his family unit together. That's all Sam wanted — his family unit back.

Heather opened her laptop and sat down opposite Sam. Tom gave a frown over her shoulder that only Sam could see. He hunched over his wife to get a closer look at the screen.

"What are you doing, darling? Looking for a toy boy? Isn't one man enough for you?"

"I'm setting Sam up on an online dating site." She smirked at Sam, then looked up at her husband, who dropped a kiss onto her lips.

"You're what?" Sam said, half choking on a tender piece of beef he was chewing.

"Come on, it's about time you got yourself back out there. I'm giving you the push. I promised Chloe I was on the case, so I'd better stick to my word. And if Joe can settle down, you certainly deserve a second chance."

"Heather…" Sam scowled.

"She's got a point, mate. It's been a while now. And Jade wanted you to live, not linger," Tom said, swigging his beer.

Sam rolled his eyes. "Did Chloe put you up to this?"

"She's concerned that you're not dating because of her."

"That's ridiculous." But was it true? Was he nervous of meeting someone else because of Chloe? What if they didn't like his daughter? What if Chloe didn't like his new woman?

"She's worried you think she won't like the idea." Heather's voice softened; the teasing dropped. "Sam, do you feel ready to date?"

Sam shrugged. "I don't know. I think I've been letting life do its thing and believed someone would come along when they're supposed to."

"I think you need to try online dating. Everybody does it these days," Heather said, her fingers tapping at the keyboard again.

Sam pulled a face. "It didn't work very well last time."

"You tried it too soon. And you were unlucky. But you should consider it again."

"Maybe…"

Once Sam had finished his dinner, Heather swung the laptop around to show him what she'd set up.

"Right, you're SamJT26," she said. The internet dating site was called Soul Mate Search, and she'd added a couple of pictures on there — pictures Chloe had taken and Heather had retrieved off Instagram. Thank goodness she hadn't made the one with him wearing an elf T-shirt and hat, holding a glass of mulled wine, his actual profile picture. He supposed it showed he had a good sense of humour, but he wasn't sure it was his most flattering.

"Heather, I could have done this."

"No, I don't think you would. You worry you're betraying Jade. And you're not." Heather pointed to the screen. "You can update your images. I think you're allowed eight for free — just don't use your Facebook profile picture."

"Yeah, yeah, I know."

He read the short profile Heather had written. It was very complimentary — he wasn't sure he would have sold himself so well, but none of it was a lie. Not only had she shared that he was a widower bringing up a beautiful daughter, she'd written he was a good cook, had an eclectic taste in music, played badminton to keep himself trim, was tidy around the house and liked things in their place.

"Does that make me sound like the obsessive psychopath in *Sleeping With The Enemy*?" Sam chuckled nervously, combing his hand through his hair.

"No, women like to know that guys are tidy and not over-mothered," Heather said. "The fact you're raising your daughter on your own is a strength women will admire."

"I'm still not sure whether you should state I'm a widower. Won't women be put off?"

"Let's start off truthful, huh?"

"If you're avoided like the plague, then maybe you could just change it to single," Tom said.

"There are other sites you can go on, but my friend recommended this one," Heather explained. "You can update your profile some more later." She narrowed her eyes, her expression stern. "But promise me you'll give this a go."

"Yes, yes…" Sam really wished he could have another beer. It was *nearly* the weekend.

"Oh, and give me your phone." Heather held out her hand and clicked her fingers.

"Heather," he said sternly. "Has Jade possessed you or something?"

"I know you're capable, but I'm not having you come up with some excuse, like you didn't have time to set it up."

With a huff, Sam retrieved his iPhone from his pocket. He unlocked the screen then gave it to Heather, who downloaded the Soul Mate Search app. She set it all up, so all he had to do was press the button, as if he was some kind of technophobe. In reality, he worked in aerospace engineering and dealt with advanced technology every day.

As he was leaving, with Chloe already running towards his car and Tom leaning against the front doorframe, holding Daisy and Scarlett back from running after her, Heather caught his arm.

"Sam, you won't be betraying Jade's memory. It won't mean you love her any less. She really wouldn't want you living the rest of your life alone."

He nodded. "I know."

Heather hugged him. "Even if you just date for a while and find your feet, it will help. The first person you meet isn't likely to be the one, but it will give you some confidence, get you out of the house."

"Are you implying I'm a recluse?"

"Of course not. But there's more to life than work and badminton." Heather chuckled. "And who knows, you might find a date for Joe's wedding." She winked.

"That's in August!" Sam hated how high his voice sounded. Heather laughed again.

"Dad, come on!" Chloe shouted from inside the car, the passenger door open.

"But your daughter won't be around forever. Eventually she'll be off doing her own thing in the world," Heather said.

Sam nodded. It didn't bear thinking about: Chloe growing up … coming home late, getting boyfriends, turning him greyer.

He still wasn't sure if he wanted to date. Heather was cajoling him into this. Would women even want to date a widower?

CHAPTER 5

Embracing the new year, Maya had joined a running club. There was a meet every day, including Saturday mornings that Maya couldn't usually make, so she intended to make the effort this particular Saturday, thanks to her parents giving her a break.

Her mum and dad had invested in an annual membership at Bristol Zoo, which wasn't far from where they lived, and both her kids thoroughly enjoyed visiting. They would probably come back with their faces painted, even if Amber was getting too old for it. Her parents deserved a medal, because this weekend not only were they taking out Amber and Lewis, they were also allowing them each to bring a friend. Amber had invited Chloe, and Lewis had chosen Emma's son, Owen. Maya supposed it was her dad's way of making use of his seven-seater car.

Maya enjoyed running on her own, but decided there would be something supportive and encouraging about running with a group of people. It might give her more motivation to get out there, with the added bonus of meeting new people too. This had been Emma's hint and probably why she'd agreed to join her this morning — to make sure Maya didn't chicken out. Being a mixed ability group, it pushed her to run faster and further. She'd only been a few times so far but had thoroughly enjoyed it. Depending on the day, the meetings were structured to practise and improve certain elements of your training. Today was a general run, with an option to run a longer distance, and take it at your own pace.

"Promise not to go too fast. My boobs aren't cut out for fast running," Emma said, stretching out her calves one at a time, then pulling up her ankle behind her to stretch her quads, copying Maya. "In fact, I'm not even sure *I'm* cut out for running."

"You just need to get yourself a good sports bra. Come on, it'll do you good."

There were about thirty runners of all shapes, sizes and ages, and about a fifty-fifty split of men and women. It being January, some wore running gloves, headbands to keep ears warm, and brightly coloured jackets. Some were in tracksuits, some in running gear, like Maya. Despite the sun being out, it was still cold, and their breath misted as they chatted. This was an easy pace run today, so she knew it would be slow enough for Emma. Probably too slow for Maya, but exercise was exercise and the catch-up with Emma would be good. As they ran with their small group, Maya told Emma about her online dating activities. It had been a week since she had taken Selina's advice and set up a profile on Find My HEA. Selina had mentioned this one and Soul Mate Search, but Maya thought it best to stick to one site for now.

The messages she had received! A lot of men only put *Hi*. Maya wasn't sure how to respond to those. Some sent 'wow, you're really pretty' kind of messages. She wasn't sure how to respond to those either. A couple commented on some of the things she'd put in her profile, and so at least this reassured her they had read it. In fact, she was starting to add to it a bit more, now she was seeing what other members had written. She couldn't be bothered with those who wrote 'just ask me' on their profile. If they couldn't make the effort to write a bit about themselves, what sort of effort would they put into a date?

After half an hour of deliberating over her username, she had chosen LoisLane38. Lois was her favourite heroine: a strong, independent woman, a risk-taker, who had Superman as her hero… Was Maya holding out for a hero…? She'd liked that line so much she'd updated her profile with it.

"I can't believe how many men have messaged me," Maya told Emma as they ran side by side.

"Of course they have, you're gorgeous. And when they find out what a fantastic personality you have…"

"I don't want to appear rude, so I've been replying to them all. It takes forever."

"Maya," Emma laughed, her cheeks rosy from the exertion now as they jogged, "I don't think you need to reply to everyone."

"Okay, that would make life easier."

"I think in this game," Emma puffed, "they've got to accept that not everyone is going to reply. Some of those guys are just fishing, probably messaging every woman on there to see who bites, and if they've been on there a while, then you're like … fresh meat."

"Thanks." Maya shuddered as she ran. But considering some of the messages she'd received, it now made sense.

They were running along the promenade now, the sea to their left, the sky clear, the wind cold and unforgiving. Maya and Emma's favourite café was to their right. It would be so easy to slip off and take refuge…

Maya giggled. "There was this guy — MrGrey19 was his username." At the time, Maya had rolled her eyes at yet another username referring to *Fifty Shades*.

"Oh, *please*, I bet he thinks women all want *that*," Emma scoffed. "You'd think he'd use something more original."

"Yes, I was tempted to write, 'sorry, not into BDSM'. But I just said, 'thanks for contacting me, but I don't think you're my type'. I didn't realise he was online, and he replied immediately, with something along the lines of 'that's a shame, I liked your profile'. Then he pretty much accused me of being shallow for having a type. I was only trying to be polite!"

"Idiot!" Emma said. "Not you, him. As if telling you you're shallow is going to help his case."

This was the first time Maya had had a hostile response. Usually they simply didn't reply or were polite, signing off, 'happy searching'. Maya wasn't shallow. Or at least she hoped not. But looks were important. She usually went for nice eyes. She'd been mesmerised by Kyle's the day she'd met him. And his cheeky smile. It had been like looking at George Clooney, in his younger *ER* days. She didn't think she really had a specific type, but MrGrey19 definitely wasn't for her.

Once back at the sports centre, they stretched and warmed down. Sweat trickled down Maya's hairline and neck, but the January chill made her shiver. She hadn't taken her water bottle with her; for such a short distance, she didn't need it. She'd stored it in a locker with her handbag. She would shower once she got home. Emma was visiting the ladies as Maya retrieved her belongings from the locker, taking a large glug from her bottle. Quickly, shutting the locker, she turned and *oomph!* Something hard jabbed her ribs, knocking her off balance. She fell heavily on her bottom and winced.

Chloe's dad. Holding a badminton racket. She held in her cry of pain as best she could.

"Oh, gosh, sorry," she said, not knowing where to look, still sprawled out on the floor, the water bottle rolling away from her.

"No, no, I'm sorry," he said, a mixture of initial shock then concern etched across his face. He held out his hand to haul her back onto her feet. She stumbled into him, her legs still not balanced. He was wearing an immaculate white cotton T-shirt and shorts and smelt clean and fresh. The stunning brunette from the pub stood beside him; his (much younger) girlfriend and badminton partner, Maya assumed, as she also carried a racket. The woman *rocked* in skinny bright sportswear, hair tied back immaculately, make-up in place.

Maya had no make-up on and was all sweaty. She stepped away from him quickly, releasing his grip, realising her hands were horribly sweaty too.

The glamourous brunette was asking if Maya was okay, too, handing back her runaway water bottle, but if Maya wasn't already red-faced from running, she certainly was now, and couldn't answer her.

"Are you really okay … uh?" Chloe's dad asked, frowning.

"It's Maya."

"Maya, yes… I'm Sam — Chloe's dad."

She knew who he was. She just wanted a portal to open, so she could escape to another time or realm.

"Yes, yes … I'm fine," she stuttered. Before either of them could say anything more to her, Maya bolted off down the corridor and out of the front entrance towards the car park. Chloe's dad was shouting something about seeing her later.

Oh God, she would too. She waved a hand but was too embarrassed to look back.

Outside, she caught sight of her reflection in a window. Ponytail askew, strands of hair all over the place, she looked like her head had been in a plasma ball. Cheeks redder than a clown's. *Shit!* She really knew how to make a good impression on Chloe's dad.

CHAPTER 6

Rejuvenated, Sam was now home from his energetic mixed doubles game of badminton with his work colleagues, Daryl and Vicky, and her wife, Zara.

Now refreshed by a hot shower that eased his achy limbs, Sam couldn't shake off thoughts of bumping into Amber's mum. Literally. Too busy looking at his phone and not where he was going. He was sure the handle of his racket had caught her in the ribs. *What a buffoon.* He knew they didn't see eye to eye, but it didn't mean it was okay to send the poor woman flying. He couldn't forget her expression of horror upon realising who he was and how fast she'd tried to get away from him. If she'd walked any faster, she'd have been running. Probably thought he'd give her another unnecessary outburst.

She thinks you're a knob, he thought. He needed to remedy that when he collected Chloe later. He'd spent the whole badminton match wondering how to. Daryl and Zara had thrashed him and Vicky due to his lack of concentration.

Sam went to store his badminton racket in his study and glanced at his laptop on his desk. He still had some time until he needed to collect Chloe.

Amber's grandparents had picked Chloe up early that morning, so he had the whole day to himself; he wasn't collecting Chloe until after tea at Amber's house. Even though he was keeping himself busy, he missed his daughter. She was growing up so fast, too. Weekends were his quality time with her now, as he didn't see her so much during the week when she was at school. When she was a baby, he'd come home from work and immediately be on bath and bedtime story duties. Now, she was happy to entertain herself. She would listen to music on the smartphone she'd got for Christmas, bury her nose in a book (just like Jade used to) or dabble in art and craft activities. The amount of glitter Sam found!

With a mug of coffee in his hand, he read and answered his emails. Apparently, he had new messages on the dating sites, so he logged into them.

Sam opened Soul Mate Search. He was still miffed Heather had created the profile for him without asking, but maybe this was the kick in the proverbial he needed.

He decided he should delete his old profile on Find My HEA. His username was PeterPan26. He typed in the password he thought it would be, and it worked. This old profile hadn't been updated in three years; he'd even deleted all the photos and details off it. It showed only his star sign, profession and that he had children, and didn't want any more.

A few years ago, he would have loved another child. But as they'd started to plan for one, Jade had got sick and it had finalised the decision for them both.

He had friends at work, similar ages to him, who were just starting a family, but Sam wasn't sure he could face the nappies, the lack of sleep and the food being thrown from a high-chair stage all over again. He could do more with Chloe now: the cinema, walks, sports, even take her shopping.

He was about to delete this account when he suddenly saw her. A stunning photo at the bottom of his screen, standing out among other women: Amber's mum. Maya. Her profile name: LoisLane38.

She looked so different to the woman he'd argued with back in October. Her profile photo showed a calm, confident woman, who looked a great deal prettier when smiling and not scowling. Admittedly, it was he who had caused the scowl.

And this morning, seeing her all flushed from her run, the hollow of her neck and chest shining with moisture, something inside Sam had stirred. For the first time in four years, he'd felt aroused. She'd looked *hot*.

Should he read her profile?

She wouldn't know it was him, as long as he kept this profile blank. And he was going to delete it anyway. He hesitated, the mouse curser hovering over her picture. Feeling a bit like a stalker, his heart quickened with a guilt. He felt as if he was spying on the woman. But intrigue made him click on the photo.

Had he misjudged her back in October? In her profile, she came across as level-headed and sensible, looking for similar things in a partner that he would want — that is, if he was seriously looking for one. Because he wasn't. He'd let Heather think he was to keep her off his back. He perused all Maya's pictures. They were all very flattering. There was a sadness in her eyes, though.

Before he realised what he was doing, Sam typed:

Wonderful profile. It's very refreshing to read. You have a beautiful smile.

However, I thought Batman was the superhero women craved?

He picked something out of her profile, hoping it would encourage her to reply. Did he want her to reply? What was he doing?

This was the same woman who'd left his daughter unattended while she'd popped out on an errand.

She was also the same woman who'd looked bloody fantastic in running leggings. Too late anyway, he'd sent it.

For now, Sam couldn't let on who he was. She might be embarrassed at the thought that someone she knew (albeit not that well) was messaging her. And he couldn't delete the account now, in case she replied…

He couldn't put a photo up now, even if he wanted to, especially as he'd messaged Maya. What would that look like?

He remembered Chloe had taken a photo of him one snowy day, a couple of years ago. He'd been wearing a woolly hat and had wrapped a scarf around his mouth, so only his eyes were visible. But those had been covered with sunglasses, because the sun had been low. He searched for the photograph and found it on Facebook. He uploaded it to this profile. There, he had a picture. He was unrecognisable, but it was him.

Or maybe he should delete this profile after all…?

CHAPTER 7

"Hello! Did you all have a fun time?"

Four children, each with their faces painted, and two worn-out grandparents trudged through Maya's front door. Emma was sitting in Maya's kitchen, nursing a glass of Prosecco. They'd headed to The Mall at Cribbs Causeway on the outskirts of Bristol after the running club, having showered and changed.

"I've got pizzas in the oven. Mum, Dad, did you want some?" Maya asked, as the kids slipped off their shoes in the hallway. Maya already knew what the answer would be. Her parents, Fern and Doug, shook their heads, leaving on their coats. "I can do you something else, if you don't fancy pizza."

"If you don't mind, love, we'll head home. It's been fun, but a long day," Fern said, giving Maya a hug.

"I understand. Thank you so much." Maya kissed her parents. "I don't know what I'd do without you two."

Maya's parents were great at giving her some respite from the kids. Single mums with willing ex-partners got a day or a weekend off, when the kids went to visit their dads. Maya didn't have this luxury often. She really had her children twenty-four-seven. Of course, she loved them, but sometimes she wanted more from life than just being a mum. And her parents, particularly her mother, understood that. When things got too much, with everything piling on top of her, all Maya wanted was someone to ease the burden, to make life that bit warmer, more loving and pleasant. Someone to tell her she was doing a good job, and to love her for it, flaws and all. For now, her own mother fulfilled that role.

"It's never a problem, and we enjoy the special time with our grandchildren," Doug said, squeezing Maya's shoulder. "It's all about making memories."

"Anytime, love, but we'll skip pizza. We're going to grab a takeaway, aren't we, Doug?" Fern winked at her husband. "And we'll put our feet up in front of the telly tonight."

"And not move, I hope!" Maya said. "Sounds like a plan." She kissed them both, then waved her mum and dad off. "Thanks again!"

Emma also shouted through her thanks, although she could hardly be heard over the excited children. Maya returned to her small, busy kitchen. She'd left Emma in charge of the pizzas in the oven.

"Wow, I handed over a son and a tiger returned," Emma said ruffling Owen's hair. Lewis had chosen to be Spiderman. The girls had delicate butterflies on their cheeks. Pretty and tasteful, and a little bit more grown up. Hopefully Chloe's dad wouldn't go ballistic.

With four impatient, hungry children around the kitchen table, Maya got the pizzas out of the oven while Emma topped up her Prosecco. She had bought enough pizzas so that she and Emma could tuck into a few slices and not have to worry about cooking later. The Prosecco was starting to go to her head, so Maya made sure she ate plenty of food.

The doorbell rang as the kids were finishing up their bowls of ice-cream. Luckily, Maya had had a Walls Viennetta in the freezer on emergency standby.

"It's probably Lucas," Emma said, finishing her drink. "I texted him ten minutes ago. I don't fancy walking home in the dark and the rain."

With her Prosecco flute in hand, Maya left Emma in charge as she went to open the front door.

"Your wife awaits… Oh! Hello…" Maya said, her tone changing from jovial to surprised. Internally she cringed. "Sorry, I was expecting Emma's husband."

"No, sadly it's just me, Chloe's dad." Sam gave an amused smile.

"Yes, of course." Automatically Maya held out her hand, switching the glass to her left, and he shook it. "As you can see, this time, I'm in. Supervising." What was she saying? She became conscious of the glass of Prosecco in her hand — it wasn't even seven o'clock.

Sam let out a nervous chuckle and his gaze dropped to the ground.

"Is it Lucas? Tell him we'll be five minutes. We've just got our second bottle of Prosecco to finish!" Emma shouted from the kitchen, laughing.

Maya blushed. She thought it best not to shout back to Emma. What would Sam think? He already thought she was a bad mother for allowing her daughter to plaster her face in make-up and leaving her unsupervised in the house. Did he now think she was irresponsibly getting drunk while looking after his daughter?

"Erm … did you want to come in for a minute? Chloe is just finishing her ice-cream."

"I can wait here — if that's easier." He stood awkwardly, hands in his pockets.

Maya frowned. "I'm not sure how long she'll be. Come through." Before realising what she was suggesting, the words escaped her. She just hoped Emma left with four kids hadn't allowed carnage to happen in the kitchen.

"Okay, if you're sure." Sam spotted the pile of shoes in the hallway. "Do you need me to remove my shoes?"

Maya shook her head. "No, you're quite all right."

She had no idea what to say to this man as she took in his appearance. He was wearing jeans and a casual grey shirt with the top buttons open, revealing the hollow of his neck. Taller than she'd realised, he had short, wavy, dark brown hair with a sprinkle of silver through the sides. His eyes were the colour of roasted chestnuts, with crow's feet creasing at the corners, giving him away as in his early forties. She realised he was actually quite handsome in a Colin Firth type of way.

Don't be deceived by his appearance, Maya, she thought. *Head up his arse, remember.*

Sam cleared his throat. "Look, um, I'm sorry about before…" he began.

"Before?" Maya frowned. "Oh! At the gym?"

"Oh, yes, and at the gym, I think I caught you with my racket. I didn't hurt you, did I?"

"Maya, the Prosecco's getting warm! You must need a top up!" Emma called again from the kitchen. Maya could hear the children giggling and imagined Emma pulling faces. She had a way of getting down to their level. But it wasn't what Maya needed right now, with Sam in her hallway.

"Oh, no, no." She shook her head, the embarrassment of bumping into him at the sports centre, sweaty and smelly, making her even more uncomfortable in his presence. "So… Shall I fetch Chloe?" She thumbed behind her towards the kitchen. "Or would you like to come through?"

"Uh…" He paused, thinking about it. "No, I'll come through. No rush."

Sam followed Maya through to the kitchen, where Emma was hurrying Owen and the rest of the children up. "This is Emma. Emma, Sam."

"Oh, hello," Emma said, smiling at Sam, holding the Prosccco bottle. Maya put her glass on the kitchen counter, and didn't encourage Emma to top it up, worried she would look like some alcoholic lush in Sam's eyes.

"Dad!" Chloe shouted, jumping up from the table and hugging her father. Sam returned the embrace. Maya noticed Sam still wore his wedding ring. She watched nervously for a negative reaction about the butterfly on Chloe's face, but to her relief none came.

"Have you had a good time?" Sam asked, still holding his daughter.

For a moment Maya forgot he was an idiot, as she could see he was a doting dad. Amber was missing so much with Kyle not being around enough. He was too loved up with his girlfriend, who he'd been seeing for over two years — a part of that relationship had been behind Maya's back. They now had a three-month-old baby girl. His focus was his new family, not his old one. She felt sorry for Amber and Lewis; their father had turned his back on them, moved further afield, to accommodate his girlfriend, and could only see them properly during the holidays and the occasional weekend.

"Yes, we had loads of fun. Amber's nanny and granddad are awesome." Chloe was hopping from one foot to the other with excitement.

Maya smiled. "I'll tell them that."

Emma was giving her a look which she hoped Sam wouldn't notice — a sort of stare with a wiggle of her eyebrows in his direction. Maya felt her cheeks flush.

"Right, are you ready, Chloe?" Sam asked. He looked from Maya to Emma and then to his daughter, smiling nervously.

"Yes, I've finished my ice-cream."

"So, what do you say?"

"Thank you for having me." Chloe beamed at Maya.

"It's not a problem. Anytime, Chloe," Maya said, then forced herself to look at Sam. She found it hard to meet his eyes. Would she have passed the test? Would his daughter be allowed over again to play with Amber? "Apparently they've all been well-behaved."

"Thank you," Sam said to Maya. He smiled at Emma, who waved.

"Lovely to meet you," she said.

Maya went to show Sam and Chloe out. She was glad to have a glass or two of Prosecco inside her; it had kept her calm. She had worried that she was blushing in Sam's presence. The memory of Amber's party still played vividly in Maya's mind. Until this afternoon, she hadn't been aware how attractive he was. Surely she could be in the company of a good-looking man and not get embarrassed? Now she worried if she had enough make-up on and whether she smelt of pepperoni pizza.

She bet the gorgeous brunette he was with earlier still smelled of roses after their game. Did she mind that he still wore his wedding ring?

"Maya..." Sam looked at her, then down at his daughter, who was fidgeting, getting her shoes on.

"Yes?" She frowned, hesitantly. What had she done wrong now?

"There's something I wanted to say ... uh ... about —"

The doorbell trilled.

"Oh, that must be Lucas." Maya hastily reached for the front door and opened it.

Lucas smiled, sheltered under Maya's porch. Behind him, streetlamps lit the cold, dreary evening, highlighting the now heavy rain. "Is my darling wife ready, or has she not quite drunk you out of house and home yet?"

"Lucas, come in," Maya said, beaming as she ushered him. Were her best friends embarrassing her deliberately?

"Erm…" Sam hesitated, then shook his head. "It doesn't matter. I'll catch you some other time." He guided Chloe out. The two men nodded at each other.

Emma dragged Owen out of the kitchen, making him sit on the bottom of the stairs to put his shoes on. "Hiya, love," she said, kissing her husband. Lucas wrapped an arm around his wife's waist. Maya envied their relationship at times — the little gestures that showed they were still in love. "Where's Finn?"

"I left him at home on the Xbox. It's only for ten minutes," Lucas said.

See, Maya thought. *I'm not the only parent to leave their child unattended at home.* Shame Sam wasn't there to hear it.

"Did you all have a good day?" Lucas asked.

"Maya and I had lunch at Cribbs, and we couldn't help having a glass of Prosecco."

"Yes, so I see," Lucas said, raising his eyebrows.

"And we've finally met Chloe's dad — properly! Contrary to expectations, he didn't appear to be a jerk." Emma gave Maya her familiar all-knowing look. "He's a bit dishy up close, isn't he, Maya?"

"Oh, no, stop right there! You know how I feel about him. I wouldn't date Sam if he was the last man on the planet!"

Emma gave a chuckle, finishing her Prosecco. She kissed Maya on the cheek. "See you in the café on Monday, usual time."

Closing the front door, Maya returned to the kitchen, catching Amber punching her brother on the arm. They were bickering.

"Hey! You two! I hope you didn't behave like this for Nanny and Granddad."

They stopped and looked up guiltily. "No, of course not."

With the kids in bed and feeling pleasantly tipsy, not drunk — okay maybe a tiny bit drunk, she'd just poured the last of the Prosecco into her glass — Maya settled down on the sofa and opened the Find My HEA app on her phone. It was still a little too early to go to bed for a Saturday night. She decided to check out her messages while she finished her drink.

MrGrey19 had finally got the message. She clicked on him and decided to block him. She wasn't shallow. She just had standards. She decided to take Emma's advice and not reply to any men whose profiles didn't take her fancy.

The couple of men she had been messaging seemed to have cooled off. Neither had asked her for her number, and she certainly wasn't going to offer it.

There were some new messages. The one that truly blew her away was from DIYDes. His profile showed him with his arm around a young woman. She assumed it was his daughter. *Hopefully his daughter.* Although smartly dressed, he had a beer belly hanging over his trousers and receding hair. He wasn't particularly attractive to Maya. But his message! Maya was sipping from her glass of Prosecco and nearly choked.

hello most women ask for superman or his looks but my reckoning is if ur waiting for him then ur gonna die a miserable old hag. I am Nige and would be happy to chat with you & to exchange the odd FCUK if you so desire? Have a nice day xxx

Have a nice day?! Maya started to reply. Then she stopped herself. She would not reply under any circumstances, even though she burned to tell him she'd rather die a miserable old hag than meet him. What a prick! *As if I'd sleep with him!*

She took a screenshot of the message. She would have to show Emma. It was hilarious. Now she'd calmed down, but she felt almost insulted. Maya wasn't the sort to blow her own trumpet — she lacked the confidence she once had — but Emma reassured her she was attractive. She knew she could do better than bloody DIYDes. And well, if she couldn't then she *would* rather die a miserable old hag, quite frankly!

Blocked! It gave Maya such satisfaction when she did that. Next message!

This one was from PeterPan26. The profile picture didn't really give much away — he was a man with a scarf obscuring the lower half of his face, sunglasses and a woolly hat, with snow on the ground in the background. He had some generic details, but the typical 'will update later' on his profile. Maya's first instinct was to ignore his message, but so far not one person who'd messaged her seemed worth replying to. His message was at least polite, even flattering and coherent; he knew how to spell and used punctuation. Maya wanted to talk to someone tonight. Was she being a little desperate? Or feeling lonely?

Hi. I don't find Batman desirable — he has no superpowers, plus he's more fallible, being human. He might be rich, but money can't buy love. I just always loved Superman when growing up, and everything he stands for. I still do. Plus, Superman can fly. He'd take me to see the best sunsets.

Thank you for the compliment about my smile. Unfortunately, I can't see yours.

Maya wondered if her last sentence would be read as rude. But she had no idea who she was talking to, although she could see from his profile that he lived in Portishead. He was the only one who'd left a decent message. It would have been nice to see his face. She didn't want to think of herself as shallow, but if she didn't think she would fancy someone, she was hardly going to want to date them, or sleep with them — which, let's face it, realistically was what this was all about. Maya shuddered at the thought. Sex with another man, albeit scary, would be nice. But she wasn't that desperate she'd sleep with someone she didn't fancy. There would have to be a connection, a spark, with body and mind. And she didn't want meaningless sex. She wanted to find someone who would hopefully become a part of her life, for good. The way her confidence was going, she would need to meet someone understanding, too. Sometimes, when she thought too hard about it all, the idea of going on a date petrified her.

Maya checked the time. She should go to sleep. The kids didn't know what Sundays or a lie in meant. In fact, they got up earlier at the weekend than they did on school mornings. Now they were that bit older, they were able to go downstairs and watch television and leave Maya in peace for a while. But she'd lie there feeling guilty that her kids were up and she was lazing in bed, so she would usually get up at around eight to eight-thirty anyway.

Putting her phone on silent, Maya decided to head up to bed. Tomorrow was a new day. The search for Mr Right could wait.

CHAPTER 8

On Sunday morning, Maya's children were up before her — no surprises there. Lewis, first up, was playing on the PlayStation, which Maya allowed at the weekends. He wasn't permitted to go on it before school — she would never get him off it. Amber woke Maya up, flushing the toilet and then slamming the lid down.

Maya rubbed her eyes, then stretched as she looked at her phone to check the time. It wasn't quite eight o'clock. She could snooze a little longer.

There was a knock on her bedroom door, then Amber poked her head around. "Mummy, would you like a coffee?"

There was a plus side to the children growing up.

"That would be lovely, Amber, thank you. Then I'll get up." Maya called out as she heard Amber stomp down the stairs. "Just be very careful. The kettle is very hot."

Maya had started to notice a difference in Amber now she was in Year Six. She wanted to be independent. In September she would be going to secondary school. It all seemed scary, but Maya was trying to let Amber have some freedom. Making her own breakfast was part of this, and some Sundays Amber remembered to ask her mother if she wanted a coffee. Maya was sure it was because she liked being allowed to use the kettle, which to Amber was probably an exciting gadget.

Maya plumped up her pillows, sitting up in bed. She was allowed the occasional lazy Sunday. She didn't used to feel like she should always be doing something with the children when she was married to Kyle. She remembered the mornings, after they'd made love, when Kyle would sneak down, hoping not to wake the kids, and bring up coffee in bed. Those were happy days. Where had it all gone wrong?

Maya looked at the empty space beside her. The king-size bed she and Kyle had owned in their old house wouldn't fit in this bedroom. Now she had a pine double bed, with matching pine furniture, in keeping with the cottage style. The walls were a dusty, pale pink, and the duvet cover was a floral Cath Kidston print — something she wouldn't have been allowed with Kyle. Some of Maya's decorating choices in her cosy new house were to stick two fingers up at her ex-husband. It hadn't been all bad divorcing him.

She was healing. She no longer hated Kyle like she had in the first months of their separation. But she would never forgive him for telling her by text message he was having an affair — a real coward's way out. She remembered the text as if it was yesterday. It had come so unexpectedly, after what she had thought was just a silly row: *I no longer love you. I've met someone else. I'm sorry.*

Then, fuelling her rage and hurt further, it had taken Kyle a few days to turn up and face her, and that was only because she'd threatened to drive to him to sort the mess out. *Coward.* He'd become a man she didn't know — spineless and deceitful. Eventually he turned up at the house because he'd run out of clothes. Surprising herself as much as him, Maya had chucked his clothes at him from the bedroom window, onto the driveway below. She'd already stripped them from the wardrobes and screwed them up into black bin bags.

She used this rage to hide her broken heart from him. He didn't see how she'd been debilitated by the grief caused by the sudden onslaught of her world being turned upside down. Her parents had supported her tremendously, and so had Emma. It took her months to regain her self-esteem, to stop missing him, to stop crying in the early hours of the morning. As time went by, the ache in her chest slowly eased. Now, only very occasionally, when she was feeling at her lowest, would tears fall for Kyle.

Maya had initially put the failure of their marriage down to the lack of sex, due to two young kids sapping their energy and their quality time together, but looking back with a clearer head, she realised that the lack of intimacy between them was entirely due to Kyle sleeping with another woman in the last few months of their marriage. That's when her love turned to rage. A hatred she had to hide from the children — he was still their father, after all.

With small, shaky hands, Amber placed the steaming coffee mug by Maya's bed on a coaster. Maya reached out to steady it, relieved to bring her thoughts back to the present.

"Thanks, love. Help your brother with breakfast, please."

"Do I have to?"

"Please … get the things down he can't reach." Maya touched her daughter's arm, stroking it, pushing her hair back. "Thanks for this. I'll be down in about half an hour. Please don't fight."

"It's not me, it's him."

Once Amber had left Maya's bedroom, she picked up her phone and checked the notifications from the Find My HEA app, telling her how many messages she had.

PeterPan26 had replied:

Sorry to disappoint, I'm not up on my superheroes. I wasn't aware Batman wasn't so desirable. But can't he fly you in his private jet?

I'm working up to posting a better picture. I'm not sure if I want to be on here or not yet.

For some reason, Maya's thoughts turned to Chloe's dad, Sam. Without thinking, she replied:

He's not desirable to me. Yet, some women do find him so. It takes all sorts, so they say. I know a man who fits the brooding, moody type. And I wouldn't touch him with a bargepole!

And imagine the messages I'd get if I had my username as Catwoman!

A better picture would be nice. I've taken to not replying to those with no profile pictures or information. You're not giving much away. How do I know you're genuine?

His profile picture made him unrecognisable, but there was something about this guy Maya liked. And what harm was there in just messaging? Plus, so far, the men with profile pictures hadn't really proved to be better.

Yes, you could attract the wrong type of guy with a username like Catwoman. Lol!

I'm sorry there isn't much information about me. I assure you I am genuine. And if you'd like to chat, then I'd be happy with that too.

A brooding, moody type? I'm intrigued to know what he did to you to merit such scorn?

Maya smiled and typed, *It's a long story...*

You can tell me, he replied.

So, Maya relayed the disastrous end to Amber's birthday party, which seemed so long ago now. She mentioned no names, and tried to keep the details to a minimum, aware she was talking to a stranger. But it felt good to get it off her chest as she explained why she'd had to rush out to collect her son, and how she'd returned to find the two girls looking nothing like how she'd left them. The situation would have been funny if Chloe's dad's attitude hadn't been so vile towards her.

I really reprimanded my daughter afterwards for going through my make-up. She lost her pocket money and had to do chores for a week! I hate that he thinks I'm an irresponsible mother. I feel like I'm going to be judged whenever I'm around him. It's hard being a single mother.

Peter Pan26 responded sympathetically:

He was probably having an off day, just like you. I'm sure he's not judging you. He'll see what a fool he's been.

Easy for you to say, Maya thought as she read.

I seem to be attracting my fair share of fools on here too. Not giving me much confidence.

Maya went on to tell PeterPan26 about DIYDes. She even copied his message out. By the time she'd drained her coffee, she was wiping tears from her eyes, laughing at PeterPan26's replies.

The man is an idiot. You'll never die a miserable old hag — not with that smile! I'm here to talk. Please don't hesitate to message me.

Maya sent another message back thanking him, and saying she needed to get up as she could hear her kids arguing. She didn't want to go into anything more personal with PeterPan26. He hadn't shared much with her, so she thought she would keep it the same. However, he was fun to chat to, even with an unidentifiable profile picture. She would maybe continue to chat until the conversation petered out. So far, he was the best the site had to offer.

Maya's phoned pinged. It was a Facebook message from Selina:

Hey, how's the online dating going? Have you started looking? I'm still going strong with Kelvin. Our weekend away was FAB! I'm so happy right now, don't give up hope.

Where did Maya start?

Sam scratched his head, then reached for his coffee, digesting the messages Maya had sent. *She's talking about you: you're the idiot.* Heather was right. He'd overreacted. He had just jumped to the conclusion that Maya was irresponsible. He hadn't even questioned why she'd had to dash out. Chloe and Amber had been in the wrong going through her make-up.

And now she thinks every time we meet you're judging her. No wonder she ran from him at the sports centre and could hardly say a word to him when he collected Chloe from her house yesterday.

Had she been worried he was judging her for drinking with the kids about?

He needed to rectify this.

One thing was for certain, he couldn't disclose who PeterPan26 really was now she'd talked to him about *him*. But he didn't want to delete the account now either — which would be the wisest thing to do — because he wanted to continue to talk to her, if she let him. She'd chatted more to him this morning, than she ever had in person.

The day Jade had died, Sam's world had imploded. The only glue holding it together was Chloe and his family. But now, as each month passed, his world had been rebuilding, gaining strength, the pain of her death subsiding. Back in October he'd been a different person to now. And maybe he needed to show Maya that. And maybe through this account, he'd find out how...

CHAPTER 9

The Sunday afternoon brought a clear sky of cornflower blue. Maya nagged her children into their walking boots and coats. The sun was low and glared right into her eyes as they walked. There was a cold wind coming off the sea, but with the wind behind them, they soon warmed up.

The beach wasn't quite as good as that of nearby Weston-super-Mare, but it was fun watching the big tankers come up the Bristol Channel, heading towards Royal Portbury Dock. They would appear so close you felt you could reach out and touch them. Huge, monstrous things. Maya wondered how they even floated. Today, they could clearly see the Welsh coast across the Severn Estuary. The park bloomed with winter flowers, particularly underneath the bare trees and evergreen s: snowdrops and crocuses in purple, mauve and yellow; yellow primroses and the green shoots of daffodils, waiting to flower with spring on its way.

Maya's phone pinged occasionally in her pocket. It was probably from the online dating app. She resisted the urge to look. She was out with her kids, and now was not the time to be looking up potential dates. Besides, the rate her online dating success was going, which was zero dates and zero men she was interested in, she didn't want to be disappointed by yet another guy like DIYDes, who could ruin her mood with a crappy message.

Amber and Lewis knew the route as Maya had walked it on so many Sundays with them. They left the woods and stopped to watch the lock on the marina, to see if a boat was going through. Only one yacht was out braving the clear, cold day.

They crossed the lock and headed around the harbour, admiring the different boats moored up in the sunshine, strolling towards the coffe

shop. Maya couldn't wait for a cappuccino, and she knew the kids would both want hot chocolates.

While Maya queued, the kids found a window seat. In the queue, she checked her dating app messages.

There were a couple from new men who hadn't contacted her before. She was mildly disappointed that there was nothing from PeterPan26.

One, whose username was FYI1234, had a profile picture of a jean-clad crotch. The message was pretty much bog-standard, along the lines of 'you're really pretty and would you like to chat?' There wasn't much information on his profile, only a rant at women who kept reporting him — so he was probably a jerk. Was that an erection under those jeans, or a couple of pairs of socks? Maya couldn't resist. She replied to FYI1234: *Is that actually your crotch or someone else's?*

Maya was at the front of the queue by now, so she slipped her phone into her pocket and placed her order. She then ignored her messages, concentrating on her coffee and talking to the kids. They finished their drinks and left the coffee shop, leaving the cosy warmth to face the icy sea breeze which bit at their cheeks and noses. They strolled around the rest of the harbour. Maya wanted to take some photos of Amber and Lewis with the marina and the clear blue sky as a backdrop. If it wasn't for the coats and scarves, you'd have thought it was a summer's day.

When Maya retrieved her phone from her handbag, she saw FYI1234 had replied: *Of course its my crotch why wouldn't it be*

Maya ignored the lack of punctuation and quickly typed back: *I've noticed on here some guys pretend to be someone they're not, by using fake profile pictures. Who's to say this really is your crotch?*

Maya giggled. She couldn't resist a wind-up at times. You needed to have a sense of humour for online dating.

"What are you laughing about, Mummy?" Lewis asked, taking her hand as they walked. She liked that he still wanted to hold her hand. Unlike Amber, who was too cool.

"Nothing, sweetheart."

"Oh, look, it's Chloe!" Amber said, and before Maya could stop her, Amber was running towards Chloe and her dad. Sam. Both walked towards them. Maya cringed internally, hoping her face wasn't betraying her displeasure.

Argh, why hadn't she put make-up on! Or worn better jeans?

Maya's phone pinged again and without thinking, she opened the message.

At the same moment, Sam approached, saying, "Hi."

Maya's eyes widened in shock at the image on her phone and she panicked, releasing Lewis's hand. But however much she fumbled to close the app for fear of her kids — and Sam — seeing what she was seeing, her phone had chosen this moment to freeze on her.

"Are you okay, Mummy?" Lewis looked at her with concern. He made a move to see what she was doing on her phone. She held it to her chest. Sam, Chloe, Amber and Lewis were all staring at her.

"My damn phone…" Maya mumbled frantically.

"Did you want me to take a look?" Sam stepped closer, holding his hand out.

"No!" Maya held her phone tighter to her chest. Sam frowned. "Sorry, sorry…" She slipped her phone into her handbag, zipping it up firmly, and tried to gather her composure.

"Are you okay?" Sam's expression still showed confusion.

FYI1234 had sent Maya another message, and by doing so he had alerted her that he'd changed his profile picture. No wonder women were reporting him! His jean-clad crotch shot had changed to an open-jean shot revealing a rather erect penis.

She'd officially seen her first dick pic! It wasn't pleasant.

"Yes, yes, just having phone trouble. Unwanted caller." Maya plastered on a fake smile and even though it was bitterly cold out, she knew her face must be shining, hot with embarrassment.

Why did some men even think women would want to see that? That part of a man's anatomy was only attractive if a woman was also aroused. And right now, standing on Portishead marina with her two beautiful, innocent children, and a man who thought she was irresponsible, Maya couldn't have felt less horny.

She needed something stronger than coffee now.

Selina had warned her. And now she had learnt the hard way that however much she was tempted to respond to these dickheads, she shouldn't. Later, when she was back home, she would go back on to Find My HEA and block FYI1234. A part of her wanted to reply with 'is that it?' But she knew better now. It would probably only encourage him to send even more indecent photos. *Do not provoke the weirdos!*

"Right, well, must get back, got to get the dinner on," Maya said awkwardly, thinking up excuses to carry on walking and get away from Sam.

"Yes, we're just taking a stroll before we head to my sister's."
Sam shoved a hand in his pocket, the other arm wrapped
protectively around his daughter. "Lovely to see you."

Was it? Really?

Maya didn't think it could have gone any worse. Sam may
have been nice to her when collecting Chloe, but she would
continue to keep her guard up. For all she knew, it could be a
front just for the kids' benefit.

"Yes, yes, bye," Maya said, plastering on a fake smile and
starting to walk in the opposite direction.

"See you at school tomorrow," Amber called to Chloe.
There were awkward waves — from Sam and Maya — and
then the party separated, much to Maya's relief.

Back home, when her children were distracted by the
television, Maya braved opening the app on her phone again. It
wasn't as if it would explode in her hand, but she dreaded what
she might see. She breathed a sigh of relief when she realised
she didn't need to block FYI1234. Find My HEA had already
done it for her.

"What a moron," she said to herself as she peeled potatoes,
preparing a roast dinner. "He wouldn't go into a nightclub and
drop his trousers, so why does he feel it's okay to do it on the
internet?"

Once the parsnips were in the oven roasting with the
potatoes, Maya decided to message PeterPan26 and tell him
what had happened. It wasn't until after dinner, when the kids
were upstairs getting ready for bed, that she could read his
reply:

Hey, Lois, it takes all sorts. But what a cretin. Another idiot! I'm sorry you had to be subjected to that level of perverse stupidity. How was your day apart from that?

The dick pic profile had made Maya think, *From now on, no messaging anyone without a decent photo.* However, PeterPan26 fell into this category. He might well be just as weird as FYI1234, only he hadn't revealed it yet. His messages did come across as sincere, though. Maya messaged back:

My day was relaxed, apart from the idiot. However, it does make me question whether I should continue to chat to you, as your profile picture doesn't give a lot away and I'm starting to distrust men on this site if they don't reveal what they look like. And any that usually message me without a profile picture I've ignored. You've been exempt from this rule.

Maya didn't know this guy, and it was best to be honest and up front. If she hurt his feelings, well, too bad — he needed to understand this from her point of view. Besides, someone who didn't appreciate her honesty would not be the right man for her anyway. And the whole point of chatting to guys on an online dating site was to hopefully find someone to date, and maybe even, if she was lucky, fall in love again.

I understand. I assure you I'm not weird. I like our chats.

"Mum, can I have…? Oh, you're on your phone." Amber, dressed for bed in her pink onesie, walked into the kitchen. "Do you have a new boyfriend?"

Maya blushed. "No," she said, sounding more defensive than she intended as she started grabbing cheese out of the fridge to make the sandwiches for the kids' lunchboxes.

"You just seem to be on your phone a lot lately. More than normal."

"No, I am not." *Must remember to put the phone on silent so they don't keep hearing it ping.* She was on her phone way more than usual.

"It's okay, Mum, if you do," Amber said. "I mean, Dad's got a girlfriend, hasn't he?"

"No, I don't have a boyfriend, and even if I did, I wouldn't let you meet him until I was absolutely certain it was going to work out," Maya said.

"Meet who?" Lewis entered the kitchen mid-conversation, as usual.

"Nobody. Okay?" Maya said, clattering the cutlery drawer as she closed it harder than intended. "Right, would you two like a hot chocolate while you read before bed?"

"Yes!" Both jumped excitedly.

She didn't care that they'd already had a hot chocolate earlier. It wouldn't do any harm, and Maya was desperate to change the subject. Did she really want to be talking boyfriends with her eleven-year-old daughter and nearly nine-year-old son? "And the magic word?"

"Please!" they said again in unison.

"Go sit in the lounge and start reading, while I make it."

She watched her children leave the kitchen, checked her phone, then decided to lock the screen and concentrate on making their drinks.

Online dating was so time-consuming. It was easy to get sucked into checking the app, perusing pictures of men, and reading their profiles — well, the ones which had bothered to write a profile. And then, when you got into messaging someone...

She had to be more careful. Amber was clearly noticing she was on her phone more than usual. Even her clients didn't message so much. Maya was hoping to keep this side of her life a secret from her kids for now. She would only introduce them to a guy if she found something serious.

CHAPTER 10

February

Maya inserted her credit card into the machine to retrieve her pre-booked cinema tickets. Saturday afternoon at Vue cinema, Cribbs Causeway, was always busy. Today was worse than usual because it was the start of February half-term. She usually preferred to take the children to the cinema after school, when it was much quieter. Or she would come midweek during the school holidays, preferably to the first showing in the morning. But this was part of Lewis's birthday treat today. He'd had a shared *Laser Quest* party with Owen last weekend, but Maya wanted to take him out on his actual birthday.

Amber gave a sudden squeal, making Maya jump. She turned around. *Oh God.* Behind her stood Chloe and her dad.

"Hello," she said, looking from Chloe to Sam. Chloe and Amber were extremely pleased to see each other. Maya didn't share their enthusiasm.

"What film are you seeing?" Sam asked, his daughter's hand slipping out of his.

Jumping up and down excitedly, Amber answered before Maya could say the name of the movie.

"So are we!" Chloe replied for Sam. He smiled and rolled his eyes.

He actually had a lovely smile, thought Maya, chiding herself for such a thought. *Shame about his not so lovely attitude, though.*

The machine chucked out the tickets. Lewis grabbed them and handed them to Maya. "Thank you, honey," she said.

Maya stepped aside to let Sam insert his card to retrieve his tickets. This felt so awkward. She wanted to walk away from him, but for Amber and Chloe's sakes she felt she couldn't.

She caught a whiff of his aftershave. He smelt great, as well as looking good in casual jeans and a sweatshirt. She gave herself a mental shake.

Sam showed his tickets to Maya. "What seats are you in?"

Their seat numbers were the same, only it looked like his were two rows below.

"Did you want to let the girls sit together, and we can keep an eye on them from above?"

This was turning into her worst nightmare. But what would it look like if she didn't let her daughter sit next to her best friend? "Oh, uh…" Amber and Chloe were already oblivious to their parents' existence, talking about… Actually, Maya didn't have the foggiest what they were talking about. "Do you mind?"

"I don't mind, if you don't."

Maya did really. But she couldn't make Lewis sit with Sam while she sat with the girls. "I suppose it would be a shame to break them up."

"Yes, they will like sitting together," Sam said.

They would. But it meant Maya would be sitting next to Sam. At least once the film started she wouldn't need to make conversation.

They walked into the foyer where the refreshments were sold.

"Popcorn?" Sam asked.

"Oh, I wasn't going to bother." Maya chewed her lip.

"Mum, please can I have some?" Lewis said, embarrassing Maya further. She hated paying for overpriced popcorn and drinks at the cinema.

"My treat," Sam said, as if sensing her anguish. "I'll get a tub for the girls, and we can share one too."

"Thank you."

Was this the same man who'd collected his daughter from her house in October? Why was he being so nice all of a sudden?

To be fair, he had been polite collecting Chloe the other Sunday...

Once everyone had visited the toilets, and Sam had returned with two buckets of popcorn, they showed their tickets and then found their seats inside the cinema. Excited to be together, Chloe and Amber sat in the two seats by the aisle, and Sam, Maya and Lewis headed towards the seats two rows above them. Maya felt less thrilled about this prospect. The cinema was already busy, and the seats next to the three Maya had booked were already occupied. Sam went in and sat in the third seat, next to the strangers, so Maya sat down awkwardly next to Sam and Lewis had the aisle seat left.

As the film trailers played, Maya found herself relaxing slightly and telling Sam which films she liked the look of and which she didn't. Admittedly, because they were watching a children's movie, the trailers matched the age range the film was aimed at. Sam nodded his agreement. Maya, being in the middle, found she had the bucket of popcorn on her lap. She offered it to Lewis, then Sam.

"Give it to Lewis," Sam whispered over the trailers, his breath warm on her ear.

The film was hilarious. Maya let out a good hearty laugh at one point, then remembered she had Sam next to her and tried to rein in her chuckles. She kept a beady eye on the two girls below, making sure they were behaving.

Afterwards, the girls waited in their seats for the cinema to clear, then they all walked out together, following the babble of the crowds.

"That was awesome," Chloe said, and Amber agreed. Lewis had enjoyed the movie too, judging by how much he'd giggled.

It was five in the afternoon by the time they'd walked out of the cinema into the cold air, and the sky was already darkening.

"Mummy, I'm hungry," Lewis said.

"After all that popcorn?" Maya ruffled his hair.

"What are you doing for dinner?" Sam asked as he gave Chloe a hug around her shoulder.

"Oh, we were… I … uh, promised the kids we'd go to Frankie and Benny's as it's Lewis's birthday."

"Oh, I was thinking of doing the same," he said.

"Please, Daddy, can Amber join us?" Chloe didn't miss a trick.

Sam wrapped an arm around his daughter and turned to Maya. "Would you like to join us for dinner? Lewis, would you like that?"

"Please Mum, please," Amber started begging, like Chloe. To be honest, it was nice for Amber to have an impromptu meet-up with her friend, and Maya could do with some adult company. Sam wouldn't have been her first choice. But hey! Beggars, choosers and all that. Lewis wasn't fussed either way and nodded happily.

"Yes, okay," Maya said hesitantly.

They were shown to a booth and the two girls sat together. Sam slid in next to them, while Maya shuffled Lewis along, so she was opposite Sam. Maya busied herself looking at the menu to avoid making conversation with Sam. What should they talk about? If the two girls were going to be 'best friends forever', then she needed to attempt to build bridges with Sam.

What harm would there be in getting to know him better? Like it or not, she would have to see him regularly, as Amber was always asking for Chloe to come over. Maybe they could put the mortifying make-up incident behind them?

In fact, it looked like Sam already had.

Only Maya was unsure why.

A waitress appeared. "Can I take your drinks order?"

"Would you like a glass of wine?" Sam looked at Maya. "I'll have a bottle of Bud, please."

"I don't know, I'm driving."

"So am I. But we can have a small one." There was a twinkle in his warm, brown eyes.

"Okay, yes… It would be rude to let you drink alone." Maya chuckled nervously and quickly perused the drinks menu. "A small pinot grigio then, please — and a jug of water."

"Of course." The waitress made a note on her pad and then took the kids' drinks order. "Would you like five more minutes to decide on food?"

"Yes, please," Maya said. She would avoid the spaghetti options, for fear of making a mess in front of Sam. He had a pretty low opinion of her already, so what would he make of her with Bolognese sauce dribbled on her chin?

The waitress set the drinks down and took the food order. The kids all chose pizzas and Maya went for a safe pasta option with a creamy sauce rather than a tomato one. Sam went for a calzone and ordered some sides to share. With the girls happily chatting and Lewis playing games on Maya's mobile phone, Maya knew she needed to make conversation with Sam.

"So, how are you and Chloe settling in?" Maya said.

"Great, can't believe it's been seven months," Sam said. "I moved in July, so Chloe's schooling wasn't disrupted too much. She's made lots of new friends." Sam looked at the two girls deep in conversation. "I'd changed jobs from Swindon to Bristol. My sister, Heather, convinced me to move closer, for an easier commute, and so she could help me out more with childcare. You know how it is."

"Yes, my parents living locally is a godsend." Maya smiled. "Where do you work?"

"Over in Filton. I'm a project manager in the aerospace industry. It can be busy, and stressful at times, but I love it. I've been in engineering all my life. I'm working on a project improving a current passenger jet. A newer model."

"Oh, like with cars, when you get the 'sport' range?"

"Yes, something like that, although this is to improve passenger comfort and fuel economy. I manage a team of about fifty."

"Wow."

"I think it's added some extra grey hairs." Sam chuckled as he combed a hand through his dark hair. He eyed the children. "So, do they see their dad regularly?" He looked awkward for a moment.

"Not enough, in my opinion, as he's moved away to live with his new girlfriend."

Maya was tempted to confide how it felt as though a switch had flicked in Kyle, making him drop Lewis and Amber, forget his responsibility to them, and concentrate on Jenna and Lola, the baby, but thought better of it.

"Where has he moved to?"

"Exeter."

"I'm sorry to hear that. I mean, I have no choice with single parenting since Jade died. I am having to raise Chloe on my own. But your ex does have a choice in seeing them regularly and being involved in their lives."

"I know. It's okay, it gets easier each day. I manage now. It's not like he doesn't support me financially. I have no problem there. He seems to chuck money at me to make him feel less guilty about swanning off. My parents are also very supportive, helping me out regularly. Emma's great too — she babysat last night."

Whoops — she hadn't meant to confess that. Maya had been out on a date. She'd been on a few now. All unsuccessful.

The food arrived, thankfully. Maya hated discussing Kyle and didn't want Sam to see how it still upset her.

There was a waft of garlic as the cheesy garlic flatbread was placed on the table and all three children made hungry groaning noises. The pizzas were placed in front of each of them, and without waiting they started to tuck in.

"So, were you out with friends last night?" Sam asked.

Maya shook her head. "Not really. Emma has convinced me to try —" she whispered the next bit — "online dating."

Sam chuckled. "Have you had much luck?"

Maya checked the kids were distracted. "Not really, I went out on a date last night," she said, keeping her voice low. Sam raised an eyebrow, to encourage her to go on. She shook her head. "He wasn't for me. There wasn't any chemistry."

"What's chemistry?" Lewis asked as he chewed his ham and pineapple pizza.

"It's a science you'll study when you're older," Sam said, bailing Maya out.

"And don't speak with your mouth full," Maya scolded.

They went back to concentrating on eating the food. "How long have you been … a widower?" The words escaped Maya's mouth before she could think about what she was asking. She watched as Sam swallowed and sipped his beer before answering.

"It's been just over four years now."

"Oh."

"Each day gets a little easier. My sister is my rock," Sam said. "What about you? How long have you been separated?"

"Nearly two years. I've lived in my new home for a year now."

"I'm sorry things didn't work out for you," Sam said.

"Yes, we drifted apart. Well, more like Kyle drifted … into someone else's bed…" Maya lowered her voice, although the kids had a good idea of what had happened, from Kyle and Maya's initial loud arguments. They'd been with her parents the day she'd chucked his clothes out onto the front lawn.

"Oh, I am sorry."

"So am I. I loved him. I thought he loved me. But it wasn't to be." Maya shrugged. She held in the *I hate him.* Hate was harsh, and it might be dying down now, but she'd never forget how he'd hurt her.

There was silence while they both tucked into their food, then Sam looked up and asked, "So how's work for you these days?"

"Other than painting nails all day?" She wiggled her fingers, showing off her own immaculate nails. "It's okay."

"I'm sure that's not all you do."

"No, I do massages too, facials, bridal make-up…" Maya instantly regretted mentioning make-up. She watched Sam's reaction. There was none. None that showed disdain towards her, anyway.

"You run your own business, while creating a loving home for your two children. You must work very hard."

Maya was taken aback by his compliment. "I suppose so. Although at times I feel like I'm losing the will to —" Maya stopped herself. She had to be thankful for her life. However hard it was, she had to be grateful she had her health, and was seeing her children grow up. Sam's wife hadn't been so lucky. "They drive me crazy, and I wonder what my next-door neighbours think some mornings. I fear I sound like a screaming banshee! And I have been known to just chuck beans on toast for tea when I really can't be bothered."

"They certainly don't appear undernourished. Or unhappy." And to prove it, Amber gave a hearty laugh at something Chloe had said. "You're doing a fantastic job."

"Thank you." Maya felt her face growing hotter. She hoped she didn't look like a beetroot. She supposed she did do a good job. Lewis and Amber both did well in school, where she feared they may have rebelled after their parents' separation. Generally, they were happy, although occasionally she would find one of them crying, missing their daddy. It was normal, part of the healing process.

"Look," Sam placed his hand on Maya's wrist. "I need to apologise to you…" Maya frowned. Realising the intimacy of the gesture, his touch was brief, but Maya could still feel the gentle pressure he'd applied. She felt sure she was blushing now. His gaze didn't quite meet hers at first, but then he focused on her. Dark brown eyes. Long eyelashes. The creases around his eyes as he smiled. She saw it all. "I need to apologise for my behaviour last year — at Amber's birthday."

Maya quickly shook her head and waved her hands. "It's okay, just a case of crossed wires."

"Yes, but I should have let you explain. Not jump to conclusions."

"They had helped themselves to the make-up, you know?"

"I realise that now. I talked to Chloe." Sam reached for her hand again.

"And Lucas was going to drop off Lewis, but he'd had to take his son to A&E."

"Yes, I overreacted. Overprotective with Chloe, I suppose. Maya, please accept my apology." Sam looked into her eyes imploringly. "I'm sorry."

Maya nervously nodded her acceptance of his apology, unable to speak. Her heart had started pounding erratically. He was handsome, and being so kind... She'd got him all wrong. She dabbed her lips with her napkin then wiped her hands with it. She excused herself to visit the ladies' toilets, where she ran cold water over her wrists to cool herself down. *Take deep breaths.* The restaurant was just so hot...

Sam has a girlfriend, remember.

Back at the table, Maya tried to relax in Sam's company, and kept the conversation on safe subjects. His easy-going manner put her impression that he was an arrogant bastard completely to rest, and she began to enjoy the evening. With Chloe in the mix, Amber and Lewis didn't bicker, which also enabled Maya to unwind. They talked about how fast the children were growing; Amber and Chloe would be moving up to secondary school in September. They'd find out soon if they'd got into their chosen school — they were both hoping to go to the same one, which pleased the girls. There were just the SATs to sit in May. The waitress interrupted them to clear the plates and ask if they wanted puddings. The children all excitedly said yes to ice-cream, but Sam and Maya both declined.

When the waitress arrived with the kids' desserts, the lights suddenly dimmed in the restaurant and the music turned up loud, blasting out "Happy Birthday". In Lewis's ice-cream was a sparkler. Sam, Chloe and Amber sang along, while Maya quickly snapped a photo of Lewis's surprised face as he watched the sparkler diminish.

Sam must have caught Maya's puzzled expression. "I had a word with the waitress when you went to the ladies," he said. "I hope that was okay?"

"Of course it was. I forgot they did that here. Thank you."

Should she invite him back to the house for a drink? She was enjoying his company and they could talk more. Would he think she fancied him? Would he see it as anything more than two friends drinking together? Why did it make it awkward because he was the opposite sex?

Maya topped up her water glass and filled Lewis's glass also. "Sam, would you like to come back to our house — with Chloe, of course?"

"Oh, sorry, I can't tonight. Chloe is going to stay with my sister, as I'm meeting someone for a drink at around eight tonight."

"Oh." Why did her heart sink with disappointment?

"Another time, maybe? I'd like that."

"Yes, okay." Maya's spirits lifted. She shouldn't take it personally — clearly, he did have plans. This meeting wasn't exactly pre-arranged.

"In fact, time is getting on." Sam glanced at his watch, making Maya glance at her own. It was seven o'clock. "We'd better ask for the bill."

The waitress placed the bill on the table, and Sam instantly pulled the little black tray towards him and placed his card on it. Maya reached in her purse to give him some money, but he pushed her hand away. "No, my treat. It's been a pleasure to have company."

"Are you sure?" Maya frowned.

"I insist. Chloe has thoroughly enjoyed catching up with Amber, too."

They left the restaurant, and there was an awkward moment — Maya thought it awkward, at least. Did she hug or kiss him, like she would Emma? They nodded a goodbye, Sam shoving his hands into his pockets, and he walked one way with Chloe towards his car, and Maya walked the other with Amber and Lewis either side of her. An unfamiliar feeling crept over her: a relaxed happiness mixed with fulfilment, satisfaction. Going to the cinema and eating out with her kids had turned out to be so much more enjoyable than she'd expected.

CHAPTER 11

Sam closed his front door quietly, then remembered Chloe was staying at Heather's. It had been a good night, sharing a few beers in Bristol with some work colleagues. His head swam a little, light-headed with the booze, but he hadn't lost the use of his faculties. Good job he'd eaten well at dinner with Maya and the children earlier. He could have done with not going out with his work colleagues, because he would have enjoyed extending the evening with her.

Fetching a pint glass of water, Sam perched on his couch and started scrolling through the online dating app. He held off messaging Maya — especially as he'd seen her this afternoon. But that's why he was on there. He wanted to contact her. They only messaged periodically; usually she'd ask for some advice, to get a male opinion. He assumed their messaging died down when she was online with someone else. Which was fine. It really was.

She was more open about her online dating experiences to him as an anonymous stranger on the site, than face to face in the restaurant. It had been difficult with the kids there, admittedly. Maya was trying to date without her children knowing. He would be the same. He only wanted to introduce Chloe to someone who would mean something to him. His daughter had no idea about his attempts at dating a couple of years ago — especially the disastrous one that made him stop altogether. The less anyone knew about that experience, the better. He'd sworn Heather to secrecy.

The woman, Annette was her name, had described herself as a widow in her profile, which had been her appeal to Sam.

However, it transpired that her husband was not dead, but in prison. Sam had nearly choked on his dinner. Annette had said he was dead to her, though. It wasn't quite the same, in Sam's opinion. He had endured three courses, paid the bill, and hadn't been able to escape the restaurant fast enough. It had been a very expensive mistake.

Heather, of course, had found it hysterical when he'd told her. But he'd never looked at the online dating account since. PeterPan26 had remained hidden.

The fact was he'd tried dating too soon after Jade's death. He hadn't given himself enough time. And then that had happened. *Putting him off for life — almost!* He wasn't even sure if he was ready now.

Sam felt a pang of dishonesty about not coming clean to Maya. But if he did, he worried he might lose the contact with her that he had started to crave. Hopefully, he'd allayed her misgivings about him today. He'd made sure he'd apologised to her. This afternoon had been a perfect opportunity to prove he wasn't a pompous, moody old git. He hoped it had worked. It felt important that she liked him. If he confessed to Maya now, would it undo all the good stuff he'd done today with her? He didn't want to ruin a potential friendship, especially as their daughters were close and he was likely to see Maya regularly.

Chloe seemed completely cool with the idea of him dating — she was almost as bad as Heather for encouraging it. It was difficult to imagine being with another woman, and he feared he'd never feel the same as he did with Jade. He still found it hard to accept that it wouldn't be a betrayal, even though she'd wanted him to move on. Before she'd died, they'd discussed it — both crying, holding each other. She'd felt so frail in his arms, as he'd promised to look after Chloe, to be happy in life. But what Jade had feared most, more than death itself, was that

Sam would be left lonely. She'd reassured him that meeting someone else wouldn't mean he loved her any less.

In the flickering light of the muted TV, his legs outstretched and his feet resting on his oak coffee table, Sam debated what to do about his profile on Find My HEA. Although not overly happy with the idea, he decided to remain anonymous as PeterPan26. Much as he wanted to delete this account now, he didn't want to lose the connection it gave him with Maya… He could support her via PeterPan26 in a way he couldn't in person. He'd stay available for her to chat to if she wanted. So as not to draw any more attention to his anonymous profile, he decided to hide his account so only Maya, because she'd been messaging him, would be able to contact him.

He switched to Soul Mate Search, which he knew Maya wasn't on. He updated the profile Heather had created for him with some pictures, including one Chloe had recently taken of him with Portishead marina in the background. Hopefully no one would think the big yacht in the picture was his. He rubbed his eyes with his palms, hoping to refresh them a little longer while he finished his water. Staring at the screen was making his eyelids heavy and his eyes dry.

He'd been messaged by several women, including a young woman whose profile was full of pouting, duck-faced selfies. Her username was SassyQueen.

More like SelfieQueen.

He imagined Jade looking over his shoulder and rolling her eyes at the women on this site. He still missed her sense of humour.

Sam finished his water and turned off the television. He thought about messaging a couple of new ladies whose profiles interested him, only to keep Heather off his back, and to keep his promise to Jade.

He rubbed his eyes and closed the app. He'd think about it tomorrow. Under the influence of alcohol, he wouldn't want to make a poor judgement call.

Unfortunately, and even more so after this afternoon, Maya seemed to pop to the front of his mind before anyone else.

But he didn't want to ruin a newly forming friendship by complicating it further. Especially if he wasn't one hundred per cent sure whether he wanted to date or not. He'd only been surfing the online dating site to keep Heather quiet.

And he'd only spent one evening with Maya. Maybe he needed to get to know her more before he made the decision to ask her out on a date. That could take their relationship on a whole new path … one where kids were involved too.

CHAPTER 12

March

"So, anything new to tell me?"

Although it was only early March, the sun streamed into Emma's kitchen, where Maya was sitting with a black nylon gown wrapped around her. Foils were being folded through her hair. Every few months, she would have some blonde highlights put in to lift her natural colour.

Maya updated Emma on her latest dating exploits. Not that there was much to tell. A couple of guys had been keen, but Maya hadn't felt anything.

"Well, I'm glad to hear you're listening to your heart," Emma said. "Attraction does grow, but there needs to be something there in the first place. I think you're going to need to kiss a few frogs first."

"The last one kissed like a frog."

Emma coughed and spluttered, trying to swallow the coffee she'd sipped in between inserting a foil. Maya giggled too.

"God, Maya, don't do that!" Emma was wiping her chin with her sleeve.

"Sorry." Maya smirked.

Emma composed herself, combing Maya's hair. "He certainly wasn't right, then. If you're going to kiss a guy for the rest of your life, you've got to at least enjoy it. Anyone else in the pipeline?"

"No, but I forgot to show you this." Maya held up the screenshot of DIYDes's message.

Emma read, mouth open, occasionally looking at Maya then back at her phone. "Unbelievable!" she said, then giggled. "Oh, that's nice that he wants to swap French Connection clothes!"

She was referring to the 'fuck' he'd spelt as 'FCUK'.

"I could see you dating him, though," Emma continued. "Maya and Nige ... K. I. S. S. I. N —"

"Shut up!" Maya turned her phone away.

"Wow, what a minefield. You couldn't make that stuff up. What a complete dickhead." Emma's tone became more sincere. "Maya, keep at it. Selina seems happy with her guy."

"Yes, I have to believe that if I'm on there, genuinely wanting to find a guy, then there must be a guy out there who is right for me," Maya said.

She still exchanged messages with PeterPan26 intermittently, but for some reason she didn't mention this to Emma, and she had resumed conversations with other guys. She had a new one messaging her now, PJWard14.

Maya shrugged her shoulders with a sigh. The foils rustled. "This guy I'm talking to now seems okay. At least he shaves."

"Designer stubble and beards are in."

"Tell me about it." Maya had always loved kissing Kyle just after he'd shaved. Soft lips, the smell of aftershave. He would be gentle, then as their passion grew his kisses would become more urgent. Maya chided herself. She kept comparing everyone to Kyle, and he was hardly a good example, cheating on her. Thinking about Kyle could enrage her, but if she looked back beyond the recent events, she could remember the good stuff.

"Did I tell you my cousin met her husband online?"

"No."

Emma laughed. "But the stories she could tell you! One guy had awful teeth. Afterwards, she realised that in all of his photos he hadn't been properly smiling."

"Oh, dear."

"His name was Ted, so from then on we referred to him as No-Teeth-Ted!"

Once Maya had stopped giggling, she said, "I won't trust anyone who doesn't smile in their photos from now on."

"No, don't!"

"You'll like this, Em. I had this younger man message me the other day; he was only in his early twenties."

"Early twenties? Why? They shouldn't need to be dating online."

"I know. They should just be out there having fun. Anyway, I pretty much figured he wanted a MILF."

"Didn't take you for a cougar, Maya!" Emma nudged her shoulder.

"He swore blind it wasn't about the sex, but then he went on to talk about nothing but sex, asking if I'd want to try something younger." Maya rolled her eyes and Emma chuckled. "Honestly. Some of them think that because I'm approaching forty, I must be desperate!"

Some men who'd messaged looked older than Maya's father. She knew looks weren't everything, but there had to be something — that twinkle in their eye, or the dimple in their chin. She wanted a man who looked after himself and took some pride in his appearance. At least Kyle did do that — maybe a bit too much. Maybe she was being too choosy, but she didn't want to settle for second best.

Why did Sam just pop into her head?

"Another coffee?" Emma packed away the bowls and brushes, then switched the kettle on.

"Yes, please."

"So, any other dates on the horizon?" Emma came into the dining room, where Maya sat with her head full of foils. She held two steaming mugs of coffee and a packet of Oreo biscuits.

"I'm now chatting with a guy called Pierce. I haven't met him yet."

"Will you?"

"If he asks." Maya smiled coyly. She may have been the first to message, but the traditionalist in her wanted the guy to ask her out on a date.

"That's my girl." Emma raised her coffee mug as if toasting.

"I'm hoping he'll ask me out this weekend, as the kids are staying with Mum and Dad."

Pierce had been quite flirtatious with Maya. They hadn't swapped phone numbers yet, but it would only be a matter of time. His photos showed he was attractive — more attractive than the others she'd dated. But she did fear the chemistry still might not be there, or his appearance in his photos wouldn't be the same in the flesh.

After Maya's foils had been removed, her hair washed through, cut and blow-dried, she set about giving Emma a luxury manicure.

"Have you got any pictures of this Pierce, then?" Emma asked as Maya placed her fingertips under the UV lamp to dry her first coat of gel nail polish.

Maya thumbed through the photos on Pierce's profile. Emma nodded approvingly.

"He's a couple of years younger than you," Emma said. "Looks handsome."

"Yes, as long as they're not old photos."

Emma handed Maya's phone back. "Hmmm… Does he have any children?"

"His profile says no, but he's undecided about children…"

"It probably means he's keeping his options open. Would you want any more?"

Without hesitating, Maya shook her head again more assertively. "No, definitely not." This morning's squabbles and the stress of the school run came to the forefront of her mind. She couldn't handle that with a new baby in tow.

"Well, a date is a date. You've got to meet him —"

"If he asks me."

"He'll ask you. He'd be a fool if he doesn't," Emma said. "Just make sure you send him a picture of you with your new hair. In fact, let me take a photo of you now."

Later that evening, with the kids asleep, Maya made herself comfortable on the sofa, her laptop perched on her thighs and a mug of herbal tea within reach on the coffee table. She updated her profile, removing an older photo, and put up the one Emma had taken of her earlier. Then she checked her messages.

Pierce (PJWard14) had left another message asking what she was up to. She could see he was online and decided to reply: *I'm in my PJs and chilling. I'm so rock and roll. (But it is only Wednesday).*

Are they sexy PJs? Pierce messaged back immediately.

Haha! I would like to tell you they are sexy … but I'd be lying. They're comfy, though. Maya was wearing her favourite pyjamas. Nothing sexy at all — they were pink and black, and had a cute kitten on the front. The kids had chosen them when out shopping with her mum and dad for Christmas presents. Obviously Pierce didn't need to know this.

Maya liked flirting with Pierce. He appeared to have a similar sense of humour to hers, which she thought was a good thing.

You're funny. I suppose we should go on a date, shouldn't we? he wrote.

Maya smiled. *If you're asking?*

Yes, I'm asking. Are you free this weekend?

She told him she was, so they swapped mobile numbers and texted one another for a bit longer, making plans for the weekend.

As Maya was getting into bed, her phone pinged. Pierce had sent her another message, with a photo attached. Maya opened it and gasped, but not in dismay. It was a picture showing just his torso, his head cut out, with a towel around his waist. A little suggestive, but tastefully done. He definitely had a great body. Slim built, he had a narrow waist, widening in a V to his shoulders with defined chest muscles and muscular arms.

Giggling to herself, Maya pushed the duvet back and rolled up her pyjama bottoms, taking a photo of her legs from her knees down to her hot pink painted toenails.

Me naked. Not. She attached the photo to her message.

Tease. But I like. Nice toes. Can't wait to meet them Saturday! Pierce wrote.

I'll make sure I'm wearing flip-flops.

CHAPTER 13

Hey, Wendy, you about for a chat? Peter.

Maya smiled at the message, and at the nicknames she and her anonymous friend had adopted. *I've got a date tomorrow. I'm a bit nervous. He's been very flirtatious texting me. Wx*

You'll be fine, he replied.

Yes, it's just the way my luck's going, I'm not sure I'm going to find anyone. I'm starting to think DIYDes was my best offer! Maya answered.

He was quick to reassure her. *Haha! You can do better than him! But in all seriousness, be like the rhino. Not the big arse, but the thick skin.*

Yes, that is good advice, she typed. *You need thick skin for online dating. You can't take anything personally. I get men being quite rude really, because they think I've got my head up my arse because I'm 'so attractive'. I don't think I'm like that … but I need to fancy them. I don't fancy dating someone who looks worse than my dad.*

Just be careful, though, he warned.

Yes, I always message my friend to tell her who I'm with and where I am. And that I get home safe. W.

Good to hear. Can't be too careful these days. P.

Late on Saturday afternoon, wearing her favourite leather boots and skinny jeans — not flip-flops — Maya walked down the hill towards The Golden Lion. The air was still cold, even though the sun was shining and there was not a cloud in the sky. She closed her eyes briefly, tilting her face up to the light, like a flower. She breathed deeply, calming the nerves that now jangled as she neared the pub. Would she ever get used to this 'first meet' feeling?

She'd texted Pierce earlier, after stepping out of the shower and worrying about what to wear, and admitted how nervous she felt. Butterflies were spreading through her tummy. They'd been flirting quite a bit online, and now it worried her. What if he wasn't what she expected?

He'd texted back: *It's okay, it's just a drink. I don't expect anything more. It'll be fun.*

She really hoped she would like Pierce. He was apparently six-foot-two and although he lived in Portishead, he worked and usually socialised in Bristol.

As she entered the pub car park, where clumps of daffodils flowered under a bare oak tree, a sudden burst of laughter and chattering turned Maya's head. She wanted to hide but couldn't. Sam was walking out of the pub garden into the car park with his sister, Heather, and a man who she assumed was Heather's husband as he was holding her hand, plus three girls, one of whom was Chloe. Before she could turn her back to pretend she hadn't noticed them, Sam caught her eye and waved. Maya walked towards them — very slowly — fearing her embarrassment was written all over her face. At least she looked a darn sight better than usual.

"Hey," Sam called out.

"Hi." Maya waved nervously. "Just meeting a friend."

"We've just had a late family lunch." Sam shoved his hands in his pockets. Heather acknowledged Maya with a wave, and she and the rest of the family walked on in the direction of the marina.

"Was it good?" Maya turned her attention to Sam, thankful she'd agreed to meet Pierce at four o'clock now. Otherwise Chloe would have spotted her in the pub and reported back to Amber.

"Yes, yes," Sam said, briefly looking behind Maya. "Right, well, best not let you run late to meet your friend. Have a good catch-up."

Maya's heart pounded harder as she smiled weakly and waved, mumbling her goodbye.

Her phone buzzed. It startled her, a reminder that she was still standing stock-still in the car park, as if frozen to the spot.

I'm at the bar. What are you drinking? Pierce wrote.

Her fingers not quite finding the letters properly and relying on autocorrect, she replied: *White wine, please. I may need it. This is where I find out you're nothing like your photos.*

Yeah, I'm the old man wearing the flat-cap at the bar, he joked.

Don't I'm nervous enough already, she quickly texted back.

It's just a drink. Two friends. No pressure.

Maya breathed in deeply then blew out through her mouth, trying to relieve her anxiety. As she entered the pub, she spotted Pierce before he noticed her and her heart lightened, relief washing over her. Unlike with her previous dates, she felt an instant attraction. He was wearing dark blue jeans and a micro-checked blue shirt with short sleeves, revealing muscular arms. His brown hair was quiffed back a little, rather like Tintin. As if his sixth sense had kicked in, knowing someone was staring at him, he turned. After a moment of recognition, he beamed at her with a gorgeous smile.

Pierce greeted her with a kiss on her cheek. He smelt fantastic. Maya's excitement went up several notches.

"Hello, Maya. Great to finally meet you."

"Yes, and you too." Maya managed an audible response, she hoped.

"Shall we grab a table?" Pierce lifted the drinks from the bar and followed Maya to a table for two.

They gabbled some small talk for a bit, then as the wine relaxed her, Maya couldn't help but blurt out, "You don't know how relieved I am. You look so much better in the flesh. Your photos don't do you justice."

"I could say the same about you." He smiled. He had an incredible smile, and blue-grey eyes she could get lost in. Wow, she fancied this man. She'd worried that after all the flirty text messages, it would fall flat when she saw him, but if anything, the opposite was true. She was excited, to the point where her back tingled and heat pooled in her lower abdomen. She could feel her cheeks blushing.

They talked more about themselves, discussing work, life and how they were finding online dating.

"I have a confession to make," Pierce said, putting his pint down. He leaned closer to Maya as he spoke, his elbows on the table. "I'm not the age I stated on my profile."

"How old are you then?" Maya frowned, scrutinising his face carefully.

"I'm thirty-nine, not thirty-six."

"Oh. Why lie?"

"I was finding a lot of 'older' women were contacting me that I wasn't attracted to, and some younger ones wouldn't give me the time of day."

"Really?"

"Yes, so a friend suggested I tweak my age."

"And it worked?"

"Yes, it did."

Maya couldn't help thinking that if they hit it off, their relationship had started on a lie. But it was only the first date.

They were getting along so well that when Maya's stomach grumbled for dinner, Pierce agreed they should order something from the bar.

After eating, a sofa became free, so they moved over to it when Pierce went to get more drinks. It was well worn but comfortable, but they seemed to have moved closer to one another, their knees touching. Before she knew it, Pierce was kissing her — gently on the lips, then his tongue found hers. He was an impressive kisser, and was stroking his thumb along her arm. Maya became lost in the sensation.

The bell rang for last orders. She couldn't believe how long they'd spent in each other's company with no awkwardness. The two of them had really clicked.

"So... Did you want to do this again?" Maya really didn't want the night to end.

"Yes, I would," Pierce said. He glanced at his watch. "I think I should order you a taxi." He made a call, and the taxi company said ten minutes, so they had time to finish their conversation. Pierce stood up, helped Maya on with her jacket, and followed her out of the pub, where a taxi was waiting.

"What about you?" Maya asked as she climbed in.

"I'll walk. Text me when you get home."

"I will."

As Maya relaxed into the back seat of the taxi, she couldn't believe how wonderful her date with Pierce had been. She bubbled with excitement. Could this be the start of something new?

CHAPTER 14

April

"Hey, Maya!"

Maya, hearing her name being called, looked up from her phone and the flirty text from Pierce that she'd been smiling at. She was waiting for Lewis to come out of his classroom. She'd been dating Pierce for nearly three weeks now and could hardly believe it. He showered her with gifts and was very attentive in bed — they'd got to the stage of sleeping with one another. She had instigated it, not Pierce. He was so damn sexy.

Sam was making his way across the school playground towards her, surrounded by excited kids breaking up for the Easter holidays. He was dressed smartly in a suit, as if he'd come directly from the office, and had Chloe and Amber with him. The way Amber was fluttering her eyelashes and putting on a pleading face, Maya could feel something coming. Probably an impossible request. Sam looked harassed.

"Hey," she said, smiling and slipping her phone back into her handbag. She wiped her lip, feeling a stray hair clinging to her mouth. She tried tucking it behind her ear, but it was windy today. All the loose tendrils from her ponytail were blowing around, and she doubted it was an attractive sight. She battled to calm her windswept hair.

"Mummy, please can I have a sleepover at Chloe's on Saturday night?" Amber burst out before Sam could say anything. His mouth opened, then shut.

"I'm sorry, sweetie, but you're going to Nanny and Granddad's this weekend. Maybe another time?" Maya looked at Sam apologetically. The girls were moaning, but she ignored them. "Maybe after the Easter holidays."

"Yes, that sounds like a better plan, rather than springing it on me when you come out of school, Chloe," Sam said, grimacing with disapproval. His expression softened as he turned his gaze back on Maya.

"Oh, did they decide during school?" Maya looked at her daughter, frowning. "They do have a habit of doing that and don't quite understand that we adults like a bit of notice." By this point, Lewis had bounded out of his classroom and was running towards his mother.

"Hi, Mummy!" Lewis said, hugging Maya. She ruffled his hair and turned her attention back to Sam as Lewis let her go.

"They forget we may have plans too. I can imagine them in the playground organising their social diaries, and then they sulk when we say no," Maya said. "It is okay to say no to them, Sam."

"Yes, I know I can. I'm not used to it, yet," Sam said. "They seem to be growing up so fast, I'm not sure what the norm is. I suppose I just want her to be happy." They all headed towards the school gate, the kids running ahead while Sam and Maya walked together. Maya felt a self-consciousness she wouldn't have if she was walking out of the school with another mother. Why was it different because it was Sam?

Stop overthinking. You're allowed to walk out of school with a man. Just because he's single and you're single, it doesn't mean anything.

"Chloe seems very happy." Amber and Chloe were skipping along together, laughing. "But, no, I don't like it either," Maya continued. "That is, I don't like things being sprung on me at the last minute. I'm not very good at spontaneous decisions to go to places, do things. Sets my anxiety off. Kyle could never whisk me away for a surprise weekend." Maybe it was the confidence she'd got from dating Pierce, but Maya was finding it easier to talk to Sam about Kyle.

"I'll remember that," Sam said, grinning cheekily. What on earth did he mean? Before Maya could ponder on his statement, he quickly continued, "The girls have a good way of laying on the old guilt trip. Which weekend would be good for you?"

"Oh, I'll check my diary, but next weekend we're away as it's the Easter weekend." Maya retrieved her phone from her handbag and started searching for her diary app.

"Yes, I am too."

"I don't want to muck Mum and Dad around this weekend. They're so good to me." Plus, Maya was meeting Pierce, and she didn't want it all to go askew by complicating the arrangements.

"Two weeks' time, then?"

"Yes, that'll be the weekend before they go back to school. Is that all right with you?" She met his warm brown eyes, and for some reason, butterflies fluttered in her stomach. He nodded while she gave herself a mental shake. "Any problems, I'll text you."

"We can agree the finer details nearer the time." Sam held out his arm, to allow Maya to walk through the school gate first.

She turned and hesitantly waved in thanks. "Have a good Easter holiday, then."

"And you." Sam gave a nod, then led his daughter away in the opposite direction.

CHAPTER 15

Sam threw his keys in the wooden bowl on the telephone table by the front door as he entered the house. Chloe was whinging in his ear that life was so unfair because Amber couldn't sleep over, and Sam could feel his temples throbbing. He'd had too much coffee and not enough water, he'd been busy at work, and now he was listening to a complaining eleven-year-old. Sam put his fingertips to his forehead and rubbed.

"Chloe, for the last time, Amber is coming to stay — in two weeks' time. It's not like I said no. Unfortunately, her mum has made plans this weekend. And it is the Easter holidays."

"But Amber doesn't want to go to her grandparents."

"Chloe," Sam said sternly, wrinkling his brow, "if you carry on like this, I'll just cancel the whole damn thing." As she grew older, it felt harder to play mum *and* dad.

Chloe stomped up the stairs, mumbling under her breath. God help him when she actually became a teenager.

Sam thought back to the other Saturday, when he'd bumped into Maya and her kids at the cinema. He remembered how much he'd enjoyed her company. Of course, he loved the quality time with his daughter, but adult conversation couldn't be knocked — especially with an attractive woman. He hadn't realised how much he'd missed the conversations he'd used to have with Jade.

He got the impression Maya really didn't comprehend how beautiful she was. Take today; her blonde hair had been tied back in a ponytail, revealing her small, delicate ears and slender neck, wisps of loose hair whipped up by the breeze. When he'd called her name and she'd turned and smiled, lighting up her whole face, he'd caught his breath, stunned by her beauty.

Missing Jade still hurt, but Sam knew he was starting to feel ready to move on now. Jade would want this. Sam still felt he would need to take things slowly, though.

Suddenly, an idea came to him. As the cinema had been so much fun, he would invite Maya and Lewis out with them for the day, and then Amber could stay over. That way, he'd get to know Maya more and spend some time in her company. He retrieved his phone and sent a text message, careful about how he worded it: *Hey, Maya, about the weekend after next — would you and Lewis like to go out for the day with us, and then Amber can stay overnight?*

Saturday was warm, with clear blue skies and a mild breeze. Spring had arrived, spreading warmth and sunshine. The weather was so good that Tom and Heather had suggested a barbecue.

It was hard to believe it was still only early April, Sam reflected, sitting in Tom and Heather's back garden with an ice-cold beer. Heather was beside him, holding a pink gin and tonic with plenty of ice. The heat of the sun through his jeans cooked his thighs, but it was too soon to be thinking about wearing shorts. As he chatted to his sister, Sam watched Chloe being very accommodating to Scarlett and Daisy, her much younger cousins, having a tea party with dollies and teddies on a blanket in the middle of the garden. It was endearing to see that Chloe still knew how to play. Too often, kids wanted to grow up too fast.

While the beer slipped down, he mentioned Chloe's antics of the previous day, guilting him into agreeing to let her have

Amber for a sleepover. He didn't know whether to confide in his sister about Maya. Was there anything to confide yet?

"I thought I could go out for the day first with Maya and her two children. But I'm not sure where to go."

"That's a fantastic idea. Isn't Maya single?"

Sam sighed. Heather didn't miss a trick. "I think she is, yes." Although Maya hadn't been messaging him much recently via PeterPan26, so he wondered if she was dating someone. "But that's not why I suggested going out for the day."

"Why don't you go to Bristol Zoo?"

"No, Amber's grandparents have annual membership. Chloe went with them recently."

Heather thought. "Noah's Ark, but that's probably a bit similar... Cinema?"

"Did that too, remember?"

"Oh, yeah, you did say... What about the place with the trampolines? And you two can grab a coffee while the kids play."

"That only kills about an hour. I'll think some more. I thought it would be nice to go out somewhere for the whole day. Plus, I've heard all sorts of tales about that place. I don't fancy an afternoon in A and E."

He wanted a relaxing day with Maya, not a stressful one.

"True." Heather gave a little chuckle. "Oh, she could be your plus one for Joe's wedding! So, has she said yes to going out for the day?"

Before Sam could answer, there was a scream. Scarlett had Daisy by her dark-blonde plaits. Chloe was trying to mediate between the two, but somehow it had gone too far. Heather flew off her seat, placing her glass on the table and storming over to break up the squabble. She returned, huffing and cursing about having two girls.

"Boys are apparently easier," she said, grabbing her glass and finishing its contents, the ice rattling. "Sorry, Sam, so what did Maya say?"

He shrugged. "I haven't had a reply yet." He finished his beer. He wouldn't reprimand her for the plus one comment. He wanted Maya to become a friend.

CHAPTER 16

Maya had been surprised to see the text from Sam on Friday evening. She hadn't known what to reply, and was then so busy messaging Pierce in between catching up with admin for her business, she had totally forgotten to text Sam back. Did she want to have a day out with him, the five of them? It would mean Lewis wouldn't get left out. It wasn't as if Sam was bad company. Would Pierce be okay with it?

Pierce and Maya had been out together a few times, and they texted regularly-ish. He would go quiet at times, but she assumed he was busy at work. She didn't like to keep constantly texting him, so she'd usually wait for him to message before replying. She didn't want to scare him off by appearing needy. It was too early to say if she was his girlfriend, but they were certainly intimate with one another — and exclusive.

Sam was just a friend, the father of her daughter's best friend. Pierce would understand. Carefully wording her text, so it couldn't be misconstrued, she replied:

Hi Sam, apologies for the late reply. It would be lovely to go out for the day. Sounds like a great plan.

The kids were off school for the Easter holidays, so today Emma had come over so the four children could play and she and Maya could have their usual Monday catch-up. Emma had brought lemon drizzle cake, while Maya had baked white chocolate and cranberry cookies for the kids.

She always scaled down her workload during the holidays, as it wasn't fair to expect her parents to babysit all the time. She usually booked Amber and Lewis into kids' clubs for a couple of days and fitted clients in for then. But the amount she earned on these days usually only covered the cost of the childcare, and proved not very profitable for Maya. She'd rather not work at all during the school holidays and enjoy the quality time with her children.

The day was sunny, although chillier than it had been over the weekend, which meant the four children could play outside on their bikes and scooters in the close where Maya lived. She kept the front door open, so she and Emma could keep a beady eye on them. A couple of the neighbours' kids had joined them, by the sound of it. Somehow, the conversation turned to Sam when Maya let slip about going out with him for the day. Emma raised her eyebrows inquiringly.

"It's not like that. We're friends — just like you and I."

"I bet you find him hotter than me," Emma said with a wink.

Maya shook her head. "Honestly, the day trip is for Amber and Chloe."

"Yeah, yeah…"

Wanting to change the subject, Maya filled Emma in on how things were going with Pierce. She decided not to mention any doubts she felt. She was probably just worried because it was all new and she'd forgotten how dating a new man felt.

"Check you out, with two men on the go!" Emma exclaimed.

"You're so not helping me." Maya sipped her coffee, giving Emma a stern look. She was feeling a niggle of guilt that she would be spending a day with Sam — and wondered if Pierce would have a problem with it. But it was hardly a date with three children surrounding them. "Pierce has asked me out on Wednesday evening. Any chance you could babysit?"

"Of course I'll babysit. I promised you I would, otherwise you'll never meet anyone," Emma said, grinning from ear to ear. The deal was Maya had to share every minute detail about her dates. "But you know, all I'm saying is it's good to have a back-up, so don't rule out Sam."

"He's just a friend. And I really, really like Pierce. Besides, imagine how awkward it would be, dating the dad of Amber's best friend. What if it went wrong?"

"I know. I'm teasing. Honestly, I'm so happy for you, Maya. Let's hope it works out."

"Thanks, honey. It's early days yet."

Pierce's texting had been sporadic for most of the day — probably due to his work being hectic. Later that evening, once the children were worn out and in bed, Maya texted him to confirm she had a babysitter for Wednesday evening. She smiled when he responded quickly, saying he couldn't wait. Knowing his sense of humour, and how they liked to joke, Maya decided to reply with something cheeky.

Fancy a threesome with an Italian?

Her phone pinged back almost immediately: *Yes! Would love a threesome :D*

Great! I'll book Bottelino's for 7.30pm Wednesday! She followed up with a winky smiley face.

Oh, that kind of Italian! Sounds great, Pierce replied.

Maya giggled. She was about to put her phone on charge and go to bed when she spotted a chat bubble from PeterPan26, showing she had an unread message:

Hey, W, just checking how things are. Hope you're okay? P

Things were good. But did she tell PeterPan26 why? Now she was dating Pierce, she didn't feel the need to chat to Peter like she used to. But she still didn't want to completely ignore him, so she decided to reply tomorrow, fearing she'd get caught in a messaging marathon and never get to sleep.

CHAPTER 17

"Your dad's here, Chloe!" Heather called up the stairs.

In response, there was a burst of giggling and then a shout: "Okay, I'll be down in a minute."

Sam walked through to the kitchen and sat down at the table, while Heather placed his dinner in front of him. His sister was a godsend, because with thirteen weeks of school holidays annually, and Sam only having around five weeks' paid annual leave, it left a lot of time where Chloe needed minding. Heather couldn't look after her the whole of the week leading up to Easter; he'd had to put Chloe into some clubs run at the sports centre. It would be easier and cheaper once she was older, but he hated the idea of wishing his daughter's life away.

"Well, have you had any dates yet?" Heather looked at Sam expectantly.

"You'd know if I had. I'd have asked you to babysit, Heather," Sam said, hating how he sounded. He was snapping at his sister because he'd had a long day at work, wanting to finish everything so he could relax over the long Easter weekend. He wanted to get away from work early tomorrow.

"You know what I mean. Are you messaging anyone?"

"One or two…" Sam ran a hand through his hair. He picked up his knife and fork. The smell of roast beef, with roast potatoes, parsnips and a mix of steamed vegetables, wafting up from his plate made his mouth water. Gravy puddled in the Yorkshire pudding. He was starving, only having had time for a cheese and tomato sandwich and a bag of crisps out of the office vending machine at lunchtime.

Heather stared at him intently. "Aren't you going to tell me about them?"

"There's nothing to tell." Sam had messaged a few women, but the conversations had fizzled out. There had been no one he fancied meeting up with. The only woman he'd clicked with online was Maya, and she didn't know it was him. He needed to remedy that, but he was afraid if he did she would blank him completely, and he didn't want to risk it. He also had a feeling she was seeing someone. She wasn't on Find My HEA much and hadn't messaged 'Peter'. None of this he would admit to Heather.

"Oh, you are boring. I wanted some juicy details." Heather sat down opposite Sam with a mug of tea. She wrapped her hands around it.

"Heather, a gentleman never kisses and tells."

"I know, I know. But you are seriously looking, aren't you? You are giving this online dating thing a proper try? Don't let what happened with that woman all those years ago put you off."

Truth be told, he wasn't making much of an effort, but Heather didn't need to know. He still wasn't sure if he was ready.

"Yeah, yeah…" Sam sighed. "Yes, I am. Where's Tom?"

"He's working late tonight." Heather glanced over her shoulder at the kitchen clock. It was ten past six. "He said he wouldn't be home until after seven. He got called out to some job earlier, and he's rung to say he can't leave until he's fixed the problem. That's the downside of working for himself. So, all set for the weekend?"

"Yes. What about you?"

"Yes, we're looking forward to a long weekend," Heather said. "It'll be great to catch up with Joe. I wonder how Rhianna puts up with him."

Sam chuckled, shaking his head. They had thought their brother Joe would never settle down. While Sam had been the sensible one, studying hard at school, Joe had been sloping off every minute he had to party. Where Sam had been classed as nerdy, Joe had been too cool for school. Heather had appeared to get the balance right, still getting her grades and being popular. "Yes, it's going to be great to catch up. Let's hope the weather holds, hey?"

"And the weekend after, have you made arrangements with Maya?"

Heather did not miss a trick. Definitely the smartest of the three of them. "Yes, she's agreed to come out for the day with Amber and her son. I still can't think where to go; it'll all depend on the weather."

"That's great!" Heather patted his shoulder. "I'll have a think for you."

Shattering the calm, the three girls hurtled into the kitchen, the door swinging and Chloe chasing her younger cousins, hands outstretched, wiggling her fingers. "Tickle, tickle, tickle."

Scarlett and Daisy screamed and giggled playfully, each running to their mother and wrapping their little arms around her legs.

"Whoa!" Heather said. She looked as if she might topple over. Chloe tickled her much smaller cousins gently.

"Chloe, be careful, please," Sam said sternly.

"Before you leave, Chloe, would you like a drink?" Heather said, prising the two children from her jeans and picking up Daisy to rest her on her hip. Daisy gave her mum an ecstatic cuddle, wiping her face into Heather's T-shirt, still giggling.

"No, thanks," Chloe replied, sitting herself next to her dad. Sam stroked her hair. Dark strands were everywhere, and it looked knotty at the back. He really needed to make her tie it back if she insisted on keeping it long. Jade would have been plaiting it...

"Right," Sam said, trying to shake off his maudlin thoughts. He pushed his knife and fork together once he'd finished the delicious roast dinner. "We'd best leave you to it. See you Thursday night."

Heather retrieved his plate, still balancing Daisy on her hip. Scarlett had snuck off, and by the sounds of it she had turned the television on and was watching CBeebies.

Sam and Heather gave each other a goodbye kiss on the cheek. Heather kissed Chloe while Sam attempted to kiss Daisy, but she hid her face in her mum's shoulder, so he ruffled her hair instead.

Back home, Sam allowed Chloe to sit up in bed and read her book for a bit, wanting her lamp off by nine. It might be the holidays, but they had an early start for kids' club, and he knew the weekend would be full of late nights for the both of them.

Downstairs, he poured himself a glass of red wine and opened up his laptop. With the memory of his sister nagging in his ear, and remembering Jade wouldn't want him to be alone, he perused Soul Mate Search to see if there was anyone worth getting into conversation with. Sam replied to a couple of women who'd messaged him, but he couldn't find anyone he fancied contacting. Why couldn't he shift Maya out of his thoughts? He opened Find My HEA and hovered over the message thread.

This was stupid. He should text her as Sam and not hide behind Peter. He grabbed his phone and started to draft a text: *Hey, I'll have a think about where to take the kids next weekend. Chloe is looking forward to it — wherever we decide to go. Have a great Easter holiday. S x*

Should he put the kiss? He removed the *S* and the *x* and pressed send.

CHAPTER 18

Maya's late night with Pierce left her jaded on Thursday morning. Emma had raised a cheeky eyebrow as she'd walked through the door just after midnight, and had insisted on hearing all the details. After Bottelino's, Pierce had driven Maya back to his for a nightcap.

"Is that what it's called now?" Emma had said, jovially. To Maya's relief, she hadn't judged her. In fact, she'd encouraged it. "About time you had some fun. You make the most of it."

Maya's tiredness was due to a combination of alcohol and lack of sleep. She had to rise early, but the kids woke her earlier than her alarm clock due to the television being on loud and them arguing about what to watch. This didn't set her up for the day in a good mood.

In the diary that morning, Maya had a couple of trusted clients who could come to the house for their treatments — she only allowed this during the holidays, being choosy about who she permitted into her home. Amber and Lewis were usually pretty good and didn't disturb Maya, but she only booked treatments that the kids could walk in on if there was an emergency, like manicures and pedicures. She didn't have room in her house for anything else, and she couldn't set up the right environment for a relaxing back massage. Privacy would be an issue, too. In hindsight, she wouldn't have booked these clients in if she'd known she would be taking the kids away for the weekend. It had been a last-minute decision when Kyle had let her down. She'd perused websites late into the night a few weeks ago, looking for an affordable seaside break — and at such short notice.

While drinking a cup of strong coffee, Maya wrote a list of things she needed to do that day. Once her last client had left, which would be at around three in the afternoon, she would load the car so they were ready to leave first thing on Friday morning, maybe catching a McDonald's breakfast at one of the motorway services.

Throughout the day Maya ticked off her to-do list in between clients, making sure she'd packed everything needed. If she was visiting Spain it would be shorts and T-shirts, but for the English coast in April — she needed to pack for every eventuality.

Pierce had texted on his way to work, and occasionally throughout the day. She liked that he kept her phone busy. His messages always made her smile. It wasn't until the afternoon when she remembered Sam had texted and she hadn't replied to it. She sent him a quick apologetic text, confirming they'd catch up next weekend.

By the end of the day, Maya was exhausted. She climbed into bed early, not long after the kids had gone to bed, ready for the silly o'clock start to her Easter weekend break.

The next morning, Maya was on the road by six a.m., her silver BMW estate fully loaded, so that she could only just see out of her rear-view mirror. She was relieved to find the motorway quieter than she'd expected it would be. They stopped at the services for their McDonald's breakfast, and Maya savoured her first coffee of the morning. The pitstop took no more than half an hour. Quickly, trying not to let the kids see, she sent a text to Pierce to say she was on the road.

"First one to see the sea buys the ice-cream!" Maya said almost two hours later, driving slowly down a narrow country lane. The sat nav claimed they were only ten minutes away from their destination.

"We don't have any money," Amber said. Maya looked in the rear-view mirror. Her daughter had a smug expression and her arms were crossed.

"I brought your pocket money." Maya smiled into the mirror.

As the road dropped down and round a bend, the beach came into view.

"I can see the —" Lewis said excitedly, then stopped, realising he didn't want to buy the ice-creams.

"It's okay, Lewis. I'm paying really."

"Wow, Mummy, the beach is awesome."

They could see the expanse of golden sand with the tide way out. Anyone mad enough to be in the water were black dots immersed in white foam. Maya hadn't been to this part of the country before and was rather looking forward to discovering a new corner of England. The beach narrowed at the top, but as it went out, with the water at low tide, the bay widened, leaving parts of the coastline reachable from the beach. Maya liked it. It was a small, enclosed beach, especially at high tide, but large enough to share with other holidaymakers without being on top of one another.

It was too early to check in at the bed and breakfast, so Maya parked up in a car park behind the small high street which overlooked the beach.

"Can we have ice-cream now?" Lewis pleaded, as they got out of the warm car. Although the sun was shining, there was a strong wind coming off the sea, and Maya fumbled in the boot to find their coats. A chilly reminder that it was still April and not August.

"Let's have an explore of the area, and then we can go buy one," Maya said, zipping up her jacket. Both children nodded eagerly, beaming with excitement. Looking at their happy faces, she knew that this Easter break was going to be just what they all needed.

CHAPTER 19

On Saturday morning, Maya jolted awake, a little dazed by her surroundings. It took her a moment to recollect that she was in a charming room in a beautifully restored, picturesque farmhouse B&B, and not in her own bedroom. Amber clambering down from the top bunk of the pine bunkbed to use the bathroom had woken her. Lewis was now stretching and sighing but remained under the duvet.

"I'm hungry," he said, mid-yawn.

Maya could easily eat breakfast, too.

Yesterday had proved to be a long day, what with hitting the road so early and the long drive down. She smiled as she recalled the fun they'd had yesterday. The Rosevear crazy golf tournament — which Lewis had easily won, much to his delight. There had been ice-creams, fish and chips for lunch on the golden, sandy beach while fighting off opportunist seagulls, and rock pooling, followed by a long coastal path walk. Then they'd watched the sun set over the ocean and had a late tea in a cliffside pub. It must have tired her out as much as it did the kids, because she felt as if she'd slept more deeply than she had for ages and was finding it hard to get up. Plus the bed was extremely comfy! It might be fun, but it was hard work holidaying with the kids on her own. This was the first break Maya had taken the kids away on since the divorce. She realised how much Kyle had made a difference when they'd been together — and even then, he hadn't done a lot. But he had been the extra pair of hands, or eyes, depending on what was required in the parenting department.

Her choice of location for this Easter break could not be faulted. She smiled to herself, remembering her children's delighted faces upon seeing the beach and its fierce waves, and then later when they'd checked into the cosy farmhouse B&B with its pretty gardens. *Well done, Maya!* The pictures on the internet did not do the place justice. She really had picked the perfect beach holiday.

She quickly checked the time on her phone. It was half-past seven, and there was still no reply from Pierce. She'd sent him a quick message yesterday to say she'd arrived safely. Maybe he didn't want to bother her when he knew she was away with her children. A glance out behind the curtains told her the sun was shining — and the chickens she'd spied yesterday were roaming the end of the garden. There were wisps of cloud, and the trees were moving with the breeze, so this might be an ideal day to let Amber and Lewis take surf lessons.

"Get yourselves dressed, while I use the bathroom." Maya pulled back the duvet, energised by the sunshine and the call of a cooked breakfast. She quickly washed and dressed, pulling a brush through the children's hair and then her own. She decided not to bother with any make-up. Who needed it in a place as relaxed as this? Besides, the sea air and good night's sleep had done wonders for her complexion.

As they made their way downstairs, they could hear the mumble of conversation and laughter coming from the breakfast room. Maya led them in and headed for the table set for four. A family were already seated at a nearby table with two young girls. An older girl was fetching juice from a serving table. There was something familiar about her, and when she turned and squealed at the sight of Amber, they were stunned to see it was Chloe. Amber squealed excitedly too, hugging her friend.

"Here's your breakfast, Chloe," a man said, entering. Maya looked up to see it was Sam. He looked as shocked as she was. "Oh my God, hello… This is a surprise," he said to Maya, stuttering. "What are you doing here?"

"Oh, er, hello," Maya replied, equally tongue-tied, the shock jangling her nerves. "We're staying here. We arrived in Kittiwake Cove yesterday." Her relaxing long weekend in Cornwall with the kids had just got complicated.

"Oh, so you must be the family staying here?" Sam said, frowning.

"Yes." Maya shoved her hands into her pockets, realising she'd been wringing them. "And you must be the family visiting?" When she'd checked in yesterday, Rose, who owned the B&B — Trenouth Cottage — had mentioned she had some of her family staying.

"Yes, this is our parents' B&B. That's my sister Heather and her family over there," Sam said, pointing.

Maya gave an uncomfortable wave. She knew Heather by sight, as she sometimes picked Chloe up from school. By now, Lewis and Amber, completely unperturbed, were helping themselves to juice, with Chloe assisting them, but Maya felt rooted to the spot. Everyone was saying hello in that awkward, polite way people did when they weren't sure how to react.

Rose entered, carrying toast, oblivious to what she was walking into. "Good morning. Sit yourself down, and I'll fetch your order in a second," she said to Maya. "I hoped you slept well."

"Yes, great, thanks," Maya replied. She could now see the resemblance between Rose and Heather. They had the same brown eyes and dark hair, although Rose's was greying. Unsure what to do next, Maya nervously edged towards the table Rose had indicated.

Sam chuckled. "Mum, we know Maya. Chloe and Amber go to the same school. They're best friends."

"Inseparable. An unknown force pushing them together, judging by the way things are going lately," Maya said, lightly. Poor Lewis looked bored as the two girls chatted.

"Oh, how funny. What an amazing coincidence," Rose said.

Sam placed Chloe's breakfast on the table Maya had chosen. Lewis had already taken a seat. "Chloe, sit here with Lewis and Amber. Do you mind?" He turned to Maya.

She shrugged. "No, not at all."

"Join me." Sam pointed to his breakfast table. "What would you like, tea or coffee?"

"Coffee, please."

Sam seemed to be taking meeting Maya in his stride. She needed to relax.

"I'm helping Mum. Be back in a minute. Take a seat." His hand briefly rested on her upper arm.

"This is great," Heather said, talking across the room to Maya. "And such luck! This is Tom, by the way, my husband." Heather pointed using her fork, and Tom nodded, chewing his food. "These two are Chloe's cousins, Scarlett and Daisy." The two girls smiled shyly, the younger one with tomato ketchup smeared around her mouth.

"It's such a small world. Years ago, we bumped into our old neighbours in Spain," Tom said. "Do you remember?"

"Oh, yes," Heather said, nodding.

Sam returned with a pot of coffee. "I've been ordered to sit down now." He took his place opposite Maya, smiling at her. He turned her cup over and poured her coffee, then his own. His face was even more handsome now he was relaxed and had some colour in his cheeks. He had a lovely smile.

Rose came back in, bringing more toast and a fresh pot of tea for Heather and Tom. "I can't believe you know my family," she said, chuckling. "Right, what can I get you? Will your two eat a kid-friendly English breakfast?" She looked over at Amber and Lewis. "Fried eggs?"

They both said yes. Maya and her children rarely had a cooked breakfast, so this was a real treat. Then Rose turned her attention to Maya. "And what would you like, my love?"

"Full English, please, but no black pudding."

"Yes, I know, awful stuff, but I have to offer it for those who do love it."

"I love it!" said Tom.

Rose smiled at Tom then turned her attention to Sam. "I'll bring yours out with our guests', shall I?"

"Of course, Mum." He looked up as Rose placed a hand on his shoulder. Once his mother had left the room, Sam asked Maya, "So when did you arrive?"

"Yesterday morning," Maya replied, still feeling a sense of shock and anxiety in Sam's presence — and trying not to show it.

Sam laughed. "I still can't believe you're the family staying at Mum's B&B. Did you know?"

Maya shook her head, frowning. "Why would I know?"

Sam shrugged. "I don't know, Chloe might have told Amber…"

"This was a last-minute treat for the kids. Amber didn't know I was booking anything."

"Oh, right, I see… So, what are your plans for today?"

"I was going to see if there was availability at the surf school for Amber and Lewis." She poured milk into her coffee and then took a sip. It was too hot, but she wanted to do something with her hands. She felt nervous, being put on the spot like this. Not that it was Sam's fault, but she never imagined he would be here. She would have put make-up on. At least she'd remembered to brush her hair.

"No need. Joe — our brother — is taking Chloe out. He was a professional surfer in his younger days."

"Oh."

"Now he's a professional beach bum," Heather said, laughing.

"Anyway, he can take Amber and Lewis too."

"Will he mind?" Maya frowned.

"No, he loves surfing. And two more won't do any harm. He'll be cool with it."

"But what about the boards and the wetsuits? I was going to hire those."

"Joe helps runs a surf school in the summer, too. He has resources." Sam winked.

Maya nodded. "Is he the same guy who owns The Cormorant?"

"That's him."

"Yes, your mum said last night. That's where we had dinner."

"Yeah, Heather is being a little harsh. Joe owns the pub which has a couple of self-catering apartments attached to it, and he helps Mum and Dad out here with the B&B in the peak season. But his routine is predominately organised around the tide, and the swell of the surf."

"Here we are!" Rose appeared carrying two plates, which she placed in front of Amber and Lewis. Instantly they stopped talking and picked up their cutlery. A tall man following behind Rose put a breakfast plate in front of Maya and Sam.

"There you go, son," he said, and Maya could see he was an older version of Sam, with white hair and a few more wrinkles around his eyes and on his forehead, but the same warm, brown eyes. "Enjoy your breakfasts. Can I get you anything else, my dear?" He turned his attention to Maya.

"Oh, no, thank you, this looks lovely." The fried egg looked perfect, ready to run once she broke the orange yolk. She took a piece of toast out of the rack, buttered it and placed it by the egg.

"Thanks, Dad," Sam said. "Have you been introduced?" Sam looked at Maya, who shook her head, then to his father. "This is Maya, by the way, Dad. She's a friend. Her daughter Amber is best friends with Chloe." Sam reached across the table for the brown sauce and poured a small amount onto his sausage and bacon.

"You mean they're inseparable, and fate seems to be keeping it that way," Maya said, chuckling. Maya liked that Sam had referred to her as a friend and not a 'mum from school.' *Or the irresponsible woman who let my daughter go home looking like an eighties rock chick.* They were past that by now. 'Friends' sounded good.

In the background, Heather mumbled something about whether it was the girls' fate that was drawing them together, and Sam frowned at his sister, which made her shrug apologetically.

"I'm Charles, Sam's father," the older man said, holding out his hand, and Maya shook it.

"Hello."

"We'll catch up properly later, I'm sure," Charles said, giving a sly wink. "For now, I've got the washing up to contend with, or Rosie will have my guts for garters."

"I will not!" Rose had overheard and whipped him playfully with the tea towel she'd pulled off his shoulder as they left the room. They were both chuckling, and the banter could be heard continuing between the two of them.

124

Sam rolled his eyes. "They're always like that."

"It's nice." Maya liked how they could laugh still. They reminded her of her mother and father. They'd also been together for years and hadn't lost that love.

For a moment, silence fell as they tucked into their cooked breakfasts. Heather and Tom were immersed in dealing with their two young daughters, although Maya was sure she'd caught some sort of eye contact between the couple, silent messaging. It made Maya self-conscious with Sam. Were Heather and Tom reading something more into their relationship? They were just friends. Besides, Maya was dating Pierce, and Sam was obviously going out with the stunning brunette from the gym.

"I didn't realise you came from Cornwall," Maya said, eventually. She wasn't sure if the silence was comfortable or not, and she felt she needed to fill the gap in case.

"Yes, but I moved away as soon as I started my engineering course at uni, and I never really returned."

Maya nodded as she listened. "So, the big question is, can you surf?" She dipped her toast into her runny egg.

"In my younger days I wasn't bad, but I wasn't a natural like Joe."

"Will we see how good you are this weekend?"

"Good God, I hope not. That water's freezing at this time of year." He chuckled, the smile reaching his eyes.

"Shhh … don't tell the kids that." Maya had to stop thinking about how attractive she found him. *Keep thinking of him as Chloe's dad and not Sam. It should work.*

"Oh, they won't care."

"Hello, everyone, good morning!" a man joyfully boomed as he entered the room.

"Uncle Joe!" Heather's daughters shrieked excitedly. Chloe ran to give him a hug.

Joe was a younger version of Sam and Charles, wearing an unzipped, fading Animal hoodie over a Rip-Curl T-shirt. He was also wearing khaki shorts and flip-flops as if it were the middle of summer. The sun may have been out, but it wasn't *that* warm. He already looked tanned. Whereas Sam always appeared smartly dressed, working in an office, it was unlikely that this man even owned a tie, or a shirt with a collar.

He kissed Heather, shook Tom's hand, ruffled each girls' hair, then turned to Sam.

"This is Joe, my brother," Sam said, though the man needed little introduction. He was quite obviously Sam's younger brother — equally as dark and good-looking. Where Sam had flecks of grey, Joe had very little. His hair was a little longer, in typical surfer style. He looked like a man who had never been stressed in his life and had a constant tan. "Joe, this is Maya."

"Hi, Maya." Joe shook Maya's hand. "Sam didn't say anything about bringing a lovely lady with him." He winked, nudging his brother.

"Oh, no, um, I didn't come with Sam." Maya stumbled over her words. "We're just friends. I booked a room here without realising the B&B belonged to your parents."

"Oh, right, well, life is funny like that."

"Chloe and Amber are in the same class at school," Sam said.

Joe grabbed a chair that wasn't being used from the kids' table and sat down with Maya and Sam. "Any more coffee in that pot?" Heather handed him a spare cup and saucer from their table.

"I've roped you in to take Lewis and Amber, as well as Chloe out surfing today," Sam said, once Joe had poured his coffee.

"The more the merrier. Fancy a dip, Maya?" There was a twinkle in his eye.

"Oh, no, I'll watch from the water's edge, if that's okay?" Joe's flirtatious manner left Maya flustered. Sitting with two such good-looking men was making her nervous. "Someone needs to take the photos."

"Ah, you don't know what you're missing."

"Freezing cold water. That's what she'll be missing," Sam said, his tone dry. Did he dislike Joe flirting with her?

Joe laughed. "It keeps the grey hairs away." He combed a hand through his curly black hair. "You should try it more often."

"There you are, Joe!" Rose entered the breakfast room to clear plates from the tables. Heather stood to help her. "We could have done with you an hour ago."

Joe stood up and kissed his mother. "Sorry, Mum, had to clear up the pub this morning from last night."

"Luckily your dad didn't burn the sausages, or the bacon."

"I'm leaving the pub in the capable hands of my staff this weekend." Joe sipped his coffee.

"Who? Rhianna has her bistro now!" Rose frowned.

"Don't panic, Mum. Lizzie and Ricky will manage. I've got extra staff in and Toby's back from uni for the Easter holidays." Joe patted his mum's shoulder reassuringly.

"I am glad," Heather said, "because it will be lovely for us to spend some time with you this weekend, Joe."

"Yeah, already cleared. And I'm only a phone call away."

"You mean you've joined the twenty-first century, Joe, and bought a mobile phone?" Tom jested from across the room.

"I've always owned one. I just don't see the need to be constantly attached to it."

Sam looked at Maya, nodding in Joe's direction. "Our brother is a bit of a technophobe."

"Phone-o-phobe," Heather teased.

"All right, you two. I don't see you for months, then the first chance you get you're ganging up on me."

"Never," Heather said, kissing her brother's forehead.

"Little point owning a mobile down here. They don't bloody work most of the time." Joe raised his eyebrows and sipped his coffee. Maya sat quietly, listening to the family banter. Even Rose and Charles teased Joe. It was endearing to watch, even as an outsider. "You won't be teasing later, when I'm in the water teaching your kids to surf."

"But we know you love it, Joe," Heather said, laughing.

"How on earth did you convince Rhianna to marry you?" Sam asked, jovially.

"Hey, hey, what is this? Pick on Joe time?" Joe held his hands up defensively, but Maya could see it was just sibling teasing.

Upon seeing Heather get up to help Rose, Maya felt she should too. She stood to check on Lewis and Amber and to retrieve their plates.

"Sit down, dear, you've paid to be waited on this weekend," Rose said. "I've got this."

"Yes, sit yourself back down, Maya," Joe said with a mischievous smile, glancing at Sam. "We haven't finished getting to know one another. Drink your coffee and let them wait on you."

Maya giggled nervously and did as she was told. Sam gave an assenting nod.

Once the plates were cleared, Charles arrived with more coffee and tea, and the kids helped themselves to more juice and pastries. The whole family, now including Maya, Lewis and

Amber, chatted about the plans for the day. Scarlett and Daisy had been given a box of toys by Rose so were easily entertained. Joe, knowing the tides, suggested the kids surfed after lunch, when the tide would be coming in. Cricket on the beach was agreed for the morning activity, with a picnic as the sun was out.

Maya hoped she wasn't imposing, but they all reassured her that she was more than welcome, and in fact the Trescotts (and the Wyatts) would be offended if she and the kids did not join them. It was settled. And to be honest, Maya would only get a sulking pre-teen if she tried to separate Amber from Chloe.

CHAPTER 20

Carrying the cricket bat, Sam wandered down to the beach with Joe and Charles, listening to their familiar banter. He might not like the cold water, but he enjoyed playing cricket on the beach. It brought back childhood memories, and it was great to now be creating the same memories for Chloe, who was walking in front with Maya and her children. What a surprise, meeting them here — but a good surprise. The girls were clearly inseparable as they skipped along the path together — it would make Chloe's weekend even more memorable. And maybe this would be his opportunity to show Maya he wasn't a stuck-up jerk after all. Perhaps on neutral ground, they could get to know one another better.

At the beach, the sun was shining but the wind was unyielding. The hard sand, washed clean by a retreating sea earlier, was cold under their bare feet. Although they were running around, it wasn't warm enough to relinquish their jumpers and hoodies.

Everyone, except Rose, who insisted she sloped off early to make up the picnic, was playing. It wasn't proper cricket. They bowled underarm — especially for the kids — and there weren't any sides; it was more about who could stay in bat the longest. And they used a tennis ball, as this bounced more easily along the sand. Scarlett and Daisy played for a while, but easily became distracted by digging sandcastles in the sand when it was their turn to be outfield. Daisy helped Heather behind the stumps, fetching the missed balls. She would run after them gladly, but wasn't very good at throwing them back to Heather, who tended to have to run for the ball anyway.

Lewis was particularly good in bat. For nine years of age, he certainly had a good eye for connecting cricket bat to ball. He gave them a good innings and enjoyed running from stump to stump, although the adults weren't counting the runs.

"Okay, everyone spread out," Joe instructed. They all laughed, and the fielders moved out further as Sam took his place to bat. He wasn't in for long. It was Charles who caught Sam out after a couple of well thrown balls from Maya. Sam had been too busy watching Maya, rather than watching the ball. Her hair was tied back in a ponytail, but wisps blew in the wind. She looked so pretty, laughing with her head thrown back. She wore a pair of skinny, light blue jeans, with a cream T-shirt under a turquoise jumper. Such joy and warmth emanated from her. She'd said, "This is it, kids, catch him out," and given a cheeky wink with her last throw, and it had distracted Sam completely. The ball had connected to the bat and had soared, high into the air, coming down easily into his father's cupped hands.

Charles shouted "Out." Joe, the biggest kid of them all, gave a cheer and ran round to high-five the palms of each child.

Cricket was halted when Rose appeared with a cool box in one hand and a bag in the other. Joe spotted her first and ran up the beach to help her. Sam followed, taking the bag from her.

"You should have called one of us to help you down to the beach." Sam frowned at his mother.

"Ha, you know how lousy the mobile signal is in Kittiwake Cove," Rose said.

"I'm sure it's deliberate, to make us leave our mobile phones behind." Sam didn't have much of a signal on his phone up in the town, but it did work better on the beach, ironically.

"Yes, to remind people they're on holiday," Joe added.

Rose shrugged, now free of her heavy burden. "It's probably not a bad thing."

Charles collected the cricket wickets together as they all made their way to the base they'd picked in a sheltered spot, over on the right side of the beach by the rocks. It curved in a little, protecting them from the wind coming off the ocean.

Rose handed out wet wipes so that everyone could clean their sandy hands, especially the kids. Then, with the party either kneeling or sitting cross-legged on the blankets, she handed out the sandwiches. "Watch out for hungry seagulls, kids," Rose said, eyeing the circling birds above. "Keep your food tight to your chest!"

Sam sat down next to Maya, but to his annoyance — and he knew he was being ridiculous to feel even the smidge of jealousy that he did — Joe sat the other side of her. His younger brother was cooler and managed to be much more at ease with the opposite sex compared to him. Even as kids, Joe the surfer dude had the girls fawning over him. Whereas Sam was the dorky, nerdy older brother, into science fiction, reading, engineering and cricket. Sam knew this feeling was ridiculous. Joe's heart belonged to Rhianna now.

As they tucked into the picnic, the sun remained kind to them. Maya and Heather applied sun cream to the children's faces and necks.

"The tide has turned. So, who's up for surfing?" Joe said, directing his question at the children.

Sam had packed a swimming costume for Chloe, but he knew he wouldn't be setting foot in the sea. He'd made that mistake once before at this time of year. Joe had convinced him to go in. His ears had frozen pink, and his lips had turned blue after about ten minutes. He smiled to himself, remembering Jade had had a good chuckle at his expense. Now he preferred to surf in the summer when it was warmer. Not much warmer but warmer than April. At least the sun could warm you up after if nothing else. Sam had never been like Joe, wanting to be in the water rain or shine.

Daisy and Scarlett screamed a yes. "Girls, you're a bit small," Heather said, frowning, and they both pouted.

"Nah, they can have a go," Joe said. "Tom, you'll come in with me, won't you?"

"If you've got a wetsuit that fits."

"Of course."

Joe was speaking to a friend at one the surf hire shops situated further up the beach, tucked over on the left near a café. He shook hands, gave a wink, and something was said about 'on the house'. Maya assumed he was giving the man a free meal or drinks at The Cormorant in return for lending them the wetsuits, neoprene socks and bodyboards. Joe owned his own wetsuit and fitted into it very nicely indeed. His legs looked a little bandy, but he had a narrow waist, widening to a toned chest and muscular shoulders. She had hoped Sam would get into one, but he'd declined. So had Maya and Heather, and Charles had headed back to the B&B to help Rose. Tom, being tall as well as solid, also looked good in a wetsuit. Heather kept eyeing her husband up and giving him a wink, and a tap on the bottom. But when he turned and playfully flicked water at her with his foot, she shrieked, running out of the inch-deep water she'd been paddling in.

"This water is so cold," Maya said to Sam, who was huddled beside her, hands in his pockets and shoulders hunched. She was only an inch deep like Heather had been, as it was impossible to roll her skinny jeans much further up her calves. Sam had rolled up his jeans to just below his knees.

"Do you mean you can actually feel it? My feet have gone numb," Sam said, swishing his feet from side to side in the clear salty water. They both stepped backwards as another wave came in.

Today the wind was bitter, making it hard to breathe. If you forgot the cold, the sun shining on the sea made it look almost tropical, the clear turquoise waters revealing the sand underneath. Further out, waves crashed, causing white lines of surf to roll along the beach. Maya loved the relentless rumble of the ocean.

"It hasn't had a chance to warm up yet. Give it a couple of months, and it'll increase by a degree or two," Sam said, chuckling. "Like that will make a difference."

"Yes, it will still seem cold."

They watched Joe instruct the older children, while Tom helped Daisy and Scarlett catch the smaller waves rolling in only knee deep. That was nearly up to the little girls' waists. Joe had the older three out deeper. They'd started on the sand at first, with Joe giving them instructions on how to hold their boards. The kids were laughing now, so he appeared to be good with them.

"Joe helps teach surfing in the summer, when it's busier. He employs more staff to manage the pub to free him up during the day," Sam said.

"Has Joe not got kids of his own?"

"Joe?" Sam shook his head as if amused by Maya's question. "Nah, he wasn't really the type to settle down with one girl. Well, he wasn't until he met Rhianna last year. They're getting married this summer. Look, he's the biggest kid of the lot!" Sam pointed in Joe's direction; he was mucking about in the water and making all three children howl with laughter. "Some years ago, we thought he'd found the one, but he either got scared, or cold feet… Something happened, we're not really sure what. Jade was ill at the time, so I focused on her more than my family, I'm afraid."

"I'm sure they understood." Maya now gazed down at her feet, stepping up and down in the water, hoping to warm them up and find a way out of the uncomfortable conversation. She had no idea how to talk to Sam about his dead wife.

"I'm sorry, I've made things awkward, talking about Jade," Sam said. To Maya's surprise, he placed his hand on her shoulder, making her look up at him.

"No, I'm sorry," Maya said. "I never know what to say. You and Chloe are obviously coping."

"God, if I didn't, I think I'd have Jade haunting me. Nagging me, from the afterlife." Sam laughed, lightening the mood. Maya was relieved he could joke about it and laughed too. But it made her wonder if Sam would ever be able to move on after Jade. *Stunning Brunette could be a mid-life crisis.*

Heather approached them at the water's edge, shivering. "I think I'm going to go back to the house. It's too cold to sit on the beach with this wind."

"We may join you soon," Sam said. They watched Heather walk off the beach.

"Shall we get out of the water and walk on the sand a bit? Do you think Joe will mind?" Maya asked.

"Yes, sure." Sam gestured for Maya to lead the way.

Maya walked past the tideline and up onto the soft sand. They found some shelter from the wind near the rocks, and Maya sat down.

"Are we still okay for next weekend?" Sam asked, sitting beside Maya, arms hugging his legs. She almost wished he'd put an arm around her, if only to keep the pair of them warm.

She hoped her cheeks were only rosy due to the bitter wind and not her blushing.

"You'll be sick of us after this weekend, won't you?"

Sam chuckled. "Never. Besides, I promised Chloe a sleepover, so I'd best stick to it."

"Well, then, it would be lovely." Maya started wondering if Emma could have Lewis for the evening, so she could arrange a date with Pierce. She needed to grab opportunities where she could. Yet, in a weird, guilty way, sitting here with Sam, she didn't want to think about Pierce. She hadn't thought about him all day.

"Just can't think what to do with them for the day." Sam scratched his head. "Any ideas?"

"I suppose it will depend on the weather. My two are happy to do anything. We can do the zoo, or Slimbridge Wetland Centre is up the road. Or slightly further afield, Devon Crealy Adventure Park. My two keep nagging me to take them there. We could pack a picnic."

Sam nodded. Maya looked out to sea, where Joe was teaching the kids. Daisy and Scarlett had already had enough. They were heading out of the water, shivering. Tom was following, carrying their two smaller bodyboards. Maya wondered when the other three would get bored, or cold, and give Joe a rest. He was very patient with the children. And she could see why they liked him. He was on their level. He was cool. Joe would demonstrate and come in on a wave, even kneeling on the bodyboard.

"He's such a show-off," Sam said, under his breath.

Maya giggled. "You're only jealous you can't do that."

"Probably."

CHAPTER 21

All showered, freshly dressed and warmed up from their afternoon in the sea learning to surf, Maya and her children had been invited to join Sam and his family for a barbecue in the back garden. The patio was much more sheltered than the beach, so the wind didn't feel so vigorous and biting. The breeze did gently ring the chimes hung around the patio though.

Maya was grateful they'd considered her and the kids this evening. She'd popped to the local Spar and bought a couple of bottles of wine and some cans of beer as a contribution. Rose had insisted they didn't need any more food. While out, and away from everyone, Maya had dropped Pierce a text to tell him about the day. Guilt played its part; she'd been enjoying herself so much being with Sam — *Sam's family* — she'd forgotten about him. However, his messages had been very few and far between, so she wondered if he wanted to leave her in peace to enjoy her holiday.

While they waited for the food to be prepared, the children played on the lawn. The older ones playing with the younger ones was always fun to watch. Amber didn't play games of the imagination like she used to, but it was amazing how the younger children would draw it out of her again. Lewis still had it. Maya would catch him in his bedroom, when banned from all electronic devices, playing with Lego and superheroes. Even dinosaurs would get a look in.

"Lovely, isn't it, to watch them play?" Sam appeared by Maya's side with a glass of white wine. He'd obviously caught her smiling at them. About to argue it was too early, Sam gave her a look as if to remind her she was on holiday. She quite liked the look he gave her. He meant business without being pushy. Their hands touched briefly as he handed her the wine glass, his fingers warm. She noticed he had strong hands, and she had a sudden fantasy of him chopping wood.

Her attention drawn back to the kids playing, as Daisy gave a squeal, Maya replied, "Yes, yes, I was thinking the same." She sipped the wine. It was crisp and refreshing.

"I'm not looking forward to September. We'll have stroppy teenagers."

"Pre-nagers, you mean. They'll only be twelve." Maya was sure she'd see a significant change in Amber as soon as she started secondary school. She was not looking forward to September.

"We'll help each other through it." Sam nudged her. Maya felt an unexpected jolt of pleasure at his touch.

"Let's hope they stay friends and don't turn mean towards one another."

Sam chuckled. "Oh, I never thought of that. Surely not. Not the way fate keeps throwing them together."

Was it fate throwing Amber and Chloe together, or Maya and Sam? She couldn't decide. She didn't mind either way. Slowly, Maya was becoming more at ease with Sam. She just needed to treat him as if he was one of the mums at school, and not focus too much on the fact that he was a very attractive, single man. He also missed Jade, and probably always would. How did Stunning Brunette feel about that? Was that why she wasn't here?

Besides, Maya was happy with Pierce — wasn't she? They'd been dating for a month now. He was generous and such good fun, especially in the bedroom. It was wonderful to be reminded that she was a desirable woman.

Burgers devoured, Maya felt satisfied and fit to burst. That last chocolate cupcake may have been the devil in disguise. And she had no idea how much wine she'd drunk — Sam had kept topping her glass up. Heather didn't appear drunk. She was sitting in a garden chair, picking at nibbles on the table. Rubbing her eyes, Scarlett asked if she could go to bed. Heather stroked her head and kissed her, then instructed Tom to carry Scarlett up to the house — in the nicest, bossiest way possible. She kissed him too and with a wink, made some quip about making it worth it for him later. Maya loved admiring the chemistry between them. From the outside, at least, theirs appeared to be an ideal marriage. Tom did everything he could to make Heather happy, and he obviously wanted to do it. Maya could see he loved her. Had Kyle ever appeared like this to their friends?

"Do you fancy a stroll, to walk off some of the food?" Sam said, coming to stand beside her and shaking Maya from her reverie. "We could go check out the sunset."

"What about the kids?" Maya glanced towards the four remaining children — five if you included Joe — who had returned to their game in the garden. Candles inside glass lanterns had been lit around the patio and down the garden path, and some sets of solar-powered fairy lights had also come on as the light faded. They hung prettily over a summer house, around the patio and in a tree.

"They'll be fine here. Mum and Heather will keep an eye on them."

"Okay, then."

Maya fetched her phone from out of her pocket and checked the time. Six minutes past eight. There was a text from Pierce. Not wanting to appear rude to Sam, she decided to read it later.

"Don't worry, we won't be back late, if you're worried."

"Oh, no, I'm not…" Was she giving off an anxious vibe? Just going off alone with Sam… What would the family be thinking?

Sam led her around to the side gate. They passed under an old rose arch with two climbing roses, buds ready to burst, clinging to it and through the cottage garden at the front of the house that Maya had admired the day she'd arrived. The tulips in various oranges, purples, and yellows that lined the path leading to the house were closed up for the evening.

Sam shut the front gate behind them, and they walked, side by side, down to the beach. A few people were about, watching the sunset. Apart from the continuous roar from the sea, Maya noticed how quiet it was. Even the seagulls had disappeared. She slipped off her pumps. The sand cooled her feet. The sea was way out now, and on the horizon the sun was low in the sky, about to dip behind the ocean, making the clouds an orangey-pink. The water mirrored the colours. Maya took a photo on her phone but it still didn't do the view justice.

"Beautiful, isn't it?" Sam said. They stopped at the edge of the sand, the expanse of sea before them.

"Yes, it is."

"I never tire of the sunsets at Kittiwake Cove." He sighed heavily. "Jade loved them too."

Maya smiled and gently nodded.

"I'm sorry, I'm doing it again. I must stop living in the past. Jade would kill me — if she was here." He laughed it off.

"I don't mind you talking about her."

"Thank you. We scattered her ashes here. Jade didn't want to be buried or left in some graveyard no one would visit. She wanted to rest by the sea. She knew I'd come here regularly with Chloe, because of my family."

"That's lovely. I think I'd want the same."

Silence fell between them for a moment. Maya let Sam be with his thoughts. Then, involuntarily, she shivered. She should have picked up her coat now they were away from the warmth of the firepit.

"Oh, you're cold," Sam said, taking off his jacket. "Here, put this on." He slipped the jacket around Maya's shoulders. It was warm from Sam's body heat and warmed her instantly. It carried his scent too, the lingering aroma of his aftershave. She appreciated the gesture.

"Won't you get cold?" Maya asked.

"No…" he said, not very convincingly. He did have a jumper on, but he probably could feel the chill. "Here, let's sit over by those rocks. It might give us some shelter while we watch the sunset."

Sam led the way, and Maya huddled beside him, feeling guilty he'd lent her his jacket. The least she could do was get close enough to share some heat.

"What happened to Jade?" Maya asked before thinking it through. "Oh, sorry, it's okay if you don't want to talk about it."

Sam shook his head. "No, it's fine, now. It's been four years. I still miss her."

"I'm sure you do."

After a pause, Sam spoke, his voice remaining steady. "She was thirty-four, and we had been trying for another baby, when she got ill. She was diagnosed with advanced colon cancer. She had a couple of operations, about twelve cycles of chemotherapy and was finally given the all clear." Sam shook his head with a huff of disbelief. He looked Maya in the eye then. "Four months later, we were told it was back. But it had spread aggressively and was now incurable."

"I'm so sorry." Maya placed her hand on Sam's arm, rubbing gently.

"She had just turned thirty-seven when she died."

"So young. It's no age."

"She had incredible strength."

They fell silent, watching the beautiful sunset. Maya was unable to find the right words for something so tragic. Sam picked up a small shell from the sand and threw it, as if setting himself free from his trance. "I used to come down here often as a kid. I loved this beach."

"So why did you move away?"

"I wanted to be an engineer — it paid better than being a beach bum. And when you're younger, you can find this stuff boring. You don't realise what you've got."

"You probably appreciate it more now because you don't live here, too." Maya pulled her knees to her chest, wrapping her arms around her legs.

"That is true." Sam made semi-circles in the sand with his trainers. "Mum's lived here all her life. She inherited the farmhouse years ago — it was our family home before she turned it into a bed and breakfast. Her brother inherited the estate."

"Estate?"

"It's not quite Downton Abbey," Sam said, with amusement. "He inherited the debt too, but Tristan, our cousin, has found a way to make it work, to keep it within the family, like mum with the farmhouse." Sam kept his gaze on the tideline, picking up small shells and pebbles and throwing them at a bigger rock jutting out of the sand. "Anyway, enough about me. Have you always lived in Portishead?"

"Kyle is from Cornwall. I'm originally from Bristol. Mum and Dad are still there, but I moved out to Portishead — it was cheaper at the time, and felt less hemmed in. I like being by the water, too. We — Kyle and I — thought it would be better to bring the kids up there. One day, we planned to move to Cornwall." Maya tried not to sound too exasperated. Kyle had got a new job and said he'd be fine commuting if it worked out — but then he'd met Jenna. He had ended up moving closer to work and Cornwall, but without Maya and the kids. "Now he's in Exeter, the kids don't see their dad often. He was supposed to have them this Easter, but he let me down — took a last-minute holiday to Spain with Jenna and Lola."

"Lola?"

"He's had another child with Jenna, his girlfriend. He says she wasn't planned. She's probably about four months old now. My two don't get much of a look in." Maya sighed. She was disappointed in Kyle and the way he'd ditched his children.

"So, your ex is a bit of a dick." Sam looked at Maya, catching her eye.

She laughed. "Yes." He was probably just saying it to make Maya feel better — and it did.

"He'd have to be, to let an attractive, fun-loving woman like you go."

Maya pulled a face. "You do realise Jenna is eight years younger than me?"

"He's still a fool... Beauty isn't just skin deep."

Maya elbowed him. "Enough with the flattery. I'm not really sure I'm fun-loving. I look a mess today — so I don't feel the slightest bit attractive." Especially when the wind had whipped her hair into knots and made her look like something a bird would nest in.

"I must say, for a woman who works in the beauty industry, you don't come across as very high maintenance," Sam said.

"I'll take that as a compliment," Maya replied, narrowing her eyes playfully.

"I mean…" Sam stammered, back-tracking, "you always look lovely."

"Thank you."

"But you're not always wearing make-up, dressed to the nines with perfect nails and hair." He nudged her.

Maya knew what he meant. Stunning Brunette looked high maintenance. Sam didn't mention her. Should Maya ask about her?

"Some of my clients are what you would call high maintenance. I'm constantly waxing brows, tinting lashes, painting nails — sometimes when they don't even really need it. I'm grateful; they keep me in business. But it amazes me how they can do the school run in three-inch heels."

"And how do they do day-to-day chores with nails like claws?"

"I have to keep mine fairly short for massages." Maya held out her hands. She didn't even have nail polish on them. She didn't have the time.

"Oh, yes, not sure I'd find it relaxing, getting the odd scratch." Sam flinched, then laughed. Maya liked his laugh. "Although in the height of passion…"

"Really?" She laughed too, not able to look him in the eye.

"Sorry, probably too much information!" Sam shook his head and changed the subject. "Vicky is what I class as high maintenance."

"Vicky?"

"Oh, she's a work colleague; we play mixed doubles in badminton together. You probably saw her with me at the gym that time."

That time I fell on my arse and made a tit of myself. And he remembers. "The brunette?" She thankfully held off saying 'stunning' bitterly, but she couldn't meet his eye now.

"Yes, that's her."

"I have to say, isn't she a little young for you?" Maya tried to make it sound like a joke, scooping dry sand and letting it rain through her fingers.

"And I'm the wrong gender. She's gay. Zara, who also plays, is her wife."

"Oh," Maya nodded, remembering the other woman she'd seen at the gym.

They then started to discuss their favourite movies — a safer subject.

"I love that moment in *Love Actually*," Maya said, her gaze still focussing out to sea, "when the guy — Mark isn't it? — rings the doorbell, and Keira Knightley answers it and he stands there, with the cue cards, telling her that he expects nothing in return but tells her that he thinks she's perfect. It's the sweetest thing ever. All along she's been thinking he hates her, and yet, he's kept his distance because he loves his best friend's wife."

"It is a good movie." Sam played with the dry sand, combing it through his fingers.

"You've watched it?"

"Are you kidding? With Jade, she loved those sorts of movies."

"Most women do. Don't get me wrong, I love action movies and sci-fi, but I love a good rom-com too — a feel-good movie to snuggle up on the sofa to watch," said Maya.

"So, you'll come see the next Marvel movie with me, then?" Sam chuckled.

"Er, yes. And if Chloe doesn't want to go, we can always take Lewis."

"It's a date… I mean, deal."

The sun sank, deepening the colours in the sky. Silence fell between them again.

"Right, we'd better head back," Maya said, standing up and brushing the sand from her bottom. She was starting to worry she'd left the kids for too long — and spent too much time alone with Sam. The sun had now disappeared below the horizon.

Approaching the farmhouse, Sam talked about his parents, and how the cottage had been in his family for centuries. Their conversation broke as they entered the garden. It was very quiet, with most of the table cleared. No children were playing.

"Where are the kids?" Maya asked, frowning.

"Daisy wouldn't go to bed, so they all agreed to go up as well, so she wouldn't be missing out," Heather said. She was sitting beside Tom and holding his hand.

"Even Chloe?" Sam asked.

"Even Amber?" Maya added.

Heather shrugged. "What can I say? They're good kids. They've only just headed up. I told them to brush their teeth and not to wake Scarlett. To be honest, I think Joe whacked them out with the surfing."

They looked at Joe, who was snoozing in a chair near the smouldering firepit, embers glowing.

"Looks like they've whacked him out too." Sam chuckled.

"I've phoned to tell Rhianna he's still here. She apologises for finishing late at her bistro and not being able to join us," Rose said. "I'd best wake him."

"I think I might go check on the kids, and go to bed myself," Maya said. She placed her hand on Sam's arm tenderly, but quickly withdrew it, worried it looked more affectionate than it was supposed to.

Sam nodded. "I might go check on Chloe too."

Maya said goodnight to everyone and headed up to her room, Sam following behind.

"Thanks for a lovely evening," she said, hovering outside her door, keeping her voice low.

"It was great to share it with you. What are your plans for tomorrow?"

"Oh, I don't know." Her heartrate spiked; she was suddenly aware she was standing in a softly lit hallway with a handsome man. The scent of smoke mixed with that beachy smell lingered on them both.

"Shall we see what the weather brings? Being by the coast, you never know what to expect," Sam said, his voice soft. "That's if you want to do something with us? You're more than welcome. Chloe is enjoying Lewis and Amber's company."

"If you're sure? I don't want to encroach on your family time."

"You're not." Sam stood close to her, so they could talk quietly.

Maya felt strangely drawn to him, like a moth to a light. "Okay, we'll discuss it at breakfast."

"See you tomorrow, Maya. Goodnight." He smiled, hesitated, then ducked into Chloe's room.

Closing her own bedroom door behind her, Maya breathed deeply, trying to clear her mind of thoughts of Sam and how first impressions could be so wrong. A bedside lamp lit up the room dimly. Both children were asleep. Not wanting to wake them, she crept softly around, getting ready for bed. She propped up the pillows and reached for her phone, typing a reply to Pierce. She updated him about her day but omitted the sunset stroll with Sam. Innocent as it may be, Pierce might not see it that way.

Maya opened her book but found it hard to concentrate. Her mind was too busy reflecting on the day. She'd enjoyed Sam's company — and his family's, of course. He was a good man. And attractive. But was he looking for a partner?

It would be a ridiculous idea to get involved with a dad from school. What if it went wrong? How would that affect Amber and Chloe? And would Maya be constantly comparing herself to Jade, his amazing wife?

And besides, she was going out with Pierce.

Sam checked on Chloe, who was sleeping soundly, her soft, regular breathing reassuring him she was having untroubled sleep. His mum had given Chloe one of her twin rooms. Her clothes were dumped in a heap on the other bed. Even asleep, she was the image of her mother. Chloe would always be a constant reminder of the love he held for Jade. It wasn't wrong to feel something for someone else, was it? That is what Jade would have wanted for him, for him to move on. Not live life alone. Not at his age. But was it too soon?

Today had been wonderful, sharing time with Maya, getting to know her. He hoped he was forgiven for his abominable behaviour last year. He knew Maya was using online dating. But he had to be careful what knowledge about her he revealed, or else he'd have to disclose his anonymous profile on Find My HEA. He was too afraid to jeopardise their growing friendship. Maybe if he gave it time, it would turn to more than friendship naturally. Maybe he needed to be patient.

He didn't want to jump into something if he wasn't ready either. He could ruin everything.

He kissed his daughter's forehead, then left the room, shutting it softly behind him. Even though he longed for his bed, his bones feeling heavy and it was an effort to put one foot in front of the other, he still decided to spend another half an hour with his family before retiring for the evening. Before he knew it, the weekend would be over, and he'd be having to head back home.

CHAPTER 22

On Easter morning they awoke to glorious sunshine, and the kids said they'd like more surf lessons and a day on the beach. Maya wasn't going to argue. This was a much cheaper option. An adventure park or something similar would have been expensive. This was free entertainment and allowed the kids the chance to explore.

Before heading down to breakfast, she received a message from Emma: *Met any hot surfer dudes?*

Maya replied with an eye roll emoji and told Emma that they were having a lovely time away. She omitted that Sam was there. It would only lead to Emma texting a load of questions. It would be easier to tell all once she caught up with her in person.

She felt a pang of disappointment that Pierce hadn't messaged. But he could be busy, too. She tried to forget about him and concentrate on her holiday. She didn't miss him as much as she'd expected. Was it because Portishead felt a long way from Cornwall? Or, being busy with her holiday, perhaps she couldn't think about him as much? The relationship was new, after all.

After breakfast, Rose gave the children a small basket each and sent them out into the garden to hunt for Easter eggs, with clues to lead to the next egg. Maya had already given her children an Easter egg each up in their room. The hunt was geared more for Daisy and Scarlett, but Rose had assured them there were some tricky eggs to find for the older children, too. It made them explore the nooks and crannies of Rose's quaint garden, including the chicken pen.

"Don't eat all the chocolate straightaway, Lewis," Maya said, her eyes narrowing on her son.

Through a mouthful of chocolate, Lewis replied, "I won't."

Maya rolled her eyes, and Sam touched her back gently.

Once all the eggs were collected and their baskets laden, the children were allowed to eat one egg before handing them back to Rose. She promised to look after the Easter eggs while the children went to the beach, storing them in her larder.

They made the most of the low tide and rock-pooled in the morning, searching for crabs and shrimps, and even the odd little fish. This kept them out of the wind coming off the ocean, although it appeared to be less forceful than the day before. Maya had removed her fleece jacket and tied it around her waist. Amber and Lewis had done the same.

They had decided not to make a base, but to stroll along the beach and explore the rocks as they went, making a walk of it. Charles showed them how to dip a bucket into the pools, to see what they'd caught, this being kinder to the little critters than fishing nets. Rose had stayed behind at the bed and breakfast with Heather to prepare a lunch, which they would go back for at one o'clock.

"Who fancies a coffee?" Sam asked. He looked up towards Tom and Charles, who were escorting Daisy and Scarlett around the rocks, while Amber, Lewis and Chloe took themselves off with less need for supervision. It still didn't make Maya relax. She watched them like a hawk ... or a seagull, hungry to steal a sandwich.

"Sounds like a great idea," Tom called from his post on some rocks higher up. Charles also agreed with a thumbs-up.

"Maya, coffee?" Sam asked.

"I wouldn't say no."

"You both go. We'll watch the kids," Tom called down. "Bring us back a biscuit or something, too."

Maya and Sam headed back up the sandy expanse in search of coffee.

"It's another beautiful day," Sam said, his arms swinging as he walked.

"Yes, shame to go home tomorrow," Maya said.

"Don't go. Stay another night. We're not going home until Tuesday."

"I can't." Maya wished she didn't have to leave, but she had clients booked in all next week. She'd booked kids' clubs and her parents to look after Lewis and Amber. "Besides, your mum might need the room."

"She doesn't. You can stay," Sam said, almost pleading.

Maya's guilt rose in her chest. "You've checked, have you?"

"Well … no, but I'm sure it would be fine." Sam frowned. "It's just we're going to Rhianna's bistro tomorrow evening. It would be lovely if you could join us." Sam and Joe had pointed out The Beach Front Bistro when they'd first strolled down to the beach together, and Maya would have loved to try the food and the cocktails. It looked so enticing, being able to watch the ocean from the veranda.

"I'm sorry, Sam." Maya shook her head. "I've got work on Tuesday. Only a couple of clients, but I still need to get back. Your family have been more than generous."

"Okay, well, let's enjoy today. And you don't have to dash off too early tomorrow."

"Oh, no, if the weather is still like this, then the kids will want to be on the beach for another round of the cricket tournament."

Not realising how far they'd travelled with their rock pooling, it took ten minutes to fetch the coffee from the beach café, then another ten to walk back.

Back at the rocks, Lewis, Amber and Chloe were keen to show off their finds in the rock pools. Sam had picked up some biscuits and cartons of juice for the kids, so they all took a breather from paddling.

"When we were kids, we used to build a sand boat on the beach, and wait for the tide to take it," Maya said, remembering her childhood holidays. "Kyle used to make one for Amber and Lewis when they were little."

"Yes, we did the same. Or we'd make a massive sandcastle," Sam said.

"We could build a boat now," Lewis said, overhearing their conversation.

"You don't have your swimming costumes on," Maya said, seeing this leading to five very wet children.

"It's too cold to swim. We'll just paddle," Lewis insisted.

They did have spades with them, as well as their fishing nets and buckets.

Sam nudged Maya. "Go on, it'll be fun. The tide has turned. If we build it close to the tideline, it should have sunk by the time we need to go up for lunch."

Daisy and Scarlett were tugging on their dad's shirt, pleading with him to build a boat.

They walked out to a spot in the middle of the beach and started digging, piling up the sand following a rough outline Lewis had made with his spade.

Daisy and Scarlett started off helping, but then decided to look for bits of seaweed and shells to decorate the boat. Tom and Charles took over with their spades. Charles was well into the boat building, as a granddad should be. As the walls got higher, he made a step for the children to be able to get in and out easily.

Engrossed in the shovelling, building and patting the sand smooth, when Maya looked up, the sea was only ten feet away. Amber and Chloe were drawing lines in the sand with their heels to measure the waves and how close the water was getting.

As the first wave hit the boat, rippling around its sides, the kids jumped into it. They all had to stand, as there wasn't enough room for them to sit. Maya got out her phone, snapping photos. She had 4G on the beach — somehow — and shared a picture via Instagram. With the blue sky and cotton wool clouds, you would have thought it was August, not April.

Caught off guard, a huge wave surged past Maya, splashing up her calves with a shock of cold. "Whoa," she heard Sam say, also caught out. She rolled her three-quarter-length trousers up and waded back to a shallower part, joining Sam. Tom and Charles were standing further back out of the water. The kids were jumping up and down excitedly — feet still dry — in the boat, undefeated, although the sides of the boat were crumbling away gradually. Tom and Charles would rush back in before the next wave hit and try to build the sides of the boat up, battling vainly against the sea, with the kids screaming and laughing at them.

Maya's feet sank into the sand as the water retreated. Not expecting her feet to be buried as deep as they were, she lost her balance.

"Whoops, you okay?" Sam said, catching her as she wobbled, his hand on her arm. She grasped his elbow. Her eyes met his, and his expression was a mix of laughter and concern.

"That caught me by surprise. My feet were stuck." She let go of Sam once she knew she wasn't going to fall.

"We'd better head back for lunch soon," Charles said, coming to stand beside Sam and Maya.

The boat started to crumble until it was only a mound of sand. Daisy had been the first to abandon ship, followed by Amber and Chloe, then Lewis. Scarlett wanted to get out too, but suddenly appeared fearful of the sea. Tom waded into the shin-deep water, hooked his four-year-old daughter under his arm, and carried her horizontally, as if she were a surfboard, turning her terrified cries into giggles.

Rose had laid out a grand picnic in the garden when they returned from the beach. Sam relished Maya's expression of surprise.

"Rose, you didn't need to go to all this trouble," she said, gazing at the huge amount of food.

"Nonsense. I love doing it for my family. And you're a part of my family this weekend." Rose ushered the children to a chequered picnic blanket on the lawn. The adults were seated around the circular garden table on the patio, Sam between Maya and Heather.

After lunch had gone down, and the kids had taken a treat from their Easter baskets, Joe arrived, ready to take them to the beach. Daisy and Scarlett decided to stay behind and play at Grandma's. Sam had to chuckle. Tom looked relieved. He clearly hadn't fancied donning a wetsuit again.

"I'm sure Joe can find a wetsuit to fit you, Sam," Tom said. Not required for surf instruction, he had a bottle of Stella open and was swigging from it, looking very relaxed and smug on his sunlounger.

"Oh no, maybe in July, but certainly not in April," Sam said. "I'm quite happy to watch from the beach."

"What about you, Maya?" Joe had mischief in his eyes. Sam recognised that look. If this had been a few years ago, Joe would have swept Maya off her feet. But it made Sam wonder if someone like Joe was more Maya's type.

She shook her head and looked as if she was about to argue, but Sam quickly said, "No, no, she's allergic to cold water too, like me."

"Besides, who will take the photos?" Maya waved her phone. "And I did enough paddling this morning."

"Okay, you two lightweights can stay on the beach." Joe turned his attention to the kids. "Looks like it's just us — the Fantastic Four."

The three older children cheered.

Sam found himself by Maya's side, yet again, standing at the water's edge, watching the children, laughing and cheering on their surfing antics. Luck really was on his side, to be spending so much time with her. She was easy-going, he could relax in her company. Getting to know her as a friend first suited his pace. He noticed she kept looking at her phone today.

"Expecting a text?" he asked. He chided himself, realising he should have pretended not to notice. Or was she messaging 'Peter' and looking for a reply? He hadn't checked in all holiday.

"Oh, sorry, it's rude of me," Maya said, slipping her phone into her back pocket and looking back out to sea, where Lewis had just fallen off his board and was splashing about in the surf. "I'm sort of seeing someone. I was checking if he'd messaged. You know what the signal is like around here."

"Oh." *Not waiting for Peter, then.* This was news to Sam. He felt a stab of disappointment. He knew she'd been going on dates, from what she'd confided in him as 'Peter', but he hadn't realised she'd started seeing someone regularly. In person, she hadn't said too much about her dating to Sam. Had she found someone already? She was a smart woman, with the added bonus of being beautiful, and she came across as a warm, loving person. Considering how her ex-husband had treated her, she didn't seem to carry bitterness and resentment. Maybe Sam's pace to dating would be too slow. "Been seeing him long?" He hoped his tone sounded cool.

Maya shrugged. "Not really, about four weeks now, but it started faster than I intended. He's probably busy with family himself. I don't want to keep on texting him and scare him off."

"You won't do that. Besides, if you do, then he's not worth it."

"Ah, thank you. I suppose I don't want to jinx anything at this early stage," Maya said, playing with the water with her toes. "It seems to be going so well, I worry it's too good to be true."

Trying his best to sound upbeat, Sam replied, "I hope it works out for you. You deserve to be happy."

CHAPTER 23

"So, how's it going with Maya?" Heather asked, catching Sam alone in the kitchen. Plates cleared, he'd volunteered to make the teas and coffees after dinner. Rose had laid the large oak dining table, and they'd enjoyed a roast beef dinner with all the trimmings after they'd returned from the beach and freshened up. It felt as if they were in an Enid Blyton novel, his mother was always feeding them. They just needed Timmy the dog.

Joe had sloped off, needing to see to the pub and catch up with Rhianna, but Maya and her children had been included in dinner. Sam's place had been set beside Maya's. He knew what his family were doing. He was grateful in some ways, but feared it might appear forced.

"Great." Sam nodded.

"We've been trying to give you some space so you two can bond." Heather leaned back against the counter while Sam poured hot water into an already warmed teapot.

He raised his eyebrows. "Well, I'm not sure how well it will work as she's seeing someone."

Heather fetched the milk from the fridge and filled a jug. "Is she? She hasn't said anything."

"It's a bit new and she doesn't want to jinx anything."

Heather nudged Sam and he nearly spilt the coffee he was stirring. "Doesn't mean you should give up. It just means you have a challenge ahead of you."

"But she might really like this guy — and he might really like her."

"It's early days. Anything can happen. Don't give up hope, Sam."

Was Heather especially insightful about these kinds of things, or were his attentions to Maya more obvious than he realised?

"I won't. But maybe Maya and I are meant to be just friends."

"I think you suit one another."

"You would, Miss Matchmaker," Sam said, his tone teasing. "Hey, while you're here, grab those two mugs, will you? They're Tom's and Dad's coffees." Sam picked up a tray with the teapot, milk jug and sugar bowl and walked through to the dining room.

"Joe was saying earlier that he's got a band playing at the pub tonight. Fancy going along?" Tom said, taking a mug from Heather as she walked in.

"I'd love to, if Mum and Dad are okay to babysit?" Heather said.

Sam poured tea into the teacups, handing them along the table.

"Yes, yes. You can all go. Sam, you can take Maya," Rose said, taking her teacup.

Sam cringed inwardly. Were his family trying too hard? Somehow, he thought Jade had played a part in this. She'd probably made his whole family promise to help him move on — when the time was right. Was the time right? Admittedly, it would be good to go out for a beer, listen to a local band. "Maya, would you like to come?"

"Oh, I couldn't. My kids…" Maya fiddled with her napkin and her cheeks pinked.

"Oh, don't worry about them, dear," Rose said, reaching across for the milk jug, which Maya passed. "Charles and I will be here. What's two more to look after? Besides, they'll probably be in bed early. They all look shattered. Go, enjoy yourself."

Showered and changed, Tom and Sam waited downstairs for Heather and Maya to emerge. Each held a bottle of lager as they leaned on the kitchen counter, talking football — their favourite subject.

When Heather had said she couldn't walk into a pub in the evening without make-up on, Maya had concurred. Sam thought he'd best wear a shirt with a collar and opted for a polo-shirt. Tom had done the same. He'd learnt long ago that if the women made an effort to dress up, so should he.

Joe had confirmed that the band weren't on until nine, so they had plenty of time. Maya was possibly fussing with her kids too, telling them to behave. Sam had seen how nervous she'd looked at the suggestion of leaving her children with his parents. It wasn't that she didn't trust them, it was more, he knew, that she wouldn't want to impose. But they could hardly go down to the pub without her. For this weekend, at least, she was one of the family. And he liked that thought.

Maya appeared before Heather, and Sam realised he and Tom had stopped talking as she entered.

"Ready," she said, nervously. She'd changed into a long-sleeved blue and white stripy Joules jumper. Her jacket was tucked over her arm. She wore her blonde hair loose, the ends curling naturally. Her make-up was light; her cheeks were highlighted pink with blusher and her eyes were lined with kohl and mascara. Lip gloss sparkled on her mouth. She looked pretty … stunning. Realising he was staring, Sam broke away his gaze and stared at his half-empty lager bottle.

"Beer?" Tom offered before he could.

Maya gently shook her head. Her hair swished, so she tucked the strands behind her ear. "No, thank you."

When Heather came down five minutes later, they said goodbye to Rose and Charles and the children. Daisy and

Scarlett were already in their pyjamas, and the five children were all seated around the dining room table playing board games and cards.

Maya kissed her children and pleaded, "Please be good for Rose and Charles. No bickering." She ruffled Lewis's hair.

"We will."

"I'm sure they'll be fine," Charles said, giving a wink for the children to see.

"Mum and Dad know where we are if there are any problems," Sam said, trying to reassure Maya as they left the house.

It was now getting dark, and the stars were appearing in the clear sky, with an almost full moon casting its light onto the beach. The constant roar of the ocean broke the silence of the night — a sound Sam missed. It wasn't quite the same in Portishead.

Heather and Tom walked hand in hand up the hill to The Cormorant in front of Sam and Maya. He would have loved to be able to hold her hand, to feel its softness inside his own, the heat of her palm against his. He missed intimate moments like this the most. But knowing she was dating someone else, he needed to be her friend. Just her friend.

As they entered The Cormorant, the band was setting up in the bay window, the tables having been removed. It was the usual band set up: three microphone stands at the front, the drums at the back. Two guitars were propped on stands, and a keyboard was to the right.

Joe greeted them, scrubbing up well in a long-sleeved Superdry shirt and jeans. It was as smart as he got. The pub was warm, so they all removed their jackets, placing them over the backs of chairs at a table that Joe had reserved for them.

"What would you like to drink, Maya?" Tom asked, going straight to the bar before Sam had a chance to offer.

"Oh, a white wine, please."

"Shall we share a bottle?" Heather stood beside Maya, sussing out the wine.

"Oh, I don't know…"

"Go on, we'll be here all night. Don't make me drink a bottle on my own." Heather nudged Maya's shoulder playfully.

"She'll probably drink most of it," Sam said in Maya's ear, loud enough for Heather to hear.

"You know me too well, brother," she said.

"Oh, go on then," Maya said, smiling.

"Do you have a preference?" Heather asked. "Sauvignon or pinot?"

"You choose. I don't mind."

"I have Prosecco on offer," Joe said, appearing beside the group. "And put your money away, Tom. This is on me."

"Prosecco?" Heather looked at Maya eagerly. "Joe's buying!"

"It would be rude not to, then," Maya said.

Joe ordered the Prosecco and three pints of Doom Bar. One by one, the bartender placed the pints on the bar. Doom Bar had been the first ale Sam had shared with his dad, when he was old enough to drink legally. He was given the job of removing the cork from the Prosecco. It popped with a hollow bang, and luckily it didn't fizz over the top. He poured the bubbling golden liquid into two flutes for Heather and Maya, then placed the bottle in the ice bucket on the table. Once the bubbles had settled, the two women tapped glasses.

"Happy Easter," Heather said. Everyone raised their glasses, and repeated, "Happy Easter."

CHAPTER 24

Once they were settled at their table, Heather turned to Maya. "So, Maya, Sam says you're seeing someone…"

Maya was caught totally off guard. Why would Sam tell Heather about her seeing someone? She hadn't gone into much detail about Pierce. It was early days.

"Yes, yes… I met him online. I've not been seeing him long," Maya said, drinking her Prosecco more quickly than intended. Luckily, Sam had returned to the bar to stand with Tom, deep in conversation with Joe. A glass of Prosecco down, Maya was relaxed enough to tell Heather about Pierce.

"I set Sam up online," Heather said, lowering her voice. Maya wondered if Heather was supposed to be sharing this piece of information. Sam hadn't mentioned anything about being interested in dating.

"Which site?"

"Oh, I can't remember now. I want him to get himself out there." Heather had already finished her glass and poured another, topping Maya's glass up as well. Maya couldn't help thinking that Heather could give Emma a run for her money in the Prosecco drinking stakes.

"Testing, testing, testing…" One of the band members stood at the mics, doing the sound check. Maya knew it wouldn't be long before the band started up and they wouldn't be able to hear one another properly. The pub had filled up with people too.

"I'm not sure how he's getting on; he tells me nothing," Heather said, leaning into Maya.

"I think it does take time. It's a great idea, but unfortunately, there are some who abuse it." Maya told Heather about the dick pic guy and some of her other disasters, which set them off in a fit of giggles.

Suddenly serious, Heather looked at Maya earnestly. "I don't want Sam leaving it until it's too late. Jade wouldn't have wanted him to live life alone. I put him on there, and nag him regularly, because I want him to find someone before he gets too old."

"I heard that!" Sam said, giving Heather a stern look. The men sat down at the table, placing their half-drunk pints before them. Sam took a seat on the other side of Maya.

Heather whispered behind her hand to Maya, "And before he loses his looks."

Maya glanced at Sam. Would he lose his looks? Not if you went by his dad. Charles was still attractive, for a man in his seventies. She quite liked the laughter lines and flecks of grey in Sam's dark hair. He wasn't quite as salt and peppered as George Clooney, but he carried an air of maturity.

"That's my fear too. I'm worried that everything will start falling south when I turn forty."

"You're stunning. You have nothing to worry about." Heather clinked her glass against Maya's. "But I do get where you're coming from. It's all right for men. They haven't subjected their bodies to pregnancy and childbirth. Tom is the only person I would allow to see me naked — or a doctor in an emergency! I don't envy women trying to find love again."

Maya remained silent, nervously sipping her Prosecco. Fortunately, more people arrived, and Maya was introduced to them. She shook hands with Tristan, who Sam explained was their cousin, and certainly didn't act like Lord of The Manor — *why had she expected him to look like Hugh Bonneville?* He was obviously younger than Sam and Joe. Heather insisted Beth, Tristan's girlfriend, joined them, pouring her a glass of bubbly.

The band started up, playing a mix of well-known covers, old and new, and it was hard to keep up the conversation. Maya sipped her Prosecco, feeling almost relieved that she didn't have to discuss any more of her dating antics with Heather, although she was intrigued to hear more about Sam being on an online dating site. She now wondered which one.

As Maya listened to the music, she reflected that she didn't envy anyone trying online dating either, but what choice did she have? It seemed to be the thing to do these days. At her age, would someone cross her path naturally? Life was too busy. And when she did go out, it was usually tagging along with her married friends on a girls' night out. This didn't really help attract the opposite sex — only the weirdos. And to make matters worse, if her married friends couldn't see the guy was a jerk, they'd encourage him, or try to set Maya up with someone else at the bar. On those nights, she'd seriously contemplated wearing her wedding ring.

This weekend, seeing Tom and Heather happy had emphasised how much Maya missed the intimacy of a close relationship. One day, it would be lovely to go out as a couple again with Emma and Lucas. She even allowed herself to fantasise about them meeting Pierce. Would he be compatible with them?

Suddenly, she pictured Sam as her date instead. Maybe she needed to delve further with Heather, and find out the site Sam's profile was on, so that she could check it out…

Maya gave herself a mental shake, realising she'd tuned out of the band playing.

Online dating was a good thing. It was just something you had to be patient with. And who knew, if it went well with

Pierce, she could say goodbye to it. Thinking of Pierce, of how he made her feel, made butterflies flip in her stomach — she wanted that again. She quickly checked her phone. One message. Disappointment quelled the butterflies. Emma was wishing her a Happy Easter and checking she was having a wonderful break. Maya smiled and texted her quickly back, still not mentioning that she was with Sam's family.

"Everything okay?" Sam asked, leaning into her ear so she could hear him over the music. Maya could feel his breath on the sensitive skin below her ear. It gave her goosebumps at the back of her neck, travelling down her arms.

She tilted her head to talk to him and caught the smell of his aftershave. She almost forgot what he had asked her. "Yes, Emma texted me. I replied that I'm alive and well."

Sam nodded as she spoke. Her mouth was inches away from his neck, and she suddenly wondered what his skin would feel like against her lips, with the roughness of the traces of stubble emerging along his jawline. Then she thought of Pierce. Maybe that was what she was missing, and being next to Sam made her ache for that affection, that touch from a man, which Pierce had ignited in her again. She'd feared she'd lost any sex drive she'd had, but Pierce had proved it was still there.

"Good. I was worried you might not be enjoying yourself."

Maya shook her head and smiled at him. "No, this if great. Thanks for inviting me out."

Smiling back, he placed an arm on her shoulder as he got up, gently squeezing. A friendly gesture — a sign of being relaxed in each other's company. For a moment, Maya felt an overwhelming sense of security. Sam checked the bottle in the ice bucket. It was empty, so he asked if Heather wanted another. She gave two big thumbs-up. Maya watched Sam go to the bar, bottle and empty pint glasses in hand.

No doubt about it, Sam was attractive and interesting to talk to... But he was her daughter's best friend's dad.

And she also had a potential relationship with Pierce ... didn't she? A relationship she needed to give a chance...

Yikes! Like buses... Nothing for two years, then two men come along, grappling within her thoughts...

At the end of the evening, after saying their goodbyes to Joe, Tristan, Beth and Rhianna, who had arrived later, Maya walked back down the steep hill with Sam, Tom and Heather, feeling merry and relaxed, her ears ringing from the loud music.

Maya smiled to herself at the memories of the last couple of hours. Heather had dragged her and Beth up to dance to a couple of popular numbers. She'd laughed so hard when Joe danced with Tom. Later, Rhianna had joined them, having been able to get away from the bistro early. Joe's love for Rhianna was plain to see. Sam had sat reservedly watching, clapping and laughing too. Kyle would have been up joining in the fun, she'd remembered thinking, though usually flirting with other women too. Would Pierce be the type to get up and dance? She still had so much to discover about him.

Maya had tried dragging Sam up, but he'd refused, making an excuse to visit the toilets. At the end, after the encore, the pub raucous with clapping and cheering, Sam had helped her into her jacket, steadied her when she'd wobbled, and even opened the door for her. She'd instinctively tucked her arm through his, to keep herself steady as she walked down the hill on tired, Prosecco-filled legs.

The four of them stumbled home and crept into the house, Heather shushing them. Maya stifled a laugh. Happily drunk and giggly, like teenagers caught out drinking late, they walked into the lounge where Rose and Charles were watching television, snuggled together on the sofa.

"How were the kids?" Heather asked.

"Good as gold," Rose said, switching the television off. "How was your night?"

"Great fun," Heather said, answering for all of them. "Maya and I even got some dancing in. Sam was the only sensible one."

"I've embarrassed myself enough recently." Sam glanced at Maya. "Maya didn't need to see my dad-dancing."

"You're not that bad," Heather said, elbowing her brother.

"See you all bright and early for breakfast," Rose said, a hint of teasing in her voice.

"Yes, Mum." Heather kissed her parents, then took Tom's hand and headed up the stairs.

"Thank you for babysitting my kids, too, Rose," Maya said, then hiccupped. *Oh, hell, where did they come from?* Now she sounded more drunk than she actually was. "Think I'd best get off to bed. Goodnight."

Sam kissed his mother, then followed Maya up the stairs.

"Goodnight, Maya," he said on the landing, outside Maya's bedroom door. They stood together, only a foot apart, his brown eyes intense, staring into hers. He pushed a strand of hair off her face. Was he going to kiss her? He leaned towards her, but Maya suddenly hiccupped, making her pull away and press her fingers to her lips.

"Sorry," she said. Then she remembered kissing Sam would complicate things. And she wasn't a cheat like Kyle. "Thanks for a great night, Sam." Hastily, she entered her bedroom. She leaned back against the door, resting her head against it and guiltily imagining what it would be like to kiss Sam. And then she hiccupped loudly again.

CHAPTER 25

Mist and fog had rolled off the sea in the night, and Maya awoke on Easter Monday morning to a much duller day. Over breakfast, they decided to go for a walk across to Penryn Point.

"Harbour porpoises were spotted a week ago," Rose said, placing cooked breakfasts in front of Sam and Maya. "You might see them if you're lucky."

Heather and Tom said they would stay behind with the two little girls, which gave Maya the uncomfortable impression that they were deliberately trying to leave her and Sam alone. Sam did his best to dispel any awkwardness, joking he'd be her tour guide. Rose insisted Maya didn't need to 'check out' and could leave her belongings in the room until she was ready to leave.

When they were ready, Sam led the way, taking the coastal path to the right of the beach. If they had time, their aim was to walk as far as the promontory called The Rumps. The path crossed land belonging to the National Trust and was typical Cornish coastal landscape: hilly and uneven and perfect for grazing sheep. First, they followed a public footpath passing a row of cottages and holiday homes with long narrow gardens, overlooking Kittiwake Cove's beach. Maya admired the houses and their perfect location, looking out over the ocean. Today, the water looked greener due to the cloud cover. Then they followed the road round, finding the next footpath, which was accessible from the end of the beach when the tide was out, through rockier terrain with short grass, thistles, heather and wild spring flowers lining their way. They crossed a stile over an ancient slate wall that enclosed a field. It had felt chilly when they'd set out, but as they strolled along, arms swinging, they soon warmed up, especially when the path led them uphill. Before long, their jackets were unzipped, and the children were running on ahead.

"Stick to the path," Maya called to them, scared that they'd fall at some of the narrower parts of the track that ran closer to the cliff edge. In places, there were freshly-dug rabbit holes and molehills.

"They should be all right," Sam said, walking beside Maya. They were both slightly out of breath, having climbed a particularly steep stretch of the path. "I used to walk along here a lot as a kid."

When they reached Penryn Point, they could see The Rumps further round to their right. The view was stunning, even on a cloudy day. On the horizon, a break in the cloud was visible; blue sky was coming. But would it reach them this afternoon?

"I don't suppose I can convince you to stay longer?" Sam said, looking out to sea.

"No, I'm sorry, I do have to get back," Maya said, catching Sam's gaze, the wind blowing the strands of hair off her face. She liked spending time with Sam, but would it be wise to fall for him?

Sam nodded. "Come on, we'd better catch the kids up, or they'll beat us to The Rumps."

"When do you go back to work?" Maya asked as they started walking again. She had to keep her nose to the ground now, watching every step, as the path had become very uneven. She was glad she'd worn her walking boots, which kept her ankles supported.

"I've taken the week off to cover the school holidays. Heather had Chloe for me all last week."

"You know, if you ever need help with childcare, please ask. I don't mind having Chloe." The offer was out of her mouth before she'd truly thought it through.

"That's kind of you. Thank you."

"It's no problem really. I tend to find it's easier with more children. Less bickering between the siblings."

"Yes, that's one problem I don't get only having Chloe. But she can do her fair share of moaning. She definitely appreciates Amber and Lewis's company," Sam said pensively. "And so do I." There it was again, Sam's smile that reached his eyes.

They came to a steep downhill part and Maya, not concentrating, suddenly tripped over a jutting rock. There must have been loose stones or earth, because the dry ground slipped away from under her feet, making her lose her balance completely.

Sam quickly grabbed her arm, his grip firm, stopping her from stumbling to the ground and making a prat of herself. Her heart raced with the shock. "Thank you," she said, once she'd regained her footing. "And there was me worried about the kids."

Sam still held her arm. "Are you okay?"

Maya nodded and he let her go. "Here, let me go ahead, and I can help you on the trickier bits."

Maya let Sam pass, then followed behind him. In some of the more awkward parts, he held out his hand, which she gratefully took to help her climb down. His hands were warm, his hold strong. He always waited until he was certain she had her footing before letting her go. The gesture was so innocent, yet his touch sent a sizzle of excitement through her, so that she felt bereft the moment he let her go.

By the time they reached The Rumps, the clouds were thinning, and the sun was trying to poke through in places. The three children had beaten them there, and were waiting patiently, sitting on the rocks.

So high above the sea, looking out over the ocean and back towards Kittiwake Cove in the distance, the views were spectacular. With little shelter to protect them, the wind blasted off the Atlantic. Maya zipped her jacket up, reminded of the old folktale she was told as a child. The North Wind and the Sun wanted to prove which of them was stronger by making the traveller remove his cloak. The more strongly the North Wind blew, the tighter the man drew his cloak around him. Whereas when the Sun shone, using its gentle warmth, the man removed his cloak, and so the Sun won. Maya felt she could do with the sun trying to remove her coat rather than the wind trying to force her off this rock.

With a small pair of binoculars, Sam looked out to sea in search of porpoises or seals, but he shook his head.

Eventually, feeling the cold of the wind, they started their descent back down the point they'd climbed.

"Down there, I did once spot seals. Two of them." Sam pointed to some rocks below, waves crashing and swirling around them. Maya could see a cove unreachable by man, unless by boat — a perfect haven for seals.

"Will we see seals now?" Amber asked.

"It was around early June, but they can be seen any time of the year. We can have a look, but they are hard to spot."

They walked off the path, closer to the edge but on more even ground. Maya took Lewis's hand, fearing he would fall. Five pairs of eyes watched the rocks below, where the water splashed, swirled and broke.

They strolled back, arms swinging, laughing and chatting, watching the children playfully run on ahead, and got back to the house in time for lunch. Sam always stopped to check if

Maya needed a hand up some of the steeper paths, and for much of the way they'd walked in a comfortable silence. She knew it wasn't awkward, as they were both happy to breathe the fresh air and enjoy the views.

Back at the bed and breakfast, the delicious aroma of baking cakes engulfed them as they entered the kitchen and Maya's face flushed warm, invigorated by the wind and the exercise. Even with a couple of windows open, the room was hot from Rose's cooking. But when Maya sat down, with a freshly brewed coffee placed before her, she felt suddenly tired and overwhelmed with anxiety, knowing she had to face the long drive home. She gave a spontaneous yawn and closed her eyes for a moment.

"Did the walk wear you out?" Sam asked, sitting beside her.

Maya shook her head. "A little. The Prosecco last night is probably catching up with me too. I'm not looking forward to the drive home."

"Stay, then." His tone was patient and caring, almost pleading.

"I can't, Sam," Maya said, looking at him, then breaking her gaze. She didn't want to outstay her welcome. Sam's family had been so accommodating, including her and the children in everything, but she knew she had to leave. "I've got to go home." She was worried she was enjoying Sam's company a bit too much.

"I know... I know." His gentle smile touched her. "What time do you think you'll set off?"

"If the weather stays like this —" she gestured to the ominous clouds outside — "I'm wondering if I'd better leave in the early afternoon." Maya tucked a loose tendril behind her ear, blown out of her ponytail by the wind as they'd walked. She dreaded to think what she looked like, windswept and with no make-up. "Otherwise, I had been thinking about four o'clock."

"That's okay, you're probably fed up with me anyway, and we have next weekend to think about too," Sam said.

"Oh, yes. Are you sure you're okay with Amber sleeping over?"

"I've promised Chloe. But I'm sure they won't play me up too much. I'll just have to be prepared to watch a girly movie with them."

"Yes, that should do the trick." Maya laughed. "Having a brother, Amber is pretty unfussy. She'll watch anything. Just promise you'll keep it to a PG."

Maya let her children watch some movies rated twelve, but she usually sat with them, or had vetted them first.

"Of course," Sam said. "I will check with you first before we watch anything."

"Yes, well, if she gives you the 'my mum lets me watch fifteens' line, you'll know she's lying."

"Don't worry, I have a devious daughter too."

"Why are they so intent on wanting to grow up fast? They'll get to our age and wonder where the hell their childhood went." Maya huffed, then laughed. She drained the last of her coffee from her mug. The caffeine was kicking in. She felt more alert now.

After lunch, the sun refused to make an appearance from behind the thick layer of cloud, but it remained dry. To have an excuse not to leave yet, Maya decided to peruse the shops along Kittiwake Cove high street with her children. There weren't many, but it would be nice for Lewis and Amber to buy a souvenir to remember their holiday by and to take something back for Nanny and Granddad. She also needed to buy a gift for Rose and Charles for looking after her so well.

There was a boutique which sold very pricey clothes but also seaside ornaments and trinkets, as well as another shop selling bits and pieces for the home and garden. She picked out some scented candles in terracotta pots for their garden, thinking they would be a good addition to their patio when they had barbecues. She thought they'd go well with the couple of bottles of wine she'd also purchased. Amber found some shells and a little something for Chloe — a friendship bracelet. Lewis wanted a toy which he found in the Spar, of all shops. Maya discovered a little something for her own home — a small piece of Cornish slate, hand-painted with the words 'Kittiwake Cove' to hang in her kitchen. She bought some traditional Cornish biscuits for her parents, and picked up a box for Pierce too, feeling she shouldn't go home empty-handed. She couldn't decide what else to get — she didn't know him well enough. But everyone loved Cornish Fairings.

Loaded with all her gifts, Maya hesitated outside a gallery called White Horses. Amber and Lewis gave a moan. Maya didn't want the kids going inside in case they broke something.

"You two go on ahead." She could peruse at her leisure then, stress-free. "You know where the B&B is. Just watch the road and stick together." Suddenly, Maya was wishing she hadn't said they could go off on their own. Crossing roads and strangers added to her worry.

They walked off happily. Maya watched for a moment, then, reassured they were safe and sensible, she entered the gallery, the bell above the door ringing. It had a light, airy feel, with wood flooring and white walls adorned with paintings and framed photographs. Abstract ornaments made from glass, metal or clay were displayed on narrow white solid blocks and there was a rack of cellophane-wrapped prints near the door. In the far corner, a young woman in jeans and a long-sleeved

T-shirt, dirty with splodges of different coloured paint, was standing at an easel, painting a seascape. She looked up as Maya entered.

"Good afternoon."

"Hello," Maya said, nervously. It was so quiet, she felt that she was interrupting the woman's concentration.

"Feel free to take a look around. Any questions, please don't hesitate to ask," the young woman said, smiling kindly at Maya. "I'm Tilly." Behind Tilly was a pram with a baby asleep, which she occasionally rocked.

Maya strolled around the gallery, enraptured by the variety of paintings by local artists. One artist, specialising in the wildlife found along the Cornish coast, had an area dedicated to his work. He painted crabs, various seabirds including a cormorant, which made Maya think of Joe's pub, and even a puffin. Maya particularly liked his detailed painting of a starfish. There were seascapes and landscapes in oils, acrylics, and pastels, depending on the artist's preferred medium, some more abstract, some more traditional, almost photographic. The seascapes were Maya's favourites, capturing the waves crashing against rocks and the sky in different shades. There was one large, prominently displayed canvas that particularly captured her attention. It reminded her of the view she'd seen the other evening, sitting with Sam and watching the sun set over the sea at Kittiwake Cove. Unfortunately, although the price was probably very reasonable given the hours it had taken to paint, Maya couldn't justify buying it.

"I've had that one made into a postcard," Tilly said. "They only came in yesterday, ready for the summer." Dropping her paintbrush into a jar of water, she went over to a stand by the till, found what she was looking for and held out a postcard of the painting Maya was looking at.

Maya admired the postcard as she took it. "I was thinking how I'd seen that view the other evening."

"Well, when you live here, you see it often," Tilly replied, standing next to Maya and looking at the painting with her. "I can pretty much paint that view from memory now."

"So, you're the artist?" Maya looked at the signature on the painting: Tilly Conway.

"Yes, and I own the gallery," Tilly said.

"You're very talented. I'll take the postcard. I would love to buy the painting, but sadly, I can't afford it. Plus, I'm not sure where I'd put it in my house. It's probably too big."

"Of course. I understand."

Maya paid for the postcard and as she was about to leave, the bell above the door jangled and Sam walked into the gallery.

"There you are. I thought you'd got lost. The kids returned, but not you." Sam chuckled.

"Oh, I was on my way back," Maya said. "I got distracted by this beautiful painting." She pointed to the seascape. "It reminded me of when we were sitting on the beach on Saturday evening. We had a very similar view." She wished she could afford the painting. It would be the perfect memento of a perfect weekend.

"Yes, we did." Sam stood beside Maya and admired the painting, arms folded. "It's beautiful."

"I've bought a postcard of it. Can't quite justify the real thing. Although, without sounding like my son, it would look pretty awesome in my living room."

"Shame," Sam said, still looking at the painting, before turning to Maya. "Mum's feeding your kids up on cake, so I thought I'd best come find you."

"Your mum has been amazing."

177

They said their goodbyes to Tilly, who was back at her easel. She gave a wave and a thank you for visiting. As they left the gallery, the bell of the door tinkled behind them.

"Did you know Tristan helped deliver Tilly's baby?" Sam said as headed back to the B&B.

"No, how come?"

Sam chuckled, relaying the story to Maya that Joe had told him: just before Christmas, when the country had suffered another bad snowstorm, Tilly had gone into labour while snowed in at Trenouth Manor. "Knowing Joe, he'd probably found a suitable excuse to leave Tristan to deal with Tilly."

Maya decided she would give Rose her thank-you gift as she was about to leave. She worried that the gifts weren't enough really. She and her kids had been truly spoilt this weekend; she'd hardly spent a penny on food or entertainment. She had paid in advance for the accommodation, so that eased her guilt a little, but all the extras had been given so generously by Sam's family.

As four o'clock drew closer, Maya packed up her car, with Sam helping with her suitcase and the holdall she'd brought. The kids were happily playing board games in the lounge under the supervision of Charles, who had Scarlett and Daisy perched on each knee. She'd even caught Lewis and Amber calling him Granddad, which was rather sweet.

When everything was packed and ready to go, Maya went to find Rose in the kitchen. Her heart was heavy at having to say goodbye, as she gave Rose her gifts.

"Oh, my dear, they're lovely, you didn't need to do that," Rose said, giving Maya a hug.

"Oh, I did. You've gone above and beyond looking after us this weekend, Rose."

"You can come and stay with us any time," Rose said, with a generous smile.

"Thank you," Maya said, then turned and addressed everyone gathered. "It was lovely to meet you all."

While Lewis and Amber gave Rose a hug, thanking her for the cake, Joe came bumbling in loudly through the back door. "Hey, everyone!"

"Maya's about to leave," Heather told him.

"Yes, I thought that might be the case. Goodbye, Maya. Fab meeting you." Joe gave her a hug and a kiss on the cheek, then winked when he let her go. "Hopefully we'll catch up again soon — maybe at my wedding." Before Maya could respond, with a twinkle in his eye, Joe had turned and ruffled Lewis's hair. "Two fab little surfers you have." Lewis and Joe fist pumped and wiggled their fingers. Lewis thought Joe was so cool. He hadn't stopped talking about him and surfing all weekend.

"Thanks, you were amazing with them." She smiled. "Right, goodbye, everyone. And thanks for everything."

Maya hugged everyone, including Sam, and kissed Heather on the cheek, then stood, swinging her hands awkwardly. She needed to leave, but as though her feet were glued to the kitchen's tiled floor, she couldn't bring herself to move.

"Right, I'll show you to your car," Sam said, as if sensing her reluctance to leave. "Chloe, come and say goodbye to Lewis and Amber."

All buckled up in the car, with a push of the button, Maya wound the electric window down, while Sam stood waving, one arm hugging his daughter around the shoulder. Chloe waved too, although she didn't look happy.

"Text me when you get home, so we know you've arrived safely," Sam called.

179

"I will."

After ten minutes on the road, as they wound through the country lanes, Maya could hear muffled crying coming from the back seat. She looked over her shoulder, then in her rear-view mirror. Lewis, red-faced, had tears trickling down his cheeks. He wiped them with his sleeve. Amber, also sombre, looked out of the window, not even teasing her brother.

"What's the matter, Lewis?" Maya asked, frowning, trying to concentrate on the road.

"I miss Kittiwake Cove. I miss my holiday," he said through sobs.

"Oh, my darling, hopefully we'll get to go back, maybe in the summer for longer. Would you like that?"

Lewis dried his eyes, nodding. Maya had forgotten how attached and sentimental he became to a location or a holiday. And they'd had so much fun, playing with Chloe and her cousins. Sam's family had adopted them as their own. Even Maya couldn't shift the grey cloud hanging over her head. She thought of home and getting back to her routine, to try and cheer herself up.

"I miss Chloe," Amber piped up.

"You'll see Chloe at the weekend, and back at school," Maya said as brightly as she could. "There's only a week left of the holidays. And you'll be spending some of that time with Nanny and Granddad." There were shrugs and grumbles, some recognition of what Maya was saying, at least. "I know, let's play I Spy to keep our minds off going home."

Maya hated I Spy and secretly hoped the kids would have a snooze in the back of the car, as she didn't want to face two and half hours of playing it. However, gone were the days of them falling asleep in the back of the car the minute she drove off.

Made it home safe. Thanks for a lovely weekend. Amber is missing Chloe. Car is unpacked. Going to have an early night myself.

Sam read the text over and over, wondering how to reply to Maya. Chloe was missing Amber, too. But she wasn't the only one missing the Rosevear family. For the last few hours Sam had felt lost, not exactly sure what to do with himself or Chloe. Before dinner, he'd ended up watching a film with Chloe on the sofa as the weather wasn't improving. The blue sky they'd seen on the horizon earlier had missed them. Now, in the kitchen, he helped his mother by loading the dishwasher — he'd been shown twice now how Rose liked her dishwasher loaded. He was half listening to Rose as she talked about Maya and how glad she was to have forgotten to book the family room off the B&B website.

Glad to hear you're home safe. Chloe misses her BFF too lol! Early night sounds like a good plan. Catch up soon. X

He'd tagged the kiss on his message before realising and sending. What the hell. If he hadn't found out about the guy she was dating, he may have made a move, and asked Maya for a date himself. The time they'd snatched alone had made him realise how much he did want someone in his life. How much he missed the adult conversation, the sharing of experiences, the love and affection, and someone to also appreciate the sunsets at Kittiwake Cove. Even though he was surrounded by his family, Sam couldn't shift the loneliness of being single. When he got home, he'd make a concerted effort to start dating. He had to.

He really liked Maya. But if she didn't like him in the same way, then it would never happen. But this weekend, spending time with Maya, he knew now he was ready to move on.

CHAPTER 26

Now Maya was home, she had hoped for a midweek get-together with Pierce, but he'd apologised that work had got pretty intense and he was busy. He promised they would catch up at the weekend. With dating Pierce, Maya wondered whether to hide her profile on Find My HEA. She checked into her own account and cleared any messages. She did drop a line to PeterPan26, feeling she needed to catch up. She liked chatting to this anonymous person. He'd become a confidant. She felt she owed it to him to tell him that she might not be on the site to talk much, rather than just suddenly disappearing. Even with her profile hidden, she could still message him. Maya typed:

How was your Easter weekend? Mine ended up being fantastic. Went away for a quiet weekend with the kids, and can you believe I was staying with my daughter's BFF's family? How was yours?

It wasn't long until she got a reply: *Great! Spent the weekend in good company too.*

Oh, that's good! Maya wrote. *Just to let you know, I may not be on here much. I'm dating a guy I met on here and as we've been seeing each other for a few weeks now, I feel I should hide my profile. It doesn't feel right to keep receiving messages from other men. It feels like I'm cheating on him, even though I'm not.*

That's fine, he replied. *I understand. And the grass isn't necessarily greener. I'm here though, if you want to chat. P x*

Maya smiled. *Thank you. I've enjoyed our chats. Happy searching, Peter. W x*

Saturday morning arrived and with some trepidation, Maya pulled up outside Sam's house early, ready for their day out with the children. Her car was loaded with everything Amber would need for a sleepover, too. She couldn't put her finger on why she felt nervous. She liked Sam and had even missed his company — although it had only been four days since they'd last seen one another. But she was excitedly looking forward to spending this evening with Pierce. He had been quiet all week, apologising that he'd been busy at work. But she'd been busy too, and she'd spent Friday evening packing and making a picnic for today.

Sam's front door opened, and Chloe, ducking under her father's arm, ran out to the car first. Amber unbuckled her seatbelt and was out of the car before Maya could say 'watch the road'. Luckily, it was a cul-de-sac.

Sam gave his familiar smile, his brown eyes warm and caring, and walked down the path towards Maya's car. He opened the passenger door to talk to her. Leaning in, he said, "If you like, we can go in the one car. I'll drive."

"Are you sure?"

"Yes, it makes sense, rather than taking two. I should have suggested it last night and come and got you."

"Well, there's all of Amber's things here. Shall we take them in then head off?"

With Maya's car unloaded, Amber's sleeping things dumped up in Chloe's room, and Sam's silver saloon packed for the day, they set off down the motorway. The three children were plugged into phones or tablets, and unaware of their surroundings outside the car. However much Maya hated playing I Spy, it did mean the kids looked out of the window.

"Lewis, if it makes you feel sick, honey, please put the tablet away," Maya said, turning in her seat to look at him. Lewis was sitting behind Sam, so she had a good view of her son. Chloe was in the middle, and Amber was behind Maya. They'd decided that separating the siblings would mean a more peaceful journey.

During the week, Sam and Maya had agreed on spending the day at Devon Crealy Adventure Park. If the traffic was good, it would only take about an hour to get there. Sam had bought the tickets online and said it was his treat, so Maya had agreed to supply the picnic.

Cocooned together in one car, it felt like they were one family. Sam looked completely at ease with this set up as Maya glanced at him, watching him concentrate on the motorway.

Maya's thoughts drifted to Pierce. Would he be happy in this situation? Pierce knew Maya had children, but would he eventually accept them as a part of the package? She wanted someone who would get involved with the kids, someone she could be a family with … as she was doing with Sam.

They arrived at the theme park in good time. The sun was shining on them as they stretched their legs. All three children were excited, discussing which ride they wanted to go on first. They were fortunate with the weather: it wasn't boiling hot, but at least the sun was out, albeit hiding among white cotton wool clouds occasionally. They queued to get through the main gates, Sam producing the tickets he'd bought online.

The children being an odd number meant one of the adults had to go on the rides with Lewis, so that he wasn't on his own. Fortunately, Sam took this job seriously. Chloe and Amber were inseparable, and Maya was happy to sit it out and watch the belongings while taking photos. They were all able to fit in the log flume — unfortunately — on which Sam insisted

Maya joined them all in getting wet. She had come prepared with ponchos and waterproof coats.

Maya was wedged in between Sam's legs, as he was sitting at the back. Lewis was in front of her, and the two girls were in front of him. The warmth of Sam's thighs pressed against her own, sending a tingle of pleasure through her — something so innocent but at the same time so intimate. As their log climbed up the flume, it was extremely difficult not to lean into his firm body, before being thrust forward as the flume dropped. The girls screamed, and then the log crashed through the water, spraying it everywhere, and Maya was forced back into Sam's body. All five of them shook out their arms and assessed the soaked damage, giggling so hard their ribs ached.

Sam managed to climb out of the log flume first and held out his hand to help Maya. She dreaded to think what she looked like — a drowned rat with wet hair flopping.

"That was fun," she said, ironically.

Sam laughed, rubbing his hand through his hair to remove the excess water. "Shall we queue up again?" He grinned.

They looked at the photos in the booth once they'd exited the ride. They all laughed at them. Chloe pointed out her facial expression, which was similar to Amber's — both had wide eyes and mouths open; an expression of terror and excitement as the flume had descended and the camera snapped the photo. Maya wasn't going to suggest they bought the photo. With her own hair flying, and her mouth caught open and screaming, it was not a picture she wished to keep.

"I think it's time for a coffee," Sam said, picking up their belongings as he led the way out.

"Can we go again?" the kids asked, jumping excitedly. They were all tall enough to go on the ride without an adult. The queue didn't look too bad either.

"Go on then, might as well get it over with, and you can dry out during the day. I'll go grab your mum and me a coffee," Sam said. "Stick together!"

"Yes, stick together. No fighting, my two!" Maya called after them, but they were already running, ponchos blowing like kites in the wind, towards the end of the queue.

"I reckon we've got another twenty minutes of peace," Sam said. He was still brushing water off and pulling at his jumper to help it dry. Maya was doing the same. "You sit yourself down at that picnic table. I'll grab us a coffee. Latte?" Sam pointed to a wooden table from which Maya would be able to watch the ride.

"Sounds like a great idea."

Sam helped Maya with the heavy rucksacks, one a cool bag, laden with food, then walked off towards a nearby kiosk. She flicked through her phone while she waited for Sam. She replied to Pierce, who'd texted to say he couldn't wait to see her. He sounded very eager. It had to be a good sign, his keenness. Then she uploaded to Facebook a photo she'd taken of the three kids on some bumper boats when they'd first arrived, while trying to keep an eye on the log flume. She would video them coming down the final drop.

"Here you go." Sam arrived, handing Maya a takeaway cup of coffee. "I'm starting to get peckish. Maybe we should stop here for lunch, as we have a picnic table."

"Yes, by the time they come off this, I think they'll be hungry."

"And twice as wet."

"We'll shove them in that dryer." Maya pointed to a big yellow and red walk-in.

Maya and Sam both videoed the children coming down the flume. All three had their hands in the air and gave a thumbs-up for the camera when they'd arrived at the bottom.

After, they ran around to where Sam and Maya were sitting opposite each other at the picnic table, giggling. The waterproofs had kept the kids fairly dry; it was mainly their jeans that bore wet marks.

Over lunch, the children discussed which rides they wanted to go on next, Chloe and Amber placing the map of Crealy Adventure Park in front of them.

"Okay, you guys head over there." Sam pointed to a play zone on the map they hadn't tried yet. "We'll catch you up."

"And stick together!" Maya packed away the leftovers, fitting them in one rucksack.

Once this was done, Sam picked up the spare bag. "You go follow the kids, and I'll meet you there in a minute. I'll take this back to the car."

Maya found the children queuing for the pirate ship ride, which had been on the way to the play zone they'd picked out.

"I think you guys better do this one once your lunch has gone down." The ride swung high, back and forth, and she could envisage them being sick. It certainly made her feel sick watching it.

They walked on, and Maya swallowed when she overheard the girls' conversation.

"If your mum and my dad got married, we'd be sisters," Chloe said to Amber.

"And you'd have Lewis as a brother. I can tell you that sucks."

"Amber!" Maya said. Scolding Amber might be the best way to defuse this conversation. Where had they got this from? A weekend shared in Cornwall, plus a day trip out, and the girls had Sam and her married off! The minds of eleven-year-olds never ceased to amaze Maya. She was relieved Sam wasn't around to hear the conversation — she'd be beetroot-red otherwise. She wanted the subject changed before he returned from the car park.

The two girls moved on to discussing being bridesmaids and what dresses they'd wear. What concerned Maya most was that they'd noticed how much time she and Sam had spent together over the weekend in Cornwall. They were more observant than she thought.

"Girls, Sam and I are just friends, all right?" Maya wanted to set them straight, and quickly. Lewis had abandoned them, running on ahead. "A man and a woman can be friends." How did she explain this to children...? "It's cool."

"What have I missed?" Sam appeared. "Has Chloe been behaving? You look cross."

Maya probably did, with her hands on her hips and pulling a frown. She shrugged and tried to relax. "Oh, it's nothing. Run along girls, catch Lewis up."

Thankfully, Chloe and Amber did as they were told and the subject of Sam and Maya getting married wasn't mentioned again.

CHAPTER 27

"You can stay for a bit, if you like?" Sam said as Maya stood on his doorstep, having said goodbye to Amber, with Lewis waiting in her car. Sam realised, with a sudden ache of disappointment, that he didn't want his day with Maya to end. He had felt so at ease with her. It had reminded him of what it felt like to be a family again, sharing little things with each other, making the monotony of life more bearable.

"Oh, uh, thanks, but I have plans. Sorry, maybe another time," Maya replied. Her expression showed remorse. "Thanks for the offer, though."

"It's been a great day." Several times, Sam had been tempted to take Maya's hand and curl his fingers between hers, wanting to feel their warmth and softness. So many times he could have stolen a kiss with her.

"It was, and thank you for that too." Maya suddenly yawned. "Gosh, I'm not going to be great company tonight. I'm shattered."

"You'd best get going. I'll text you tomorrow when I'm ready to drop Amber home, but it won't be before ten."

"Yes, it's the last lie-in before they go back to school."

Sam watched Maya give one last wave before she drove off. He knew she had a date. She hadn't disclosed much information during the day, but in their messages on Find My HEA, she had told him more than she'd confessed in person.

He should just go ahead and ask her out on a date, but the thought of her new boyfriend stopped him. He also felt very conflicted about whether to confess about his Peter Pan account. How would she react? He didn't want to lose her trust or friendship. And maybe their online conversations would dwindle naturally now she was dating.

"Daddy, what film shall we watch?" Chloe called from the lounge, waking Sam from his reverie. He slumped on the sofa, wrapping an arm around his daughter while she and Amber searched Netflix for a film.

Tucked beside the sofa, wrapped in bubble wrap and tissue paper, was the canvas of the sunset at Kittiwake Cove — the painting Maya had been admiring in the gallery last weekend. He wanted to give it to her but wondered if she'd consider the gift too generous.

When he'd caught Maya staring at the picture, it had also reminded him of the evening they'd spent together on the beach, watching the sunset. He wanted to give her that memory and knew this painting would help do just that. Maybe he'd have to ask Amber when her mum's birthday was.

"How was your *date* with Sam?" Emma asked Maya eagerly as Lewis ambled through to the lounge to join Owen and Finley, who were in the middle of playing Minecraft. He'd dropped his overnight bag at the foot of the stairs with his shoes. Maya knew Emma wanted gossip. But what was there to tell?

"It was good." Maya knew by Emma's expression she was hinting at something. "And it wasn't a date. It's not like that. I know what you're thinking. We're just friends."

"You did spend a weekend with him."

"It wasn't planned."

"And then today. Are you sure there's not something there?" Emma asked, frowning. "Do you have time for a coffee?"

"No, sorry, I've got to go." Maya glanced at her watch. Only two minutes had passed since the last time she'd checked it, but she could feel anxiety pressing on her shoulders. She needed to shower and put fresh clothes on. "I like him, that's all, Em. He's very thoughtful, and generous. But…"

"But?"

"He's Chloe's dad."

"So?" Emma put her hands on her hips.

"I couldn't get involved with him. What if it didn't end well? It wouldn't be fair to jeopardise Amber's friendship with Chloe."

"He comes across as the kind of guy who would keep things amicable. And you don't have to rush headlong into anything. You're overthinking things. Keep it simple, one date at a time."

"Precisely. And in case you'd forgotten, I'm dating Pierce. Who just happens to be gorgeous. I'll see where this leads first." Again, Maya glanced at her watch. "Which reminds me, I have to dash." Maya went into the lounge and kissed Lewis goodbye, but he was too engrossed in Minecraft to notice. "Be good for Emma." She received a grunt in response.

Emma showed her out. "Have fun tonight. I'll drop Lewis back tomorrow when you're ready."

"Thanks, Emma."

"You deserve to be happy." Emma hugged Maya, kissing her on the cheek.

At home, Maya ducked into the shower, hoping the hot water would wake her up. A day walking around a theme park, plus the hour's drive each way — even though she hadn't done the driving — was tiring. She hoped she wouldn't fall asleep on Pierce.

An hour later, sitting on her sofa, wearing a smart, sparkly top and a pair of black, skinny jeans, and worrying she was overdressed, Maya glanced at her watch. What time had he said he would pick her up? She checked her phone. She'd been dashing around so much to get ready she hadn't thought to check her messages.

She had an unread text, and tapped it open with dread.

It was from Pierce. He had texted while she'd been showering to say he had to cancel. Something had come up.

Really?

Could he not have called her rather than sending a lame text? Why hadn't he let her know earlier?

She could have accepted Sam's invitation to stay for dinner! And she hadn't needed to offload Lewis onto Emma and Lucas. She could have had an evening with her son. Now she was sitting here all dressed up with nowhere to go. And she was exhausted. She wasn't sure she had the energy to call Emma or another friend to see if they fancied the pub. She went to the fridge and poured herself a glass of wine, then plopped back down miserably on the sofa.

All week her phone had been quiet with only the occasional text from Pierce, but she figured he was busy and didn't have time to be constantly looking at his phone to message her. It had been the same during the Easter weekend, after all. But considering his attention before that weekend, it really had dropped off. Maya found herself pulling out her laptop and going online. Maybe she could ask Peter Pan for some advice.

Her eyes widened, her mouth falling open in shock. She could see Pierce was online. Anger bubbled in her chest. He had time to check his messages online … but he was too busy to keep their date! A date with the woman he'd been sleeping with for the past few weeks!

What an absolute arsehole!

She took a deep breath, trying to calm herself and her thoughts. She took another gulp of wine. Okay, she had to think this through rationally; she had only been seeing him for four weeks — nearly five. It didn't mean they were girlfriend/boyfriend. That hadn't been discussed. However, each time they'd met, they had slept with one another. In Maya's opinion, that showed a level of commitment to someone. He'd seemed so keen when she'd last seen him. She hadn't noticed any changes in affection. But this week he had distanced himself…

She understood some people were better at texting than others. Emma was sporadic in replying at times, but Maya appreciated she led a busy life, like she did. Pierce worked full-time, so she realised during the day he could be quiet.

Had he cheated on her over the Easter weekend and couldn't face a scene?

She wasn't putting up with this. She'd vowed, after Kyle, that no one was going to treat her like shit again. Fumbling with her phone, she rang Pierce. They never had conversations on the phone — another weird thing, now Maya came to think about it.

"Hello?" Pierce answered, sounding surprised.

"Hello, Pierce. Look, I'm sorry, but I'm a little annoyed you couldn't call me to cancel," Maya said, regretting her haste and the way she'd blurted it out. She knew her voice betrayed her. She sounded angry. Her throat had tightened as she held back her tears, and her hands were shaking with determination and the fear of confrontation.

"Yes, I know. I'm sorry."

"It's not good enough, Pierce. If you're so busy, why can I see you're online on Find My HEA? I think you can make the effort to at least call the woman you've been sleeping with these past few weeks…" Enough was enough. Her eyes were pricking with tears, yet she tried to hold it together. "Do you like me? What is this we have? I'm so bloody confused."

"Maya, I do like you. I like you a lot. But I think we're looking for different things."

"I'm looking for a relationship. And it says you are too on your profile."

"Over this past week, and while you were away, I was thinking about us. And whether this is what I want... I'm not sure if I believe in the whole happy ever after. I'm sorry."

"What do you mean?"

"I'm not sure I can give you what you want ... long term."

"So where do we go from here?" Did he expect they would just continue having sex? Was that what Maya wanted? No, she'd gone online in the hope of finding a partner. She understood not everyone worked out for life, but eventually, she hoped she'd find someone to grow old with.

"I think it would be unfair of me to carry on seeing you, Maya." She heard Pierce sigh.

Had it just been sex? Maya couldn't bring herself to ask that question. She had to believe Pierce had liked her. He had treated her to dinners out, and even gifts. She didn't think she could take the emotional blow, the knock to her self-esteem otherwise. "I think you need to update your profile, Pierce. It's very confusing. It says you're looking for a relationship, and clearly you are not." He didn't reply. "Goodbye, Pierce."

"Goodbye, Maya. And I'm sorry. You're really lovely. I do like you."

"I liked you too. But I think I liked you a bit more than you did me."

Maya hung up and burst into tears, throwing her phone onto the sofa and reaching for the box of tissues. She sobbed, awash with anger, hatred, sorrow and disappointment.

She hadn't known Pierce long enough to be in love with him, but an affection had formed. Hell, this dating malarkey hurt.

She hated herself when she had to break it off with someone she didn't fancy. And she hated it when they broke it off with her. Although this hurt more, she preferred it this way. She didn't feel guilty. Only sad. Very, very sad … and lonely.

What was wrong with her? Good job she hadn't deleted her profile — only hidden it.

Drying her eyes, she reached for the laptop and set her profile back to visible. She had hidden it, not wanting to waste anyone's time while she'd been dating Pierce. She went in and blocked his profile. Maya did not need to be reminded of his handsome face. She decided to message PeterPan26:

And another arsehole bites the dust. Lord knows what is wrong with me. Can't seem to hold a man down. I'm starting to wonder if there really is anyone genuine on this bloody site.

CHAPTER 28

While Maya waited for Sam to arrive with Amber, she leafed through her beauty magazines at the kitchen table, catching up on the new treatment trends. Emma had messaged to say she would pop Lewis back for her. She'd slapped on minimal make-up, hoping to hide the fact she'd been crying on and off. But her skin felt taut even after applying facemasks and creams galore. Last night, she'd ended up finishing the bottle of wine and watching the television. She'd felt too tired to go out and too upset to even call Emma. She would talk to her when she dropped Lewis off. She fancied a sofa day with the kids.

Sam arrived with Amber before Emma.

"Hey, did you have a good evening?" Sam asked as Maya invited him in. Chloe and Amber climbed the stairs to Amber's room. Maya had given her daughter strict instructions to unpack her bag.

"Yes, thank you," she lied, unable to look Sam in the eye. Did she divulge her broken night's sleep? The tossing and the turning, and the conversations she'd had in her head, the things she wished she'd said to Pierce. No, it was a conversation to have with Emma. "Did the girls behave?"

"Yes, Amber was great. Very polite. Maybe a little shy."

"Doesn't sound like the child I dropped off." They both laughed.

"Yes, I often think that when I read Chloe's school reports."

"Oh, yes. I'm sure their personalities transform the minute they walk through the school gates." Maya poured the coffee, swirling in some milk then handing it to Sam. They became at ease with one another much more quickly now. "What time did they go to bed?" Maya gestured to her kitchen table. Sam took a seat one side, and Maya sat opposite, bringing the biscuit tin with her.

"Well, I sent them to bed after the movie, at half past ten. I thought that was late enough even for a sleepover."

"Yes, I'd say the same."

"But I don't think they actually fell asleep until gone midnight."

"Early night for them tonight, then, with school tomorrow."

"And me. I'm back to work tomorrow." He combed a hand through his hair, and his expression betrayed a hint of stress.

"Yes, and me." Pedicures and manicures, and a couple of massages.

"Maya..." Sam looked at her, his eyes suddenly intense. He cupped his mug.

Maya's heart sped up with the anticipation of what he was about to say. Anxiety, worry... What had happened last night? Did he have to tell her something about Amber? "Yes...?"

"HELLO!" Emma's voice boomed from the front door. Maya had left it open so that she could let herself in.

Maya looked back at Sam questioningly, but he shrugged as if to say it could wait. "We're in here," Maya called.

Sam stood up, draining his coffee. "I'd better go, get out of your hair."

Maya stood too. "No, don't feel you have to rush off."

Emma entered the kitchen. "I want to know all the explicit — oh!" She stopped, seeing Sam standing in Maya's kitchen, pulling his car keys out of his jeans pocket. "Hello, Sam."

"I'm just dropping off Amber, but I'd best go."

"I've brought Owen and Finley with me, as I will probably be here an hour gassing to Maya."

"Help yourself to coffee," Maya said. "I'll just show Sam out."

In the hallway, Sam called up to Chloe. In a typical display of child behaviour, she didn't come immediately, but called back, "I'll be down in a minute."

"Was there something you needed to tell me? Was it about Amber?"

Sam shook his head and rubbed his chin. He had a morning shadow where he hadn't shaved yet. Something was on his mind. "No, no, nothing like that. It can wait. The girls were fine. Gosh, sorry, I didn't mean to worry you then." He went to the bottom of the stairs. "Chloe, come on. *Now.*"

Chloe thumped down the stairs, Amber following.

"See you at school tomorrow," Amber said.

"Yeah, awesome." The girls did some sort of fist pump shake they'd made up — it looked similar to the one Joe and Lewis had done — then hugged, and Maya closed the front door behind Sam and Chloe. Amber went off to play with the three boys in the front room.

"Why the frown?" Emma said, sitting at the table where Sam had sat, stuffing a biscuit into her mouth.

"Sam."

"What about him?"

"I don't know. Just as you arrived he was about to ask me something or say something, and well, he's said it can wait."

"Can't be important, then. Unless he wants to ask you out!"

"No..." Maya said, plopping back into her chair. Her coffee was lukewarm, but she drank it anyway.

"Maybe." Emma shrugged, then popped another biscuit in her mouth. Once she'd swallowed, she said, "Tell me about last night. Where did Pierce take you?"

Maya burst into tears. Thank God the children weren't in the kitchen.

"Oh, Maya, what's up?" Emma reached across the table for Maya's hand.

"He dumped me."

"Really?" Emma frowned. "I thought he was keen."

"So did I." Maya then went on to tell Emma the full extent of the conversation.

"What an utter bastard. You should have called me!" Emma said.

"I was exhausted from the day out with Sam, and to be honest I just needed to be alone." In her own self-pity party.

Emma nodded, taking another biscuit. "Right, well, from now on you're on a three-date rule."

"What's a three-date rule?"

"You've never heard of the three-date rule? You don't 'put out' until after the third date. That way, if they're interested in you, they'll at least take you out three times."

"Oh, I see. Another way to sort the wheat from the chaff." Maya wiped her eyes.

"And the players," Emma said.

"Do you think Pierce is a player?"

"Yes, absolutely. He bloody used you, Maya!" Emma said sharply. Then, more calmly, she mused, "Who'd have thought meeting men on the internet would be such a minefield?"

"It is a minefield!"

"Right, well, I mean it, Maya. Doesn't matter how hot a guy is, you've got to keep him at arm's length initially. When I get home, I'm checking if I can buy chastity belts, and I'll be the one in charge of the key." Emma laughed.

Maya laughed too. "You can trust me."

"Maybe, but I can't trust them!"

Maya didn't want to sound whiney, but she needed her friend's opinion. "He said he liked me but wasn't into happy ever afters. Didn't believe in them. So what's he saying, he doesn't want to commit? Yet on his profile it states he wants a relationship. What did I do wrong?"

"It's nothing you've done; the guy is a player. Maybe he's learnt that if he puts he's not looking for a relationship, he doesn't get much bite. Or the quality of bite is very low. Therefore, he pretends he is after a long-term thing."

How deceitful. "But players don't stick around after the first date — do they?" Or two, in Maya's case. "I could handle a one-night stand — especially if he'd been honest with me, but I can't handle the way he dragged this out."

"He probably did really like you, Maya," Emma said, her tone softening with sincerity. "You are gorgeous. Maybe he's had a rabbit in the headlights moment."

"A what?"

"He's panicked. Maybe he started to realise he liked you too, but it wasn't what he wanted, what he'd planned, so he's pulled away before getting too close. His loss. Not yours. Move on."

"Easy for you to say," Maya said.

"I know, hun. But I think you've got to approach this dating lark with a tougher skin."

Maya sighed. "Yeah, be like the rhino. Not the arse, but the thick skin."

"Exactly! Who said that? I like it."

"A guy I chat to online sometimes." Maya leaned against the kitchen counter and wondered what to do next.

"Why don't you date him?" Emma asked, sipping her coffee.

"I don't even know what he really looks like. We seem to gel anonymously. I'm afraid I'll ruin it. He's good to go to for male advice."

The kitchen door banged open, and Lewis wandered in. "Mummy, I'm thirsty."

Maya, swiping the last tear off her cheek, got up and fetched him a glass of water. He gulped it down.

"What are you talking about?" Lewis frowned at his mother. Hopefully he wouldn't notice she'd been upset.

"Nothing that concerns you, sweetie," Maya said, ruffling his hair.

"I heard you say something about meeting men from the internet."

Emma stifled a chuckle. Maya blushed.

"It's nothing to worry about, baby," she said, taking the glass from his hand and trying to usher him out of the kitchen.

"But Mummy, you're not meant to meet strangers from the internet," Lewis said, refusing to budge. "That's what we got taught at school."

How come if she called Lewis for his dinner, he wouldn't hear her, yet from the lounge he'd ear-wigged her and Emma talking about dating.

"Yes, you're right. But Mummy is always careful, and I'm an adult, so it's different."

"How?"

"Because at school they're warning you about a different sort of stranger danger, darling." Maya bent down to level with Lewis. His expression was confused. "I do tell Emma where I am going, who I'm meeting. That way, if something does happen to me, she knows the last person I met."

"What could happen to you?"

Maybe Maya shouldn't have admitted the last bit. It was meant as a joke. She hoped there weren't any serial killers lurking on the internet, using online dating. "Nothing, nothing can happen to me."

"Lewis, do you want a biscuit?" Emma stepped in, offering him the biscuit barrel.

His eyes lit up. "Yes, please," he said, taking the jar.

"Take it into the lounge and offer Owen and Finley one." Emma waved him off with a smile.

"And your sister," Maya added.

Lewis shot out of the kitchen. Maya sighed with relief. "Thank you. That was awkward. At least he didn't ask *why* I was meeting men on the internet."

Maya thought she'd got away with the dating conversation. Unfortunately, Amber brought it up at teatime, while the three of them were tucking into their roast dinner.

"Mum, Lewis said you were meeting men on the internet. Are you dating?"

Maya swallowed her mouthful and took a sip of water, wondering how best to explain this to her daughter. "Yes, I am."

"Is it Sam?" Amber asked.

Maya nearly choked on the roast potato she was chewing. She shook her head. "No, it's not Sam."

"Oh. Will you introduce us to them?"

"No, not unless it becomes serious."

"Why?" Lewis asked. Amber looked at him and then at Maya, as if seconding her brother's question. They were ganging up on her. They did say never let kids outnumber you. Which was fine if you happily remained with your partner, but as soon as you became a single parent the odds were immediately stacked against you.

"Because I don't want to introduce you to everyone I meet. I need to make sure they're serious about me first, and I need to get to know them, to make sure they're safe for you to meet."

"Safe?" Lewis picked up on the word before Amber. He was more astute than Maya gave him credit for.

"Sweetheart, I want someone who'll love us all, if that makes sense. We come as a package really. But so I don't scare the poor man off, I have to get to know him first."

"Have you met someone, then?" Amber asked, fork poised, about to stuff roast chicken into her mouth.

"Would you be cross if I did?"

"No, it's cool. Dad's got Jenna, so you need someone too." Amber sounded so grown up suddenly. "You need to be happy too, Mum."

"Ah, thank you, Amber." Maya smiled gently at her daughter. "Come on, eat up! Ice-cream for pudding."

"Yay!"

"That's to make up for the early night you're both going to need. School tomorrow."

"Boo!" they said in unison, scowling.

Maya knew her children loved school. It was the prospect of an early night they didn't like. However, after the sleepless night she'd had, she wouldn't be far behind the children in going to bed.

CHAPTER 29

May

It was the Wednesday after the May Day Bank Holiday. Chloe had been back at school for a couple of weeks. Sam stared at the message Maya had sent to his PeterPan26 profile — just over two weeks ago! He hadn't bothered checking it recently, after her last message saying she was dating. He hadn't thought she would message him again. Did this mean she was single? That Sunday morning, when he'd dropped off Amber, he had sensed something was up but didn't feel it was his place to ask. Now he wished he had. He read the message over and over. He could feel her anger and hurt as he read it. Poor woman. She was beautiful and warm — a wonderful mother and friend — and she had an infectious laugh. How did he tell her she was all he wanted?

He began to type: *Hey, I'm sorry for the late reply. Turned out to be another frog, huh? Or a toad? You have to remember that there are genuine men out there. And when you find the right man, you'll realise he'll do whatever it takes to make you happy. P x*

He could see Maya was replying, so he waited.

I was deceived. Definitely a toad. Thank you, you just put a smile back on my face.

Good. I only ever want you to smile, he wrote. *Tomorrow is a new day. Mark him down as a learning experience. He didn't deserve you if he couldn't see your beauty inside and out.*

Fetch me the sick bucket lol! she joked.

Okay, too far ... lol! But you do deserve better. P x

After ten minutes deliberating over this new information, Sam decided to grab the moment and text Maya — this time as himself: *Hey, are you free this afternoon? Fancy a catch-up before the school run?*

Five minutes later, Sam fist-pumped the air. Maya had replied to his text agreeing to meet for lunch. She had until two o'clock, when her next client was scheduled. They arranged to meet at the coffee shop on the marina.

He had to remember that Maya hadn't told *him* that she'd split from the guy she was dating, she'd told *Peter*. But now he wanted to see her. With the kids back at school, he'd been looking for an excuse to get Chloe and Amber together, so that he could see Maya. He hadn't been collecting from school much, Heather had. A deadline loomed at work, and it meant spending many hours working overtime in the office. Heather had suggested a barbecue this weekend, so he thought if he and Maya met up, he could drop this into the conversation. He'd taken the afternoon off work for a dentist appointment, only to have them call and cancel at the last minute. He figured he could go back to work, and would have, but now Maya had agreed to meet him. A much better option.

Taking the path down to the marina, the sea air filled his lungs. The day, albeit cloudy, was warm, hinting that summer was on its way. He'd lived here for nearly a year now, and Chloe had settled into her new school. He didn't doubt he'd made the right decision. This was turning out to be a new start for them both. Portishead wasn't quite Cornwall, but it was better than living the suburban life in Swindon. He loved the sound of the wind through the boats in the marina, making their sails and rigging rattle and ting, reminding him of Padstow. He and Chloe often spent Sunday afternoons watching the lock fill and empty, letting boats in or out of the harbour. It felt good to be near the sea again.

Sam walked across the lock gate, which was currently shut, and headed towards the coffee shop. He could see Maya walking towards him. Her blonde hair was tied back in a chignon, with tendrils blowing loose in the wind. Clearly dressed for work, she wore a midnight-blue tunic with an asymmetric V neck collar, and matching trousers.

"Your timing was perfect. I wanted to escape the house. I was just making work for myself," Maya said as she approached. Her smile was bright, her lips glossed pink.

"Yeah, I was supposed to be going to the dentist. I'm glad you agreed to meet up, otherwise I was considering going back to work."

"The sun is trying to come out. It would be a shame to lock yourself away in an office."

"I agree." Sam held the door open, and they entered Costa. They chose a panini each and walked to the counter. "What coffee would you like?"

"A skinny-latte should keep me going," she said. She reached inside her handbag.

"Put your money away. My idea, my treat."

"Are you sure?" Maya frowned.

"Of course. Do you want cake?"

"No, I'd better not."

"Grab a seat by the window, and I'll be over in a minute with the coffees."

"Yes, okay," Maya said, and made her way over to a circular table with three comfy tub armchairs around it. Sam watched as she took a seat facing the window. From this table, they would be able to enjoy the view of the harbour and watch the people passing by. Sam placed the coffee orders, handing over the paninis to be toasted, and picked up a bag of mini rocky road bites which were by the till.

Sam brought the coffees over, placing the latte in front of Maya. He took the seat next to her, which also faced the window. They both sipped their coffees, sitting in companionable silence for a few moments, as they watched the seagulls fly around the many boats moored in the marina.

Sam decided to come straight out with it. "It's supposed to be good weather next weekend, so Heather and Tom are having a barbecue on the Saturday afternoon to celebrate her birthday. She's asked me to invite you and the kids. Mum and Dad should be coming up from Cornwall, too."

"Oh, that'll be lovely, thank you." Maya fetched her phone out of her bag. Sam was relieved he didn't have to try and convince her to come. "I'll put it in my diary now. You'll have to let me know where she lives."

"Her house isn't that far from mine." Sam retrieved his own phone from his pocket and looked through his contacts to give Maya Heather's address.

The barista arrived with their paninis, toasted and halved, hot cheese oozing out of them.

Maya frowned at her phone. "Oh, Mum and Dad have the kids next weekend." She looked up and met Sam's gaze. "They like to take them out for the day for me occasionally. Enables me to get on with things I need to do or squeeze in some occasional Saturday work. I've got some appointments in the morning: a manicure and a bridal make-up."

"Your parents can come too. The more the merrier," Sam said. He was certain Heather wouldn't mind.

"Oh, I think they'd like that. I'll check with them and get back to you, though." Maya continued tapping at her phone.

"Thanks for meeting me for lunch. I actually didn't think you would be free this afternoon," Sam said.

"I'd had a cancellation from a client. It's rather annoying." Maya placed her phone on the table and picked up her panini. "Some clients think that because I'm self-employed they can just phone for an appointment and I'll be free, and equally they can cancel at the drop of a hat. They don't seem to realise I do have a living to make, and it's quite stressful as a single mum. This is my business."

"Those with a regular income probably don't get it."

"Some are mums from school, who don't work, or some are retired. They have all the time in the world, so they assume I have."

Maya's phone beeped. Sam watched her as she navigated through her phone to read the message. She huffed.

"Here you go. Someone who thinks I'm available twenty-four-seven. She's wondering if I could fit her in at half-past three this afternoon for a manicure and pedicure. She's going on holiday tomorrow and totally forgot to book." Maya rolled her eyes. "Honestly, she knows I have kids."

Sam reached out and stopped her as she was texting a reply, her hand soft and warm under his touch. He lingered there for a moment, before taking his hand away. "Say you'll do it. I'll fetch the kids. I've got to get Chloe anyway."

"You don't have to do that, Sam. I'll just tell her I can't do it."

"No, I don't mind getting the kids. Do it."

Maya frowned, thumb poised over her phone. "Are you sure?"

"I wouldn't offer if not, Maya. Besides, Chloe has been angling to have Amber over for tea, so I'll kill two birds with one stone," he said. "This way, you don't lose any money and you keep a customer happy. And I keep my daughter sweet."

"As long as this client doesn't think she can do it all the time." Maya gestured to her phone.

"She won't. Tell your client you can do it this once, as a friend has just offered to have your kids." Sam winked.

"Thank you. That would be handy."

"And I'll cook tea for all of us, so you don't have to worry about dinner tonight either."

"Really?"

"Don't get too excited. I'm an engineer, I'm no chef," Sam said, holding his hands up. "Do your kids like pasta?"

"Of course."

"That's settled, then."

Maya sent a text to her client. "Oh, I'd better call the school, so they'll release the kids to you." She picked up her phone again, and Sam carried on eating his panini while mentally trying to prepare a dinner in his head that the kids would eat and he couldn't get wrong, if he wanted to impress Maya with his culinary skills. He had better visit the supermarket before picking up the kids, too.

Maya pulled up outside Sam's house, stomach rumbling. She'd gone from her two o'clock client, straight to her three-thirty appointment, which had taken longer than anticipated. When Maya had mentioned she offered waxing as a mobile service, her client had asked if she could have her bikini line done too. The wax was already in the car from the previous customer, so Maya dragged in the massage bed, towels and set up the wax pot, allowing it to heat up while she painted her client's nails and buffed her feet. This extra treatment had delayed Maya, and she had been stuck in the rush-hour traffic. She had texted

Sam and he'd told her it was fine, but she had worried it looked as if she was taking advantage of his generosity. He reassured her the children weren't killing each other and told her to take as long as she needed.

Sam opened the front door with a smile, the corners of his eyes creasing warmly, and boyish dimples forming in his cheeks. Maya's heart quickened. Did he realise how he affected her? He welcomed her through to his kitchen after she had poked her nose in on the kids to say hi. They were watching television in the lounge. Both replied without taking their eyes off the screen. She secretly observed Sam's clean and tidy house, confirming the man didn't live idly.

Maya sat at his small breakfast bar. Behind her was a door leading to the dining room, with patio doors open, allowing a breeze into the house. She could see he'd already laid the table.

"How was it?" Sam asked as he put another larger saucepan filled with water on another ring on the hob, turning on the gas.

"Not too bad." Maya could smell the sweetness of garlic and onions. "What's for dinner? It smells delicious."

"Spaghetti Bolognese. I figured it was something the kids would eat." He popped a tray of garlic bread into the oven and set the timer. "I thought I'd wait until you arrived before I put the pasta on. The sauce is ready."

Maya watched as Sam made her a mug of tea, and continued with the dinner preparations, all the while occasionally catching her eye with a smile. It was nice to be waited on, Maya mused, especially by a good-looking man.

"Thanks for this," Maya said. "I'm sorry my appointment took longer than anticipated. When she found out I offered waxing as a service too, she asked if I could do her bikini line. And the way she asked, I felt I couldn't say no."

"She knew you wouldn't say no."

Maya sighed. "Why do people leave things to the last minute? She flies out on holiday in the morning."

"You're the sort to be packed a week before, aren't you?"

"What's wrong with that?"

"Nothing. Jade was the same," Sam said, then dropped his gaze, concentrating on the pans on the hob. Maya didn't feel any discomfort at the mention of Jade's name. He had nothing to be embarrassed about. "The kids have been great, by the way. Haven't really heard a peep out of them. Bribed them with biscuits and a drink when we walked through the door, then they've been watching TV or playing on the Wii."

Occasionally, Maya could hear the children's laughter from the lounge. She sipped her tea. "Is there anything I can help you with?"

"No, you relax."

She didn't need telling twice.

Ten minutes later, five pasta bowls were filled with spaghetti — smaller portions for the children — and Bolognese sauce was spooned over it. Slices of garlic ciabatta bread, smelling divine, was retrieved from the oven and placed on a large plate, which Sam handed to Maya.

"Please can you take that to the table? And maybe round up the kids," Sam said.

"Wash your hands, kids," Maya called out, after placing the garlic bread in the centre of the table. The three children, drying their hands on their shirts, came running into the dining room and took their seats, leaving Maya to sit next to Sam, who would take the end of the table.

"Oh! Wine!" Sam went back into the kitchen.

The kids all grabbed a piece of garlic bread as if they would miss out if they didn't, even though there was plenty there. It felt like the days when she was married to Kyle, and they all sat around the table together. It was important family time. She wished for those times again.

With Sam? The thought popped into her head.

Sam returned from the kitchen with two small glasses of red wine, placing a glass before her.

"Thank you," Maya said. She waited for him to sit down, then clinked her glass with his. "Cheers."

Sam and Maya let the children lead the dinner table conversation, recounting what they'd done in school that day. Sam would glance across at Maya, with that twinkle of laughter in his gaze, and would give encouragement to the children. It felt good to share this with someone, the day-to-day stuff which got taken for granted.

The food was devoured quickly by the children.

"Can we play another game on the Wii, Mummy?" Lewis asked as he was about to get down from the table, the last to finish.

"Erm, what do you say first?" Eyes narrowed, Maya gave him a stern look.

"Please may I leave the table?" Lewis asked, looking at Maya and then Sam. The girls had already asked to leave.

"Yes, but we can't stay too long, darling," Maya said, getting up from the table to help Sam with the plates.

"Yay!" Lewis was gone.

"I don't want to eat and just leave, but it is getting late." Maya glanced at her watch. It was seven. "We'll have to go soon."

Unfortunately. It would have been nicer to stay, to cuddle up on the sofa, watch a film, finish the wine. That's all Maya wanted; to be loved.

"Of course. It's a school night." Sam took the plates from Maya, rinsed them under the tap then placed them in the dishwasher.

They both returned to the dining room, to clear anything remaining on the table. Both wine glasses were empty. They gathered up the discarded pasta bowls, laughing and joking comfortably together. In an unguarded moment, Maya caught Sam by the arm.

"Sam, I just wanted to say thanks for this. Babysitting the kids, the dinner... I really appreciate it. You're a real friend." She dropped her gaze, nervously tucking a strand of hair behind her ear that had worked itself loose from her bun.

"Any time, Maya. I've enjoyed having you here."

CHAPTER 30

Maya decided to give the online dating a rest. She occasionally messaged PeterPan26, but other than that, she kept her profile hidden so she couldn't be contacted by anyone else. She did not need to be subjected to any more depressing messages from the likes of DIYDes to knock her self-esteem. She still ruminated over Pierce and how he'd conducted the whole relationship. She couldn't help obsessively analysing it, trying to work out if she'd said or done something wrong, kicking herself for sleeping with him too quickly. She didn't regret it — she was a grown woman. She'd given birth to two children and was a responsible adult. Emma reassured her it wasn't her fault. But late at night, lying in bed in the darkness with only her thoughts for company, she still questioned herself.

This weekend was Heather's barbecue, giving her something to look forward to. Her parents were taking Amber and Lewis out for the day, and would come along to the barbecue in the late afternoon, delighted to be invited.

Maya had seen Selina's Facebook status over the weekend, changing from happy, positive thoughts to much more emotional ones, hinting that something was amiss. Her relationship status had switched back to single, too. Maya sent her a personal message to ask if everything was okay, and Selina replied that Kelvin had suddenly ended their relationship. Shocked, Maya thumbed a reply: *I'm sorry to hear this. I thought he was the one. If there's anything I can do, let me know.*

Since their initial discussion about online dating, Selina had regularly checked in with Maya, interested in how she had been

214

getting on. Now Maya wanted to be a friend Selina could lean on.

While busy checking her stock and monitoring Lewis doing his homework at the kitchen table, Maya's phone pinged. It was Selina: *Hi, Maya, I wondered if you were about this Friday. I could do with a night out and a chat.*

Let me see if I can organise a babysitter, Maya replied. The way she was feeling about Pierce, she believed Selina would be good to talk things over with. Sometimes their married friends didn't understand the trials and tribulations of being a single mother. Emma was a great support, but maybe Selina was what Maya needed right now.

Her mother, Fern, didn't do texting, so Maya telephoned her.

"Hi, Mum, it's only me," she said. "You know you've got the kids on Saturday? Well, I was wondering if you'd mind having them overnight on the Friday?"

"I can't see why not. It would mean you're not disturbed on Saturday morning; you'll be able to go straight to work," Fern replied. And if Maya had a hangover from the Friday evening, she could recover in peace. "We could treat the kids to a Frankie and Benny's breakfast."

"Oh, they'd love that." Lewis always talked about the pancakes with maple syrup and bacon. "Yes, and I've been invited out on Friday night —"

"Ooh, another date?"

"No, no, no more dates. I'm just going out with a mum from school. She's split up with her boyfriend, so I think she needs some company."

"Oh, no," Fern said, sounding concerned. "Yes, well, that's fine. We'd love to have them. Would you like us to collect them from school?"

"Do you mind?" With the phone to her ear, Maya checked out her appearance in the mirror in the hallway. Her eyebrows needed attention. This week, she'd let herself go. Not good for a beauty industry professional. "It would be a great help."

"That's settled, then."

Maya waited outside The Golden Lion early on Friday evening. The clouds were as grey as her mood, and she hoped Selina wouldn't keep her waiting too long. They'd never socialised before. They always said hello in the school playground — Toby was in the same class as Amber — and they chatted via Facebook, more so since Maya had first asked about online dating. And although Selina had become a new client for treatments, too, they'd never been out for a drink together.

"Hi, sorry I'm late," Selina said, running down the hill, her blonde hair streaming behind her like a kite's tail in the wind. She wore skinny black jeans, heels and a floaty, flowery top underneath a black leather jacket. She appeared to have made much more of an effort than Maya, wearing her make-up heavier too. Was Kelvin old news already? Perhaps Selina was putting on a brave face. Maya wished she'd put heels on too, and not opted for flip-flops.

They entered the pub chatting nervously, as if it were a first date, and heads turned. Maya noticed Sam immediately. He was here again with his friends, casually dressed, sports bag by his feet, pint glasses half empty. Vicky — the stunning brunette — was also there. Now Maya knew who Vicky was, she didn't feel any resentment or jealousy towards her.

Maya smiled at Sam and gave a feeble wave. Selina found them a table.

"Who's that?" she asked as she handed Maya a menu.

"Just a friend. Chloe's dad from school."

"One hot dad. Why haven't I noticed him in the playground before?" Selina asked. "Probably because I was so loved up with Kelvin."

"He rarely does the school run." Maya tried to brush off Selina's comment, hoping it looked as if she'd never noticed how hot Sam was.

"Shall we share a bottle of wine?" Selina looked up from her menu. She had lovely blue eyes, accentuated by dark kohl, and long black eyelashes. She was so pretty. Was Kelvin mad? Why had he let Selina go? From the photos Maya had seen of him on social media, she'd always thought the man was punching above his weight. "White or rosé?"

"I think they have Prosecco on offer."

"Oh, yes, let's do that." Selina sounded very cheerful, but Maya wondered if it was a front. When they'd spoken in the week to finalise their meeting, Selina had become quite tearful. Hopefully they both wouldn't be sobbing into their Prosecco glasses later.

Leaving her card at the bar, Maya set up a tab, ordering the bottle of Prosecco and their food. While she waited for the bartender to fetch her bottle, she felt a tap on her shoulder.

"Don't panic, I'm not stalking you. Daryl and I sometimes have a pint after badminton," Sam said, standing beside her. "Vicky and Zara joined us."

"Undoing all your hard work exercising," Maya said, trying to keep the conversation light.

"Yes." Sam chuckled, rubbing his stomach. "Anyway, we're off now. I thought I'd say goodbye and see you tomorrow?"

The bartender serving Maya placed an ice bucket on the counter with the bottle of Prosecco and two glasses tucked inside.

"Thank you," Maya said, then turned to Sam. "Yes, see you tomorrow. Bye."

"Have a good evening."

"And you."

When she returned to the table, Selina said, "He likes you."

"No, he doesn't." Maya frowned, unconvinced. "It's funny how things turn out, though, because he was vile to me when we first met — but we're over that now. We've become friends due to our daughters being best friends." Maya wanted to change the subject to the reason they'd met up. "So, come on, tell me, what happened with Kelvin?" she asked, unpeeling the foil from the cork.

"I don't know. He decided he wasn't good enough for me." Selina's demeanour changed from cheerful to gloomy instantly.

"What? Shouldn't you be the one to decide that?"

They spent the evening — over a couple of bottles of Prosecco and good pub grub — swapping relationship notes and online dating horror stories, boosting each other's self-esteem.

With desserts devoured and thinking it wise not to invest in a third bottle of Prosecco, they settled the bill and visited the loos before leaving the pub. Still giggling, they trudged up the hill to walk home. They came to a fork in the road, where Selina needed to take the left and Maya the right.

"This was so much fun." Selina hugged Maya and kissed her cheek. "We must do this again."

"Absolutely. Single friends together." Maya hugged her back, reaching up on tiptoes as Selina towered over her.

"Take no bullshit!"

"Ditto." They high-fived.

"You never know, Mr Right might be right under our noses," Selina said, wistfully. "Text me when you get home safe."

"You too." Maya waved and headed off, her heart lighter and happier. It felt great to let off steam with Selina. Maya had thoroughly enjoyed herself. And she hoped Selina had too. Hopefully, both women had walked out of the pub with their confidence restored — *ish*.

When Maya entered her house, she remembered she had it to herself, so she could clatter around without fear of waking the children. Once in bed, her make-up removed, she texted a 'home safe' message to Selina, who replied with a thumbs-up emoji and a 'me too'.

Maya scrolled through her phone, looking at Facebook and Twitter notifications, and noticed she had a message in Find My HEA. The only person it could be was PeterPan26. She had informed him earlier she was heading out.

Hope you had a good evening out with your friend and you've made it home safely. P x

Home safe, Maya replied. *Fab evening slagging off sad men. Feel so much better. Although that might be the Prosecco. W x*

Lol! Poor guys, he wrote. *I bet their ears were burning. P x*

CHAPTER 31

Maya's head thudded as her phone alarm went off, a dull ache at her temples reminding her of how much Prosecco she and Selina had drunk the night before. They had certainly cheered each other up. She resolved, too, to keep her profile hidden and take a break from online dating. What if she was trying to force something that wasn't meant to be yet?

Much as she liked Sam, she worried whether it was worth jeopardising their friendship. With a sigh, Maya threw back the duvet, knowing she couldn't lie in bed any longer. She needed to make the most of the morning, getting a run in before meeting her first client.

The running club met early now the weather was warmer and the mornings much lighter. Running first thing was quieter, too, especially on a Saturday, when most people stayed in bed later. The run cleared her head, and after a quick breakfast and shower, Maya donned a clean, deep purple tunic, tied her hair back and applied her make-up. Ready for work, Maya loaded her car with what she needed for the morning.

Maya's first client was a new customer who had been put in touch with her through a friend of a friend. Ingrid was a woman in her early fifties and came across as snooty. She took longer than Maya wanted to deliberate over which colour nail polish to choose, and Maya had to fend off a few cats, but otherwise she was running on time to reach her next client, a bride.

They'd gone through a make-up trial a week earlier, so Maya knew exactly what she was doing. The bride, with her hair already set and pinned, and with flowers and jewels dotted in the twists and curls, wore her pink, silk dressing gown to cover the fact she only had her underwear on underneath. The dress was going on last.

Three other young women — the bridesmaids — flitted about, chattering and giggling. It was noisy and the excited tension was palpable in the room. They were each doing their own make-up, helping one another in what could only be described as organised chaos. There were pain au chocolat and croissants on the table, and four glass flutes, each with champagne bubbling in them and lipstick marks on the rims. Every now and then, one of the young women would return to their glass and take a sip. The bride's glass was the fullest.

Among this bedlam and noise, as Maya's head started to thrum, the bride reached for her champagne flute and knocked it over, spilling its contents into the eyeshadow palette. Maya's stress levels lessened as the girls rallied round, a team effort, and Maya was able to apply eye make-up to the bride, but not quite how they'd originally planned.

Later than scheduled and feeling like the morning had been one big rush, Maya pulled up on her driveway, yanking up the handbrake before the car had even stopped. Thinking she wouldn't last until the afternoon and not wanting to start drinking on an empty stomach, she slapped together some lunch. She then unloaded her car, drank coffee and scoffed a sandwich — a fine example of how women could multi-task — before jumping in the shower again.

The weather looked clear, but blowy — the usual downside to living by the coast — so Maya opted for three-quarter length denim blue jeggings, a dusty pink floral top and a matching jacket for the cooler evening to come. With a glance at her watch, Maya locked her house, popped on her sunglasses and started her route to Heather's house.

"Oh, bugger!" Halfway there, she realised she'd forgotten to buy Heather a present, plus a bottle of wine to take with her. She'd meant to call into the supermarket on the way home from her last client, but what with the spillage of champagne over her make-up, and the hysteria of the bride and bridesmaids, she'd clean forgotten and driven straight home.

Maya detoured back towards the supermarket, grabbing a basket as she entered. Not knowing Heather very well, she opted for a pretty bouquet of yellow and orange flowers, a mix of roses, lilies and gerberas with gypsophila scattered between them. Always Maya's favourite. Then she picked up two bottles of Prosecco and a giftbag.

Laden down with the two bottles of Prosecco and trying to cradle the bouquet of flowers without breaking the stems, as if holding a newborn baby, Maya's arms felt like lead by the time she rang the doorbell. She had walked around for twenty minutes trying to find Heather's house. And her legs were reminding her she'd gone for a 5K run this morning, too. As soon as she heard the doorbell chime, she spotted the note taped to the door saying, *back gate open.*

"Hello!" Maya called, struggling to open the gate. She had to put the bottles down with a clink. With her thumb, she manoeuvred the latch on the gate and pushed, and to her relief she was through. Blowing her hair out of her face as she reached down for the bottles, suddenly feeling hot from the walk, she stepped forward, and *oomph!*

"Sorry!" she said, bumping straight into Sam. Solid, firm torso — Maya relished it for one brief, pleasant moment.

He looked and smelt divine, wearing dark denim jeans and a blue checked shirt.

Why did he always look bloody amazing when she looked harassed, stressed and usually sweaty!

"I heard a hello and thought I'd come see if you needed a hand. It sounded more like a call for help." Sam was holding a pint of beer.

"It was, really. But shouting 'help' might have sounded pathetic."

Sam welcomed her through. "Can I help you carry anything?"

"The bottle in the carrier bag is my booze contribution." Maya held up her hand, arm aching, and Sam took the bag from her. She still cradled the flowers and the other bottle. "I'll go give these to Heather."

"I'll put this in the fridge and get you a drink. There's an open bottle of Prosecco already in there." Sam led Maya into the small garden, where a gas barbecue was being fired up by Tom, who was chatting to Charles. Chloe and her cousins were playing on the lawn. Plenty of garden chairs were placed out around the patio, and there was multicoloured bunting — pastel pink, green and yellow — strung from hanging basket to hanging basket, all newly planted with bedding flowers. It all looked so pretty. Maya found Heather sitting in a chair, talking to Rose.

"Happy birthday," Maya said as Heather stood to greet her.

"You didn't need to do this, Maya. They're so pretty." Heather gestured to the flowers and then the giftbag containing the extra Prosecco. She kissed Maya on the cheek as if they were old friends. "Thank you — I'll go put them in water."

"Come and sit down," Rose said, patting Heather's vacated garden chair beside her. "Lovely to see you again. You're looking well."

"Yes, and you." Maya's healthy glow was probably due to the exertion and stress rather than the sun.

"Hey, Maya." Joe came through the patio doors, looking like he'd just come off the beach in knee-length shorts, a T-shirt and flip-flops. He gave her a hug before she could take her seat. "Great to see you."

"And you," Maya said. "I didn't expect to see you here." She realised now it was Rhianna sitting on the other side of Rose and gave her a friendly wave.

Memories of Easter in Cornwall with all of Sam's family flooded back to Maya, a weekend she wouldn't forget. Their warmth and hospitality were palpable. They always made her feel like a part of their family, even though she wasn't. But could she be?

"I'd better help Tom with the barbecue. Don't want burnt burgers." Joe thumbed behind him.

Tom shouted, "Hey, I heard that!"

"Who's holding the fort at the bed and breakfast?" Maya plopped down beside Rose, envisaging not being able to get up for a while. "As Joe's here."

"I roped in my nephew, Tristan," Rose said, sipping from a tall glass. "He's usually terribly busy, but it's only for one night." There was a glint of mischief in her eye, the same twinkle Joe had.

"And who's managing the bistro, Rhianna?" Maya asked.

"Yasmin is my second in command. And the season hasn't really picked up yet," Rhianna replied. "So they should manage without me for a weekend."

"Can't be all work and no play." Joe appeared, standing behind Rhianna, and gave her an affectionate kiss on the cheek.

"Have you got a drink?" Heather called from the open patio doors, where Maya could see a dining room table pushed against the back wall, loaded with food, including fresh salad and buttered burger buns.

"No, Sam's getting me one."

And as if on cue, Sam appeared with a full pint in one hand and a glass flute in the other, the golden liquid bubbling.

Handing Maya her drink, he took a seat beside her. "How was your day?"

"Don't ask." After her morning and the walk here, Maya was glad to be sitting down. "From trying to paint some mad cat lady's fingernails, to four overexcited women getting ready for a wedding, spilling champagne everywhere, including into my make-up palette... Let's just say I need this." She took a sip of her drink, and it was like liquid gold lining her throat. Each swallow felt medicinal.

"You can relax now," Sam said, reassuringly. "When are your parents arriving?"

"They said they'd leave Bristol Zoo at about three-thirty." Maya glanced at her watch. They would be here soon enough. Maya thought she should make the most of the quiet before her children were returned to her and she'd have to resume her mum role.

Sam and Maya soaked up the sun in the corner of the patio. Relaxing in his company, she told him about her morning. Sam laughed. Occasionally he would pat her knee, or she would tap him as they spoke, especially if he teased her, and it would send a zing of excitement through her.

Lewis and Amber arrived before Maya's parents appeared, having run from the car to the garden. They found their mother, hugged her, and as fast as they'd said they were here, they were off to find Chloe.

"Rose, Charles, this is my mum and dad, Fern and Doug." Maya introduced her parents. They shook hands and welcomed each other. Charles and Doug stood chatting with a bottle of beer each, handed to them by Joe. The thought suddenly entered Maya's head that if she and Sam did date, at least their parents had met. She quickly shook off the thought and concentrated on Rose and Fern's conversation, listening with Rhianna.

"So what part of Cornwall are you from?" Fern asked, as Sam handed her a glass of white wine.

"Kittiwake Cove, in North Cornwall," Rose answered in her usual warm tone. "We run a bed and breakfast. We converted our family home once the kids grew up."

"It's beautiful, Mum. And you'd love staying at Rose's farmhouse. All original features, quaint and rustic. Rose bakes the most fantastic cakes, too." Maya couldn't help interjecting her thoughts on the place. Sam returned to his seat beside her, giving her a warm smile, completely at ease with the situation. Would Kittiwake Cove be the same without Sam there — and Chloe, of course?

Garden Jenga had been set up on the lawn and this amused the five children endlessly, with the aid of the grandads, allowing Maya to relax. She soaked up the warm May sunshine in Heather and Tom's back garden with a glass of Prosecco. Being in such good company was the perfect way to spend a Saturday. It felt like everyone was one big happy family.

At around seven, a small firepit was lit, to keep everyone warm. Heather came out armed with skewers and a bowl of marshmallows. The children were closely monitored, but had so much fun toasting marshmallows and squashing them between milk chocolate digestives.

Heather sat down next to Maya, topping up her glass once again. "Thanks for coming, Maya. I thought we all had such a lovely time in Cornwall, it would be nice to do it again."

Heather was looking at Sam, who turned, caught Maya's eye, and smiled.

Yes, they certainly had had a lovely time in Cornwall. Warmth, sand, sea and surf. And a sunset.

"Are you still seeing that guy?" Heather asked.

"Oh, he ended it a couple of weeks ago," Maya said. "I think I'm going to give the whole dating thing a rest for a bit."

"There's someone out there, I'm sure. He might be right under your nose and you don't even realise it." Heather clinked her glass with Maya's and they both laughed.

Whoever was out there, they would have to wait. Maya needed her heart to heal from Pierce's rejection. She didn't want to rush into anything else too quickly, fearing it could be a rebound. But she couldn't stop thinking about Sam.

At eleven o'clock, lightheaded and giggly from the Prosecco and the atmosphere, Maya had to say her goodbyes. She had two very exhausted children to take home, and her mum and dad were ready to leave. She went around as the others did, saying goodbye with a kiss or a hug.

"Remember you must come and visit us at Kittiwake Cove," Rose said, kissing Maya on the cheek. She'd said the same to Fern and Doug.

"I will."

"Yeah, don't be a stranger!" Joe hugged her after Rhianna. "You're more than welcome at our wedding."

"Oh, I don't know..." Maya said hesitantly. This was a step too far into the Trescott family, maybe.

"Yes, there's room for more," Rhianna agreed.

Sam walked out with Maya to her parents' car.

She hugged him like she had Joe, only Sam held her longer, his hug firmer. She could have sworn her family went silent in the car. She kissed him on the cheek, and he kissed her back, and as she withdrew — reluctantly — she couldn't quite make eye contact, only smiling at his shoes. He felt so good to hold and even with the mixed aroma of barbecue and smoke, she could still smell the lingering scent of his aftershave.

"Goodnight, Maya," Sam said, holding the car door open. She slid into the back with the kids.

"Goodnight, Sam," she said, pulling on the seatbelt. "See you soon." He closed the passenger door, and her father pulled the car away. Maya watched as he stood and waved.

"Sam's nice," Fern said, from the front of the car.

"Yes, he is," Maya replied, hoping her tone appeared neutral.

"They're all lovely. What a wonderful family," Fern continued. Maya could tell she was a little tipsy. "I've had a lovely afternoon; I'm so pleased they invited us."

Doug, the designated driver, nodded in agreement.

Fern was not the only one tipsy. Maya blamed the alcohol for the mixed emotions she felt about Sam swirling around her head.

He was more than nice.

He's...

He's Chloe's dad! It would get complicated.

CHAPTER 32

The next two weeks flew by. Maya, busy with clients, never saw Sam and hardly bumped into Heather on the school run either, as Lewis and Amber went to after-school clubs. Her work usually picked up at this time of year with people booking holidays and wanting waxes, manicures and pedicures to be beach-ready. Maya couldn't believe the kids only had three more days left before they broke up for May half-term. Before she'd had children, Maya was certain time didn't fly like this. Nowadays, she spent her days counting down the school weeks until the next term break.

Having heaved the massage bed into the boot of her car, she was ready to pull away when she remembered to check her phone. It was something she always tried to remember to do, as on several occasions she'd had clients cancel on her but had turned up on their doorstep, not seeing the text message first.

There was a message from Kyle. She frowned, then rolled her eyes in disbelief as she read it: *Hi Maya, as I didn't have the kids for Easter, I've booked a holiday for us all. I'll come and collect them on Saturday morning and deliver them back the following Sunday in time for school.*

"Maybe, Kyle, you should be asking if it's okay for you to take them away for May half-term," Maya said angrily at the phone screen. Okay, it was great he wanted to spend a week with them, but giving her three days' notice — what if she'd made plans?

Thankfully, she hadn't as such. She had kept her work diary free for a couple of days, including her birthday, which was on the 29th May, so she could take Lewis and Amber out on some day trips. Now it would mean she could work over the half-term and not stress about childcare.

But it would mean not having the children around to celebrate her birthday, she thought more glumly. It was only her thirty-ninth. It wasn't special. Just typical of Kyle to forget about her birthday.

She would hold off booking more clients until she was absolutely certain Kyle wouldn't cancel on her at the last minute.

She texted back: *A bit of notice would have been nice, but the kids will love seeing you. I'll make sure they're packed for a week. See you on Saturday.* Maya couldn't resist giving a dig.

This was a prime example of what Kyle didn't get. As he hardly saw the kids, he didn't have any of their clothes at his house. She usually packed a bag to send Amber and Lewis off with. So that meant tonight's job was making sure everything was washed and ironed.

Thanks, Kyle.

Kyle turned up at around eleven on Saturday morning. Maya had packed the children's bags the night before, so she didn't have to rush around like a headless chicken to get Amber and Lewis ready. Each bag was by the front door, with a week's worth of clothes.

"I think I've remembered everything," Maya said as she handed over the two holdalls.

"How much have you packed?" Kyle was unshaven and looked like he'd put on weight, the skin under his jaw saggy. Although still attractive, he appeared to be slowly losing his looks, or at least losing his appeal to Maya. Maybe baby Lola was taking her toll on him? Maya had ensured she looked fabulous this morning, even wearing make-up.

"You never know with the weather. It's not as reliable as Spain." She'd packed outfits for both warm and cold weather, underwear, toothbrushes, towels, swimwear, spare shoes, flip-flops, sun cream (which she hoped Kyle would think to use) and she'd given them each some spending money. She'd probably overdone it, but they were her babies. They were prepared for every eventuality. She smiled brightly. "Where are you going?"

"Just a caravan in Devon."

Maya rolled her eyes. That wasn't exactly the way to sell it to the children, although they'd be more than happy in 'just a caravan in Devon'. A holiday was a holiday, and they loved the beach. "Are Jenna and Lola going?"

"No, I thought it would be nice with just me and the kids."

"Oh, okay." It would do their children good to have quality time with their dad and have him focus on them rather than Jenna and Lola. Yet, they did need to bond with their new half-sister. But that was Kyle's worry, not hers, she decided.

"I'll bring them back on Sunday, is that okay?" Kyle said.

"Yes, not too late, though, as they have school the next day."

Kyle nodded. "Come on, munchkins. Say goodbye to your mum."

"Have a lovely time." A lump formed in Maya's throat as she kissed first Amber and then Lewis, giving them each a hug. "Be good for your dad." They were always good for Kyle. He even said he never had problems — and couldn't understand what Maya was going on about. However, Amber had confessed one time that they were afraid to be naughty in case he didn't want to see them again. It seemed Kyle only saw the best side of the kids on the few occasions they visited him.

Maya watched Kyle drive off, the kids strapped in the back, waving. She closed the front door and rested her head against it. A tear escaped, rolling down her cheek. She wiped her face with the back of her hand. There was a silence, an emptiness. She hated it when Kyle took the kids away, yet she loved the freedom it gave her. Then she would berate herself for the selfish thought, but she knew it made her a better mother if she had a break. She could recharge her batteries and come out a more patient person. Hopefully.

By late afternoon, with the housework completed, Maya had made some phone calls and sent some texts. She'd updated her Facebook page to say she was available for treatments over the half-term period, giving away some special offers, hoping to generate extra bookings. The house was eerily quiet and still, even with the radio on in the background. Kyle texted to say they'd arrived safely at the caravan site in Devon.

Before making dinner for one, which she felt uninspired to cook, she decided to go for a run. The exercise would release endorphins and lift her spirits. Breathing in the fresh air and taking in the scenery of the marina both helped improve her mood and motivation.

After dinner, she decided to watch a film. Something grown-up, that she couldn't watch with the children. At the back of the cupboard she found an unopened box of chocolates. With everything to hand, including her laptop, Maya settled down for a lazy evening on the sofa. One day, she hoped her Saturday nights would be more exciting. And less lonely.

While deciding on which movie to watch, she thought about trying to find herself a date to make the most of this week alone. Even if it turned out to be dinner for one night only, it would get her out of the house — especially as it was also her birthday week.

She'd toyed with the idea of texting Sam. But without Amber and Lewis here as playdates for Chloe, she wasn't sure she had a decent enough excuse to catch up with him.

Why did she keep thinking of Sam? *Because you can relax in his company. He's the kind of guy you would like as a partner. Easy-going, someone you can talk to and laugh with, and who you're attracted to physically...*

She huffed. Being single was a vicious circle. On the one hand, she had the freedom to do what she liked, but on the other, all she wanted was to find someone to share her days with. Loneliness crept up on her, thinking of the highs and lows life can bring and having no one to share them with. Even her best of friends couldn't be there for her all the time — they had lives of their own. Whereas a partner created the cement within a house, sticking everything together, filling in the cracks of life, to make your life feel whole. Having a partner didn't mean being with them twenty-four-seven. Just knowing they were there was enough. Even when Kyle had gone out for a night with his mates, he'd come back to Maya ... *until Jenna.*

But not everyone was like Kyle. And there had been good times. At least ten good years with Kyle

Putting Netflix aside, she logged into Find My HEA and unhid her LoisLane38 profile. She tweaked some of the stuff on there and swapped a photo for a more recent one taken by Selina from when they'd been at the pub. It made her chuckle, remembering how well they'd got on that night, sharing their online dating antics. Maybe she'd find someone to take her out for her birthday? She even sent PeterPan26 a message. He'd gone quiet on her these past weeks, too. Maybe he'd found a date?

She returned to Netflix to choose something to watch. Maya decided against watching a romance — it would only leave her disappointed — and opted for an action movie with a hunky hero, which would have some romance in it, no doubt. She would pause the movie if she started chatting to someone.

The first message Maya received made her wonder if she was doing the right thing, going back online. She huffed and shook her head as she read: *Hey, beautiful, how are you finding this sight?*

Maya resisted the urge to tell him her eyesight was fine, thank you. He'd only see it as encouragement if she replied. Determined, after her conversation with Selina, not to put up with less than she deserved, she hit delete on the message button. She returned her attention to the film. What had she expected? The first man to message be an intelligent hunk of a guy?

The laptop pinged again and Maya paused the movie to read the message. She had learnt that if she stayed online within the dating site, it generated more messages. She doubted it was a good thing, for she was becoming frustrated. The message was from a guy in the US — an army general, no less: *Hello, Lois, you are a beautiful woman. I would love to get to know you better. My name is Grant.*

"Why is he messaging me?" Maya talked to the screen. "He's from the USA. Unless he owns a private jet, don't bother!" *Delete.*

Another guy messaged, and Maya did respond to him as his profile appeared half decent. Sadly, the messaging soon came to an end when he replied: *LOL!*

Maya waited to see if anything else would follow, but it never did, so she decided not to continue messaging him. *His loss.* She refused to keep the conversation going if all she was getting in response was a laugh out loud — continuously. It was just lazy and crap, and too one-sided. She deserved better.

By the end of the film, and with most of the chocolates devoured, Maya climbed the stairs to her bedroom, feeling disheartened and dejected. So much for going for a run earlier to make herself feel better.

CHAPTER 33

That week, Maya persevered with the online dating site and now she had a date with MrPisces123, real name Craig. He was single with no children, which worried her slightly, but she wasn't looking for a marriage proposal, just a date. He lived over forty minutes away in Gloucester. He seemed a normal enough guy and his profile picture was attractive. Possibly a little too-good-to-be-true attractive, when she considered the quality of the other men who had messaged her. Craig was a similar age to Maya, with dark hair and the designer stubble look. She'd kept to her rules — sort of — chatting on the site, then moving it to text messages. Quickly into the texting, he suggested meeting up on her birthday, although she hadn't disclosed this piece of information. Fed up with twiddling her thumbs, she accepted the date.

Maya met Emma for lunch to celebrate her birthday, and she gave her approval.

"He looks nice. Tell me how it goes, okay?" Emma said, nodding at the screenshot of Craig's profile while Maya opened her birthday present. They'd met at Cabot Circus shopping centre in Bristol and were sitting in their favourite Italian restaurant after browsing the shops. Emma had bought Maya some pretty costume jewellery, which she would wear on her date.

The Golden Lion was the agreed venue for a drink tonight — at this rate, Maya would get a name for herself, but she wasn't sure of the reputation of any other pubs. She knew it wasn't full of cliquey locals and if the weather remained pleasant, they'd be able to sit outside and watch the yachts sailing past. It being half-term, and warm, there would probably be plenty of boats out.

Maya was standing in front of her wardrobe with a towel wrapped around her, choosing her outfit for the evening when her phone pinged to notify her she had a message on Find My HEA — she'd changed the sound to distinguish it from her other notifications. She smiled at her phone. It was PeterPan26: *Hey, sorry, I haven't been ignoring you. I've been away with work and not been able to get online. How are things with you?*

She thumbed a reply: *Kids have gone away with their dad, so it's been quiet. I decided to give the dating malarkey a bash again and actually have a date tonight! We're only meeting at my local pub for a drink.*

I hope it goes well, he replied. *Message me later if you like.*

Sam stared at his phone, disheartened. A dull ache formed around his heart and nausea rose in his stomach as he read Maya's message. She was dating again. He'd thought he should give her some time after her relationship had ended with *that guy*. Then, out of the blue, an urgent job had picked up at work, which had meant working all hours, then flying out to Toulouse for more meetings. He'd been stuck in France for over a week. Heather had looked after Chloe for him. He'd been pretty much out of contact with everyone. He hadn't been able to access the online dating site, and then he hadn't been sure about texting Maya directly, without the pretext of making a date for Chloe and Amber. And now here he was reading she was meeting another man!

He'd told himself to bide his time, but now he was losing patience and was worried he'd lose out completely. Since Jade, he'd never felt so certain about someone, and the past weeks had only made him more so. These days, if Chloe wasn't at the forefront of his mind, Maya was.

You should have just asked her out!
Be the rhino...

It had occurred to Sam that Maya might not be attracted to him. Well, he would deal with that scenario if it was the case, and move on. But he couldn't ignore the nagging instinct that Maya would make him happy.

And, given the chance, he would do everything in his power to make her happy, too.

He wanted to text her right now, to tell her everything, share his feelings for her. But it would be best to do face to face.

Be patient.

Dressed for her date, Emma's jewellery sparkling, Maya arrived at The Golden Lion before Craig. As the evening was mild, she bought a glass of white wine and returned to the beer garden. She found a central picnic table, enabling her to spot her date but also giving her a good view of the sea. She sent him a text to say where she was sitting. He hadn't replied yet.

While she waited, she scrolled through Facebook and Twitter, and checked her phone for messages. After fifteen minutes, and drinking her wine very slowly, she turned her mobile on and off, fearing messages weren't getting through. But the network was good; she had four bars and 4G. Still no message from Craig.

How long should she wait? What if he wasn't going to show up?

She perused the messages between them. They'd definitely agreed to meet here at eight. She sipped her wine, wishing she'd opted for the large now. He was coming from Gloucester. He could be stuck in traffic. And if he was driving, he'd be unable to message her.

Her phoned beeped. It was Craig: *Sorry to be a pain, still at my folks'. Can we postpone?*

Anger boiled inside Maya. She blew out her breath to calm herself. *Really? I'm already at the pub.*

Yeah, sorry, stuck at my parents', unable to get away, he replied. *Didn't realise Dad's had a new pacemaker fitted, and Mum's been explaining it all to me in great detail.*

If he was telling the truth, and this was a legitimate reason, Maya felt she couldn't tell him off. How unreasonable would she look? Then again, he could be just making excuses. Extreme excuses. How could he not know his dad had had a pacemaker fitted? And surely he must have been aware of the time? *No problem,* she typed. *Would have been nice to get this message half an hour ago, though.* She inserted the eye roll emoji. Her favourite.

I'm sorry. Don't make me feel worse. I'll make it up to you, he replied. *Are you free tomorrow?*

No, sorry, I'm working, Maya wrote. To check her theory, and to see if Craig was sincere, her fingers trembled as she navigated through the Find My HEA app.

"The bastard!" she said aloud.

Craig was online.

She blocked him instantly. She didn't want to hear any more pathetic excuses. He'd probably got a better offer closer to home — maybe guaranteed sex on a first date — who knew? But he was obviously a player.

Her woman's intuition had known it — too good to be true. Overwhelmed with rage, she messaged PeterPan26: *Cannot believe it. I've been stood up. On my birthday too! He's sent some sorry excuse, but I can see the bastard is online on this site! I am so angry right now. Why do I have no luck? Do I go home or order another glass of wine?*

She didn't have to wait long for a reply. She'd just finished her wine when her phone pinged: *Oh, that sucks. I am sorry. Where are you?*

The pub, she wrote.

Order another wine, he suggested.

No, I feel miserable. I'm going to walk home.

Tears started to well in Maya's eyes and her throat tightened. Why did she keep meeting men who mucked her about? What was wrong with her? They all said they wanted to meet genuine women, yet none of them were genuine themselves. Maybe she really did need to take a leaf out of Selina's book and take a step back from dating. Maybe she was trying to force something the Universe wasn't ready to provide her with yet. She wasn't even forty. She had time on her side. She checked she'd emptied her wine glass, then rose from the table and walked away from the pub.

She needed to get drunk, but alone in her own home. She didn't do drowning her sorrows publicly.

As she stormed up the hill, she was mentally going through the contents of her fridge. She had no white wine chilling in there. Switching to red could be lethal. She turned around and walked down the steps, past the RNLI, hoping the shop on the marina would still be open.

By the time she arrived at the store, her tears had dried. She dreaded to think what state her face was in, though. She probably looked like a puffy-eyed monster, but who cared? She avoided eye contact with the shop assistant as she paid for her wine. She'd bought two bottles — they were on special offer — and a BIG bar of chocolate. She strode purposefully along the harbour, not caring how beautiful and majestic it looked that evening, striding past the Italian restaurant at the end, the sight of all the happy couples seated at tables for two adding salt to her wound.

Turning into the high street, she was only ten minutes away from her house when a car pulled up beside her. She carried on walking then hesitated, realising the driver might be asking for directions.

"Maya!" The driver had wound down the passenger window.

She turned. "Sam?" Although for a moment she was pleased to see him, anxiety took over. She dreaded what she looked like. She wiped her face hastily with the back of her sleeve.

"Erm… Would you like a lift?"

"I'm only ten minutes away…" She gestured with the carrier bag in her hand, making the wine bottles clink together. The last thing she wanted was for Sam to see her in this state. She couldn't look at him properly.

"Maya, please…"

"I'm okay. I can walk."

"I can't drive off without giving you a lift home." Car still running, he ran around and opened the passenger door for her. "Please, get in," he said, softly. He gestured to the passenger seat.

She decided it would be easier to accept his offer and got in. The car was lovely and warm, smelling freshly valeted.

"Are you okay?" Sam asked, concern etched across his face as he got back in the car and pulled the seatbelt over his shoulder.

"Yes, yes…" Maya really didn't want to admit to Sam that she'd just been stood up. "Where have you been? Haven't seen you in ages."

"Work got stupidly hectic, then I had to fly out to Toulouse for emergency meetings. I only got back this morning." Sam checked his mirrors and pulled the car away. He was smartly dressed, still wearing his work clothes.

"Oh, right." The journey back only took a couple of minutes in the car. Maya sat silently, the wine cold on her lap.

Sam pulled up outside her house. "Where did you go? I thought I'd find you walking up the hill from The Golden…"

Maya frowned. "How did you know I was at The Golden Lion?" The only person she'd told was Emma at lunchtime.

"I just assumed. I've seen you there before." Sam glanced down at his lap, then back at Maya, combing a hand through his dark curls. He looked so serious and nervous that a chill of anxiety crept up Maya's back.

"What do you mean? Have you been driving round looking for me?" It didn't make any sense. Oh God, was he going to tell her someone close to her had died? Were her kids okay? Why had he come to find her? It had to be serious. "Did Emma ask you to get me?"

"No, no…" He shook his head.

"What, then?"

"Maya, I have a confession…" He still couldn't look her in the eye. Maya's heart hammered inside her chest. Then, taking a deep breath, he turned to face her. "I'm Peter Pan."

"What?" She shook her head in confusion. Some sort of relief washed over her. Her children were safe. But the news confused her. Peter Pan? Who was he talking about? She felt disorientated and dizzy. She rubbed her temple. "I don't understand."

"I messaged you from that account before I'd decided whether I wanted to be on there or not. And before we'd really got to know one another in person. And then we messaged and messaged, you telling me about how badly I'd treated you." Sam rubbed his face. "You know, that time we first met?"

"Amber's birthday…" she whispered. Maya's addled brain was filling in the gaps. PeterPan26.

"And so then, I couldn't bring myself to tell you it was me. I know it was wrong, I know it was deceitful, but I liked you messaging me, telling me things you probably wouldn't have confessed if you'd known who I really was. I really like you." Sam's brown eyes implored Maya's. "It was nice not being the poor old widowed single dad, too."

"Oh my God!" Maya couldn't understand the ramifications. All this time she'd thought she'd been chatting to some stranger, when all along it had been Sam. Now she wondered what she'd told him, what she'd confided… "Oh my God!"

She panicked, gathering up the wine from her lap. Fumbling, she shoved open the door and scrambled out, slamming the door shut behind her.

"Maya!" Sam shot out of his side of the car. "I'm sorry. I know I should have told you sooner. It got out of control. I was worried how you'd react."

"Well, obviously I'm going to react like this. It *was* deceitful." Standing on the pavement, clutching the carrier bag and pushing the strap of her handbag over her shoulder, she burst into tears. Sam, the one man she'd learnt to trust, a man she'd thought was her friend, had also been lying to her. Did he think this was some kind of sick joke? This was too much.

"Look, I'm sorry, how can I make this up to you?" Sam stepped closer, coming around his car, but she held her hand up and shook her head, her tear-filled eyes narrowing on him, daring him to take a step further. He stopped, eyes glistening, and hung his head, hands in his pockets. "Maya, please... I'm so sorry. This is the last thing I wanted to happen. I never wanted to hurt you."

Maya stormed up her driveway, and with trembling fingers she fumbled the key into the door, cursing it wouldn't open quickly enough so she could get away from all the bad things happening to her that evening. Once inside, she slammed the door behind her and let her tears flow.

Thank God she'd bought two bottles of wine. What a crappy birthday!

CHAPTER 34

Maya bolted upright, waking with a start, making her head hurt. Her hand flew to her forehead, and she winced as she calmed her breathing. She'd forgotten to set her alarm and panicked about what time it was. Then she relaxed back into the pillows, remembering she didn't have a client until late morning.

Opening the second bottle of wine had not been the wisest idea, but she'd been determined to numb the pain — the feeling of rejection from being stood up and then the shock of Sam's deceit.

All along PeterPan26 had been him! And he'd known he was talking to Maya. Last night, she had been consumed with fury and had spent the evening sobbing into a box of tissues, texting Emma everything.

Now, she took time to reflect — more soberly. She checked her phone. There was a text from Sam: *I'm so sorry, Maya. Please believe me, I never meant to deceive or hurt you. Please tell me what I need to do to fix this and I'll do it. I don't want to lose you. X*

Since their first misunderstanding, as Maya liked to think of it now, he'd made every effort to make up for his behaviour. He'd always been a true gentleman towards her and given her the confidence boost she needed — in person and online. And now, reading between the lines, she realised how much he must like her.

And he had tried to be the hero by rescuing her from being stood up.

Emma had even mentioned this last night — she'd phoned Maya in the end, and they'd talked into the early hours of the morning. She'd agreed that Sam should have told Maya who he was earlier on, but she could also understand how it had got harder the more they'd communicated.

Sam's heart was in the right place. They'd become good friends where the children were concerned. But maybe it was more than that too? She kept remembering sitting on Kittiwake Cove beach, watching the sunset with him. She'd become at ease in his company. And maybe she could understand him remaining anonymous. It was difficult being a widowed man, and many women might be put off by that fact. She hadn't pitied PeterPan26, or treated him any differently, because she hadn't known that he was a widower. Whereas when she was with Sam, at times she'd found herself treading on eggshells because of his dead wife, afraid to say the wrong thing.

But he'd deceived her. Was that any way to start a relationship?

Relationship? she thought suddenly. Maybe Sam only meant he didn't want to lose her friendship. He'd said nothing about a relationship…

Feeling emotionally drained and unsure what to do next, Maya pushed back the duvet and turned on the shower in the en-suite. She raised her face into the spray, the hot jets of water massaging her temples and easing her self-inflicted headache.

After a long day of appointments, Maya slumped on the sofa and closed her eyes. She needed to change out of her tunic. She still hadn't replied to Sam. She hadn't spoken to anyone really, except Emma, who'd texted to check how her head and heart were.

Maya missed her children. They'd been gone nearly a week now, something she never got used to because Kyle had them so infrequently, leaving her feeling empty and lonely. She needed them more than ever right now. Her stomach grumbled, reminding her that she hadn't eaten properly all day, so she forced herself off the sofa and into the kitchen.

Maya pottered about, opening and shutting cupboard doors, trying to build up the motivation to cook. Just then, the doorbell rang.

She answered and gasped. Sam, dressed in a suit and tie, as if he'd come straight from work, was standing on her doorstep, holding large sheets of card.

He pressed his finger to his lips, then reached down to a boombox by his feet. He pushed the play button and Dido started singing 'Here With Me'. The scene in front of her was familiar. It suddenly dawned on Maya that the song was from the *Love Actually* soundtrack. She remembered she'd told Sam that the cue card scene was her favourite part in the movie. She chuckled nervously, holding her hand to her mouth as, card by card, Sam slowly revealed his message to her:

Maya, with these notes I want to tell you

I'm sorry.

Really sorry!

For being a complete jerk. He pulled a face as he revealed this card.

I should have been honest all along

And asked you out on a date

Because the night we watched the sun set together

I knew I was falling in love with you… Maya gasped, her hand flying to her mouth.

I want you to have this as a gift

to you from me

Instead of another cue card, she noticed he was holding the painting she'd loved — the Kittiwake Cove sunset from the gallery. The one that reminded her of that evening. He'd bought it.

Ignoring Maya's attempts at refusal, Sam handed her the painting, awkwardly trying to keep the cue cards in order, which made her giggle again, and as she wiped a tear from her cheek, she realised she'd started crying.

She wanted to speak, to protest that the painting was too extravagant a gift, but he held his finger to his lips and continued with the messages on the cards.

I never meant to hurt or deceive you.

Please forgive me for my stupidity.

And let me ask you out on a date… He paused before revealing the next card, hesitating.

Will you have dinner with me, Maya?

Maya wiped her eyes some more. Afraid of dropping the painting, she hugged it tightly. She found herself nodding. "Yes, yes, I'll let you take me out."

"Would tonight be pushing it?" Sam said over the music. He turned the volume down.

Maya shook her head. "No, no."

"Have you eaten?"

"No," Maya said. "I was just thinking about what to make, with no motivation to actually cook."

"Can I take you to dinner, then?" He stepped closer, discarding the cue cards, resting them against the wall of her house. She could see he was still nervous, rocking on his heels.

Maya chewed her lip, brushing a hand down her tunic while the other hugged the painting. She didn't want to go on a date with Sam while dressed for work. "Can you give me an hour? I need to shower and change." She sniffed and wiped her eyes.

Sam's face lit up. "Of course, me too. I'll be back at seven-thirty," he said with a nod, then swiftly kissed her cheek. Eagerly, he picked up the cards and the portable CD player.

"Sam," she blurted, "I can't accept this painting."

"Yes, you can. Consider it a birthday present, if you need a reason. I bought it for you." With everything gathered he walked back down the driveway, not letting her argue. "See you in an hour," he called over his shoulder.

Maya shut the front door and placed the painting on the sofa, admiring its sunset orange hues, then raced upstairs, undoing her tunic as she went.

CHAPTER 35

On the dot of seven-thirty, Sam rang Maya's doorbell, his heart beating erratically. He took a deep breath to calm his nerves, holding his hands behind his back. He had ironed his favourite Ralph Lauren casual shirt and tucked it into his dark blue jeans, then untucked it, unsure what looked better. He was freshly shaved and had splashed on aftershave too. He hadn't been on a date in years. Yet he knew Maya. He'd spent time with her. Why should tonight be any different than the evening they'd shared in Cornwall?

Maya opened the door. Sam looked up and his breath caught in his throat. She was wearing a fitted, pastel blue, floral dress and sparkly heels that accentuated her slender legs, and she held a cream cardigan in her hand.

"Will I do?" she asked, swishing her golden hair back off her shoulders.

"More than do." Should he kiss her now or would that be too weird? This was a first date. "You look stunning."

Her gaze didn't meet his, and she gave a nervous laugh, brushing off the compliment.

He walked her to his car and opened the passenger door for her. As he walked around to the driver's side of the car, he breathed in deeply through his nose and let the breath out through his mouth, trying to calm the excited teenage boy inside him. Heather was having Chloe over for a sleepover, so he didn't need to rush this evening.

Sam took Maya to a little bistro on the marina, The Lock and Harbour. Knowing the restaurant had a reputation for being popular, he had booked the table before he'd asked Maya out, hoping she would say yes. He thought it best to guarantee somewhere special for their first — and hopefully not their last — date.

They were seated by the window, which looked out over the lock and the marina, the evening sun reflecting in the water. Their table had a white tablecloth lying diagonally across it, with the cutlery and glasses already laid, and there was a red candle burning inside a miniature glass bowl.

The waiter returned after a few minutes to take their drinks order. Sam let Maya choose the bottle of wine. She opted for a pinot grigio. The waiter returned with the bottle and a stainless-steel ice bucket on a stand, which stood beside the table. He poured the wine, allowing Maya to sample it first.

"Happy birthday, albeit a day late," Sam toasted, tapping his glass of wine gently against Maya's once the waiter had left them to read the menu.

"Thank you," Maya said, taking a sip of her wine. "It hasn't turned out to be too bad."

"I want to make it a vast improvement on yesterday." Sam put down his glass and picked up the menu. "Look, I don't want to go over old ground, and I certainly don't want to ruin this evening..." Sam leant forward, resting the menu against his chest. "But I do want you to know I am deeply sorry for not telling you sooner about the Peter Pan account. I never wanted to hurt you."

"I realise you didn't do it maliciously."

He shook his head. "I'm just hoping you can forgive me — again — like you did when I was an absolute monster the first time we met."

Maya smiled as she shook her head, which put Sam's mind to rest a little. "So why did you have the Peter Pan account?"

While they chose their food, and their courses arrived, Sam divulged the whole sordid story of his attempts at online dating too soon after Jade's death. From now on, he was going to be always honest with Maya.

Their initial awkwardness was soon lost, their usual relaxed state returning, strengthening Sam's conviction that Maya was the one for him. Maya listened with gestures of encouragement and disbelief as he told her of his horrific date years ago. He disclosed how he'd been deceived by Annette; how she'd lied about her appearance, her age, even her marital status, and how he had hated deceiving Maya by remaining anonymous, knowing how it felt. He wanted to replace his tainted memories of dating with good ones. He was already thinking of all the places he wanted to take Maya.

"Admittedly, that account did have a purpose, because if you hadn't chatted to me through Peter Pan, I wouldn't have learnt how you felt about me, and that I so strongly needed to rectify it," Sam said, pushing his knife and fork together.

"This is true," Maya said with a chuckle, finishing her own meal.

As the waiter brought out their desserts and topped up the last of their wine from the bottle, Sam wished the evening would slow down.

Maya gave a smirk, swishing her blonde hair back off her shoulders. Her blue eyes looked at him intently.

"What?" he said, his eyes narrowing with intrigue.

She held her spoon over her chocolate mousse. Icing sugar and strawberries decorated the square plate. "I might have to bring up Peter Pan occasionally. It'll make great dinner party banter." He could see by the mischief in her expression that she was teasing him. He loved her mouth: glossy, full lips he was dying to kiss.

"Please don't." Sam placed a hand over her other hand resting on the table. She didn't pull it away, so he relished the touch of her skin, entwining his fingers between hers. "I don't think I could bear the embarrassment."

"How much is it worth?" She twisted the spoon between her fingers, before delving into the chocolate mousse. Her lips smoothed sensuously over the spoon as she ate, savouring the rich dessert.

Sam wanted this woman. For the rest of his life. "You've got me over a barrel, basically. You might need to name your price." Sam had opted for the vanilla cheesecake and took a bite. He wasn't particularly hungry, but he hadn't wanted Maya to eat dessert alone — plus he didn't want the evening to end and was doing everything in his power to prolong it. "But does this mean I get another date, if you're thinking of dinner party banter?"

"Absolutely. If you want to, of course? Unless I've showed myself up?"

"Well, you do keep putting your elbows on the table," Sam said jokingly.

Maya quickly tucked her elbows into her waist, then laughed.

He loved her laughter and her beautiful smile. Peter Pan had told her often enough.

After Sam paid the bill, he said, "Shall we go for a walk?"

"Yes, I'd like that."

As Maya walked out of the restaurant, her heart full of joy and her stomach full of delicious food, she thought of yesterday, and how it now felt like a distant memory. The upset and the heartache felt surreal compared to being here with Sam.

It being the end of May, it didn't get dark until late, and so as they strolled alongside the marina, they could see the golden remnants of the sunset on the horizon. The stars were brightening as the sun sank. It wasn't quite Cornwall, but it would do. A warm breeze blew, gently rattling the riggings of the boats moored in the marina.

"What are you thinking? You're quiet," Sam said, taking her hand. How long had she wanted him to do this? How good did it feel?

"The overthinker in me is worrying about the children, and what they will think."

"Don't worry. We already know they get on great, even Lewis with Chloe. She likes him. And we don't need them to know yet."

"How do you mean?"

"I assure you, we'll have quality time just the two of us together, but we can still do days out with the kids. Only, we'll keep 'us' a secret, until we're ready to tell them. If that will make you happier?"

She nodded gently.

Maya leaned on the railings overlooking the lock. Sam stepped closer. He softly pushed some loose strands of Maya's hair back behind her ear. Then, his eyes intent on hers, he combed his hand through her hair and, finding the back of her neck, pulled her towards him. He kissed her, like she'd fantasised him doing too many times to count. Her body melted against his, her arms looping around his neck as she kissed him back.

How long they kissed, Maya didn't know, but feeling the heat between them, she gently pulled out of the kiss, pushing at Sam's chest.

"What?" Sam said, keeping a firm hold of Maya's waist. "I was only getting started."

"We're in public." Not that there were many people milling around the marina, but there were enough. Plus, houses looked out onto the harbour.

"So?"

"I'm on a three-date rule." Maya laughed, her hand softly resting on his breastbone, not fully wanting to disconnect.

Sam nodded, releasing his grip, even stepping a foot away from her. "Of course you are. What are you doing tomorrow? Can I pick you up at around two?"

"Make it three."

"Great." Sam kissed her, then moved his mouth to her ear, his breath sending butterflies down her spine. "And because I know you like to be prepared," he whispered, the hairs on her neck responding to him, "pack for a night away."

Her eyes widened, and her mouth opened to ask, what, why, where ... but Sam placed a finger to her lips and said, "Let's get you home safe before I insist we break the three-date rule."

CHAPTER 36

As promised, Sam collected Maya at three o'clock on Friday afternoon. After a lingering kiss, and smelling absolutely gorgeous, he placed the small carry-on case she'd packed in the boot of his car.

"Where are we going?" Maya asked as Sam joined the M5.

"It's a surprise."

They chatted casually in the car, conversation flowing easily between them. If Sam was nervous, he didn't show it. Maya's nerves were on edge, but more with the anticipation of where Sam was taking her.

It soon became apparent when they passed the 'Welcome to Cornwall' sign along the A30.

"Are you taking me to Kittiwake Cove?" Maya asked excitedly.

"Maybe." Sam smiled, giving Maya a quick glance before concentrating on the road ahead.

Just over three hours later, as they'd hit some traffic on the A30, Sam pulled up outside Trenouth Cottage.

They were greeted by Rose and Charles, hugging and kissing them both, before being shown to a room each. Maya wouldn't have minded sharing a room with Sam but liked that he hadn't been presumptuous. It was chivalrous of him.

"Take your time freshening up. I'll meet you downstairs when you're ready. We have a table booked for seven-thirty." Sam kissed Maya on the cheek then disappeared into his own room.

Sam escorted Maya to The Beach Front Bistro, Rhianna's restaurant. It was perfectly situated on Kittiwake Cove high street, with an uninterrupted view over the beach. Rhianna greeted them, and Maya couldn't help thinking she had a knowing smile about her. As Rhianna took Maya's light jacket, she gave a nudge and said, "Looks like you'll be coming to our wedding after all." Maya inwardly grinned. She couldn't think of anything better than being involved with Sam's family.

Due to the warmth of the evening, they were seated at a table outside, so they could watch the sun descending over the ocean. The tide was out, and they could see surfers as black dots, still in the water. It was as if Maya had never left.

"Joe reserved us a table," Sam said.

"Joe knows about this, then?"

"He always had an inkling." Sam laughed. "It's funny, because back during Easter, when we were here last, he was deliberately flirtatious with you, and it riled me."

"Why?" Maya stopped perusing the cocktail menu and met Sam's gaze.

"He's always been the cooler, trendier one, with his natural ability to surf and flirt. He's also younger. Possibly better looking. He always got the girls better than me when we were teenagers. I was worried he was more your type of guy." Sam raised his eyebrows. "And I know he's smitten with Rhianna, but I didn't like seeing him give you attention. He confessed he did it only to force me make a move on you."

Maya tilted her head, smirking at the thought of a jealous Sam. "I won't argue, he is an attractive man..." Maya held up a hand as Sam frowned. "But so is his brother." Smiling, she chewed her lower lip. "Besides, Joe's way too laid back for me."

Sam looked very handsome with the top button of his shirt undone. He'd changed into smart trousers as well. Maya had luckily packed another dress to wear, as the one she'd been wearing earlier was rumpled from the long car journey. "And I prefer my men older."

"Excuse me, I'm not that much older than Joe."

She laughed at Sam's incredulous expression.

Rhianna's warm voice interrupted them. "Hey, are you two ready to order?" Rhianna smiled at Sam and then Maya. "Or do you need a couple more minutes?"

"A couple more minutes, please." Maya had been too busy taking in the view and enjoying Sam's company to even peruse the menu yet.

"Can I get you a drink while you choose?"

"Yes, please, Rhianna," Sam said, then turned his attention to Maya. "Would you like to share a bottle of wine?"

"Yes, that's a good idea."

"You choose. Pick what you like."

Maya chose a pinot grigio. By the time the wine arrived, they were ready to order some food.

Sam could not have taken Maya anywhere more romantic for their second date. The village was becoming her favourite place on the planet.

The food turned out to be heavenly. They laughed and relaxed in each other's company, their friendship expanding further than Maya ever believed it would. Now, opposite this man, listening to his every word, letting his deep brown eyes charm hers, she wanted nothing more than to share everything with him.

From their table, sharing the bottle of cold white wine, they were able to watch the sun gradually descend over the sea. As the sun dropped, Rhianna brought out blankets and turned on the patio heaters. Sam moved his chair once they'd finished eating, so he could sit beside Maya, holding hands and snatching a kiss while watching the waves tumble until the sun set.

"Everything okay for you guys, or can I get you something else?" Rhianna returned to clear away the dessert plates.

Maya shook her head. "No, we're fine, thank you." Sam squeezed her hand, his thumb rubbing gently over the back.

"Okay, enjoy the view." Rhianna sighed and stood there for a moment, appreciating the view. "I never tire of it."

Maya leaned her head into Sam's chest, and he wrapped a comforting arm around her. "This is lovely," she said.

Sam gently turned her head and kissed her. "I already know I want to spend the rest of my life with you," he murmured, lips still brushing hers. "We can come here as often as you like." His words warmed Maya's heart. She wanted this too.

They walked back to Trenouth Cottage hand in hand, Sam occasionally pulling Maya in for a kiss. She could feel Sam's arousal when their bodies met. Even though the sun had disappeared below the ocean, it wasn't yet dark, providing enough light for them to see their way up the garden path. They couldn't get through the front door quickly enough.

The farmhouse was dark, except for a couple of lamps in the hallway, to allow guests to see their way up to their rooms. They were both relieved that Rose and Charles had retired to bed, and they giggled like naughty teenagers as they climbed the stairs.

Outside Maya's bedroom, neither wanting the evening to end, their passion grew as they kissed, Sam's tongue softly finding hers, his arms tightening their hold, his fingers searching for bare flesh. Maya could feel heat pooling between her thighs, a sexual tension needing to be released. Sam was hard, pressed against her, equally turned on.

Only their clothes were in the way of flesh touching flesh…

"Come in." Maya rummaged for her key, opening her bedroom door. She hauled Sam inside and he kicked the door shut behind them, their mouths barely disconnecting.

Maya fumbled with Sam's shirt buttons as he tugged the zip at the back of her dress.

"Wait." Sam stopped, pulling away. Maya felt bereft without the heat of his firm body against hers. "What about the three-date rule?"

"Sod the rule." Maya tugged him back, urgently pressing her lips, breasts, and stomach against him, wanting the heat back.

"Oh, thank God." He embraced her harder. She tore at his shirt, now unbuttoned, revealing his strong shoulders.

"Besides, if we count the cinema, Easter…" Maya murmured between kisses, while unbuttoning his fly, "we're pretty much there."

"Good, because I don't think I can wait much longer." Sam pushed the straps of her dress off her shoulders and it fell to the floor. "Seriously, you're beautiful," he whispered.

Without hesitation, he dipped his head, tenderly kissing each breast cupped in her lacy bra. Thank goodness she'd had the sense to wear matching underwear. His touch sent all sorts of feelings through her body and her mind, turning her on, her arousal becoming as urgent as his. Nothing else mattered tonight, just Sam, making her feel alive and loved. Swiftly, he twisted her around, pressing her back into his torso as he kissed the hollow of her neck, along her collarbone, sweeping her hair over her shoulder. His hands gently roamed the front of her body, sometimes firmly, sometimes as if brushing with feathers, smoothing over her stomach, hips, breasts… His fingertips trailed along the top of her underwear, then dipped gently inside.

A moan of delight escaped her, but she needed this to slow down. She wanted to savour every tender second.

"Gosh, I'm sorry if I'm a bit rusty at this," he said.

"You are far from rusty..." Maya closed her eyes, relishing the delight and sensations Sam stirred.

And as if Sam knew, also wanting this night to last, he slowed the pace, becoming less urgent. He took his time touching her, with his lips and fingers, not rushing a single thing, so that Maya ached for him. Slowly, Sam led Maya to the double bed, kissing and caressing her, unable to let her go, wanting the heat to remain between them.

Between the twisted sheets, Maya became lost in the pleasure Sam was giving her. Her fingers combed through his hair, wanting to feel the softness of it...

"Make love to me," she said softly.

As they made love, she felt nothing but completion, the two of them becoming one with their bodies entwined. She sensed nothing but pure adoration for this man.

Eventually, they both lay breathless and sated. Cuddled together, the sheets entangled around them, Sam continued to kiss and stroke her skin, his fingers trailing over the curves of her body, his gentle touches making her sleepy.

She felt his breath behind her ear before she heard his words. "I love you, Maya."

A lump formed in her throat and a single tear escaped. That was all she wanted. "I love you too, Sam."

EPILOGUE

Dinner devoured and warding off hungry seagulls, Maya and Sam were now cuddled up together on a blanket on Kittiwake Cove beach, laughing at Lewis, Amber and Chloe playing in the sand. Sam had fetched fish and chips for them to have supper on the beach, so they could watch the sun go down.

It was the end of the summer holidays; the weather was being kind — today at least — and they'd tagged on a couple of extra weeks in Kittiwake Cove after Joe and Rhianna's wedding. This was the bonus of dating a man whose family owned a bed and breakfast in Cornwall. Sam's words. Not Maya's. But he did have a good point, she reflected, as she soaked up the coastal atmosphere.

The wedding had been a small, intimate affair at Trenouth Manor with family and close friends. Tristan, as well as hosting the event, had been Joe's best man. Joe and Rhianna had gone away together for a couple of nights, but were going on their honeymoon once the summer holidays had ended. It had felt special to Maya to be included in this beautiful occasion and fully immersed in Sam's family.

The three children, still in their wetsuits after surfing with Joe, were digging a huge sandcastle. Joe had sloped off now, saying he had a wife to please and a busy pub to run. They all had a healthy glow after being out in the sun, wind and rain.

Considering the busy time of year, Sam and Maya had been given a cosy double room. Rose and Charles had housed the children in a room together, next to them — which appeared to be working. If Sam and Maya tired them out with activities during the day, they fell into their beds and didn't keep each other awake. Fern and Doug had also stayed for a long weekend after the wedding, having gone home yesterday, along with Heather and Tom, making parts of these two weeks together a real family affair.

Now it was back to the five of them. Rose and Charles gave the couple space, catching up more in the evenings. They would sit in their garden with a glass of crisp white wine, candles burning and nightlights twinkling, recalling the events of the day. With the summer holidays in full flow, the B&B was full to the brim too, with any spare rooms booked out, which kept the pair busy. Rose refused Maya's help, insisting she enjoyed her break.

The sun still had a couple of hours to travel before it set. The tide had about ten feet before it would reach the sandcastle Lewis, Amber and Chloe were frantically adding to.

With the sun on her skin, a warm breeze in the air, Maya was … happy. That was the simplest way to describe it. All three kids were content, and they hadn't been all that surprised when Maya and Sam had sat them down to tell them about their relationship.

She knew life could throw its curveballs, but right here, right now, she was going to treasure every moment. She tucked in closer to Sam, and he gave her a responsive squeeze, hugging her more tightly.

"This is just perfect," she said.

"It is. And I've been thinking…" Sam said.

"Careful. You might strain yourself."

"Haha!" He poked her in the ribs playfully.

Maya squealed with laughter. "Stop!"

"No, seriously, Maya…" He glanced over at the kids. They were too busy shovelling sand and running in and out of the shallow water to concern themselves with their parents.

Maya shifted away from him, staring in horror. "I can tell you now, we're not having a baby!"

Sam laughed loudly. "Hell, no, I never dreamed of suggesting a baby."

Maya breathed with relief. She loved that Kyle was stuck changing nappies — Jenna had another on the way — and Maya was enjoying life with Sam. Lewis, Amber and Chloe, being that bit older, did allow Sam and Maya to steal some quality time together, just the two of them. More time than a baby would allow. "Phew, what then?"

Sam cupped her face, kissing her. "This *is* perfect. Move in with me." He gently pushed a strand of hair off her face, his fingers brushing her cheek. "If Jade's death has taught me anything, it's that life's too short. Let's do this, let's start living our lives together. Start making memories together — as a family."

A lump formed in Maya's throat, leaving her speechless.

These past few months together had been thrilling, especially when they were first dating and keeping it a secret from the kids. They'd shared so much laughter, with and without the children. They probably had more ups and some downs to face, and bickering from the kids, but they'd overcome everything together. Maya couldn't imagine life without Sam.

"Maya?"

Maya nodded. "Yes, yes, okay, let's do it."

"Fantastic." Sam scooped her into both of his arms and kissed her.

Oblivious to the kids and the faces they pulled every time they caught Sam and Maya kissing, she closed her eyes, savouring his touch.

Emma was right. You had to enjoy kissing the person you wanted to spend the rest of your life with. And she did. Maya and Sam kissed as if they were made for one another. Soft, gentle kisses, deepened with passion and longing, their bodies pressing together tightly.

Maya never need kiss another man again. She'd finally found her happy ever after.

A NOTE TO THE READER

I hope you liked *Sunsets and Happy Ever Afters*, and it has given you that escapism we sometimes all need.

If you enjoyed reading this book, the best way to let me know is by leaving a review on **Goodreads** and/or **Amazon**. It's also a great way to share with other readers too! And I will be forever grateful to you.

I love hearing from readers, so please feel free to contact me on any of my social media platforms. I'd love to chat with you. You can follow me here:

Facebook / **Goodreads** / **Amazon** / **BookBub** / **Blog** / **Website** / **Instagram** / **Twitter**.

I also have a monthly newsletter that you can subscribe to **here**. I sometimes run competitions open only to subscribers. You'll get all the gossip there first.

Once again, thank you. You are the reason I love to write romance.

Kind regards,

Teresa

www.teresamorgan.co.uk

Sapere Books is an exciting new publisher of brilliant fiction and popular history.

To find out more about our latest releases and our monthly bargain books visit our website: **saperebooks.com**